JUSTICE OF THE WILD

Michael Du Preez

First published in 2016 by
FARAXA
www.faraxapublishing.com
Email: info@faraxapublishing.com

Justice of the Wild

ISBN 978-99957-48-52-4

Printed in the UK.

JUSTICE OF THE WILD

Michael Du Preez

30-12-2017

To Pierre
from
Helène
with love !

→ do read !!

Michael [signature]

Dedication

To those who devote their lives to Wildlife Conservation and to animals that pay the ultimate price to satisfy the greed and brutality of ruthless poachers.

ONE

WEDNESDAY 14H15.

Rampha Singh looked across the classroom. What's he up to now Paul wondered as he caught his eye? He watched his crazy, mad scientist friend slip a folded note to Princess Debbie next door. With her half smile that drove him to the brink of insanity and a quick sleight-of-hand movement, she passed it smoothly along the well-travelled route four desks to her right. He deftly palmed it from Boetie Nkonayni, his immediate neighbour.

Opening it stealthily beneath his desktop Paul read, 'Storm 10 mins on the dot. Five bucks.' He glanced at his digital watch, his sixteenth birthday present. It showed 14h15.34. He picked up a pencil and wrote, 'You're on. Now 14h15 and 52 seconds.' Undetected the crumpled reply returned along the same route.

Rampha opened it, smiled, checked his watch and nodded.

Paul looked outside. A dense black, sinister-looking mega-cloud-driven forward by gale force winds loomed and sped with menace across the heavens, darkening the sky.

Paul loved it. A serious monster rainstorm was headed this way. The earthy rainy smell triggered his younger days. His parents never knew how he would prance around in their secluded garden at home, naked in the rain. As an only child, he spent a lot of time by himself.

Now his family was falling apart.

He had another quick look outside. The cloud wave approached rapidly, stitched together stray patches of cotton wool and annihilated shards of blue sky. Flashes of lightning produced triple forte tympani. No rock band at a concert with their latest electronic sound gear could wish for a more satisfying din.

A large stray drop splashed against the window pane, carving a meter-long path through the dust.

He glanced at Rampha who was trying hard to appear calm and collected.

Well, guess what? Paul thought. For once his friend was wrong and he knew it. It was a dead giveaway how he ran slim fingers through his thick, jet black mop and kept checking outside. Even the wink he tossed was just another nervous sign.

Paul resisted squeezing the new emerging pimple on his chin and turned his attention to the tedious, afternoon history lesson he and the rest of the class were embroiled in. It dragged with no end in sight.

History teacher Buster Lister spoke his own version of Shakespearian English and could be an amiable person outside of class. Sometimes. But when he waxed lyrical on his favourite topic, the 'History of The Struggle in South Africa', his voice submerged into a monotonous tone that brought about a sluggish soporific effect on his learners.

Groans of rebellion were pointedly heaved and breathed around the class. Grade eleven students were far too young to recall the events of 1994, the year South Africa held its first democratic elections. To Paul and his colleagues, history was best left buried in the past. There were more important things to focus on like Princess Debbie the absolute secret love of his life, his music, the latest cell phone technology, Facebook and of course animals.

But to Paul's parents, Bernard and Martha Patterson and indeed most grownups of Mr. Lister's era, the elections were a life-changing experience. Some spoke of it as a miracle day, to be nurtured in memories forever.

That's like okay and cool, Paul reflected. Right now, there was an exciting, brutal storm out there to be relished and kept at bay just long enough to win his bet and rub Rampha's hawked nose in it.

WEDNESDAY 14H20

The Lion Park was located five kilometres away as the crow flies. There, in one of the camps, a group of lions moved restlessly beneath wildly thrashing clusters of very old and very tall blue gum trees. The nervous young male of the pride, larger than the rest with a huge dark tawny mane, padded back and forth alongside the four-meter-high double Bonnox fence. His family of five agitated females watched his every move.

At each thunderclap, he would recoil and growl softly. Highly-strung and greatly on edge, he sought in vain for an exit through the fence for shelter to wait out the ominous electric storm. There was scant cover in this five-acre enclosure that was home to them. The camp consisted of a small field of tall thatching grass, dotted with blue gums and acacia trees. A narrow dirt road wound around the perimeter and back to the gated entrance.

WEDNESDAY 14H25

A short distance away seated at his desk in the administration block, Martin Resnick winced at the clamour of the storm. He stared through his office window at the trees in the camps bending and twisting about in the wind. He pressed a button on the intercom.

'Joseph,' he shouted. 'Don't feed them just yet. Tell the guys to wait till the worst is over.'

'Okay, Boss,' the voice crackled back. 'This is a big one.'

'Looks like it,' Martin said. He knew how irritable lions became in weather like this. At best, when the food truck entered they were aggressive. At times they would leap onto the back to snatch their choice share of the spoil. No, they were best left without food in these conditions.

You don't mess with these guys, Martin thought. Hungry lions are vicious. When the storm was over, he would make sure his wardens were extra careful feeding them. Even though when their bellies were full, he was one of the few who could walk with impunity among the friendlier ones. But he would never dare approach them under these circumstances. No way.

Martin enjoyed the fact that scores of eager city dwellers and tourists, whose closest brush with wild animals usually comprised an assortment of zoo creatures behind bars, experienced a sharp reaction within the confines of the Lion Park. Here their blood pressure shot up considerably. The scary in-your-face proximity to the legendary king of beasts on his own turf caused a rush that was both exhilarating and quite unique.

The Park is safe, thought Martin, provided you remained securely in your car. Reaching out the window to stroke one of these oversized pussy cats was never a very good idea.

He recalled a few years back when some lionesses had indeed attacked and killed two unfortunate and unwise Taiwanese tourists. The reckless pair had left their car to get a closer look and take pictures. More recently, an American woman was leaning out of the window for a better picture, when a lioness crept up unseen alongside the car and bodily dragged her out. Unfortunately, she did not survive the attack.

Those tragic episodes were entirely due to gross foolhardiness plus a total disregard for the Park's strict rules. The publicity these attacks spawned far outweighed the negative connotations. The Lion Park usually scored a surge of morbidly curious visitors following similar episodes. There is really no such thing as bad publicity, Martin thought. But today, with lightning and thunder roaring about heralding the imminent storm, there were no visitors. No people, no cars, no cameras, no food, nothing to distract the pent-up animals.

WEDNESDAY 14H30

'… and that,' declared Mr. Lister solemnly, 'concludes our lesson for today.'

His favourite conniving ploy thought Paul. The man's got a double Ph.D. in deceit. Time without number he would make that wished-for eagerly anticipated announcement, then with hardly a decent pause for breath, he would proceed to bend the ears of his long-suffering audience a further ten to twenty minutes, depending on his perverse, mean mood, especially during the last period of the day. Even the looming storm outside would not deter his resolve to wind up the lesson to his absolute satisfaction.

'Lest we forget,' he continued without missing a beat, as Paul rolled his eyes and the class loudly shuffled their feet in protest, 'the most important aspect of any country's history is to learn from it. What's the point of history,' he uttered the word with deep reverence, 'if one cannot benefit from it?' He looked around the room enquiringly.

Did this mentally challenged moron really expect a response?

Rampha put up his hand. Here's fun, thought Paul.

'Well, Singh?'

'Please, may I leave the room, Mister Lister, sir?' Not a muscle moved on his face. Oliver Twist was asking for more with lilting rhyme in rap format. Nascent giggles rippled around the classroom as the beadle narrowed his eyes and rewarded Rampha with one of his notorious 'looks'.

'And me sir,' said Paul, putting up his hand quickly, taking advantage of the pause. A clap of thunder, with perfect timing, shook the classroom, rattling windows dramatically. Giggles crescendo to suppressed laughter.

'Et tu, Mister Patterson? Weak bladder no doubt?' Mr Lister said, measuring each syllable while adjusting his specs. He contemplated holding the two to ransom a little longer, but in a sudden u-turn briskly waved them out and fixed the rest of the class with a challenging stare.

'Without a country's past, it has no future,' he continued, warming once again to his closing sermon, ignoring the rumbling thunder blended with loads of tangible hostility, 'Take Nelson Mandela for example...'

WEDNESDAY 14H32

They reached the door together and hurried out. Paul thrust his watch into Rampha's face.

'You've got forty-five seconds.'

'I make it sixty,' Rampha said, checking.

'Huh, fifteen seconds.' He glanced up at the sky. It was black. Strong gusts tugged their uniforms. 'You're such a loser.'

'Let's go,' shouted Rampha. They dashed across the quadrangle towards the covered walkway leading to the dormitory block.

'Okay, cough up,' announced Paul, sticking out his hand. 'Look Ma, no rain.'

At that, a sudden shattering flash brightly lit the sky. An ear-splitting blast and clamorous roar like a rocket launch followed a split second later. The boys ducked instinctively as Heaven opened her floodgates.

The walkway was simply not wide enough to prevent sheets of water lashing in on both sides. They charged for the dormitory but were drenched to the skin as they arrived, laughing breathlessly.

'Loser, am I, duh. Who owes who?' shouted Rampha triumphantly, stamping water from his shoes.

'Luck!' said Paul. Was there no end to Rampha's good fortune? They looked bedraggled. 'Did you see that lightning?'

'Near the Lion Park.'

'Yup,' said Paul. 'It was there, alright.'

'Hey! There're Ayesha and Debbie,' said Rampha. 'Wonder how they managed to escape?' He waved to the girls standing under the veranda roof at the far end of the quad. Cupping his hands, he shouted, 'Let's grab a coke when the rain stops.' The girls waved back. Suddenly the rain increased. The torrent became a deluge.

'Those two are destined to spend the rest of the afternoon standing right there,' said Rampha, 'Any bets?'

Before Paul could retort suitably, another almighty flash more devastating than the first, exploded across the heavens.

'Wow! Definitely the Lion Park,' Paul muttered.

He wondered how animals there reacted to violent storms such as this. He thought about Soldier, the fearless Rottweiler they had when he was younger. How nervous the dog would be whenever thunder and lightning were about. He would shiver, shake and scratch at the door to get into the house, and then make a muddied paw beeline for the foot of the bed where he would remain curled up, shivering for the duration. Unfortunately, when he was fourteen years old, he contracted a rare muscular disease that crippled him. He had to be put down. Paul had wept bitterly for days after he and his father buried his beloved Soldier among the roses in the back garden.

Life was less complicated then.

Paul was passionate about three things in life, four if you counted Princess Debbie. One were his parents, two was music; three the welfare of animals. His mind was set firmly on becoming a vet or a ranger one day, or both with music as a sideline. Music would probably be his first choice if it weren't for his acne. No performer in his right mind would appear in public with a monster pimple face like his.

'Let's get changed and wait for the girls,' said Rampha.

'Okay, but I've gotta do some practicing,' Paul replied. 'Music teachers are merciless.'

'You just want to impress Debbie,' Rampha laughed. 'I know your type.'

'You should take it up,' said Paul. 'It's good for the brain.'

'And for getting girl fans, I've noticed,' said his friend. 'Besides, there's nothing wrong with my brain.'

'And all that scientific stuff you keep cramming into your head?' said Paul. 'It'll make you crazy some day. But hey! It already has.'

They hurried into their room with a wave towards the girls who ignored them as they waited for the storm to abate.

WEDNESDAY 14H35

At the Lion Park tension peaked as the intensity of the heavy storm continued unrelentingly. Hurricane force wind lashed the trees and tall grass where the young lion, amber eyes smouldering, crouched low. He was an alpha male. In a mighty territorial battle, the week before, he had defeated two older males in that very camp. He would have killed them both had Martin Resnick not intervened, separating them.

nKunzi, meaning 'bull,' a name given to him by one of the warders, remained a problem. An undisputed leader he unfortunately sometimes, without warning, presented a bad attitude despite his progress under Martin's training. Decisions for his pride were paramount and unchallenged. He could influence his females whichever way he chose.

Suddenly a brilliant mammoth flash illuminated the entire camp. The heavy electrical charge, carrying millions of volts, tore upwards through the trunk of the tallest blue gum tree, vaporizing its sap en route, ripping it in two. The lightning surged its way upward to the low cloud directly above. All oxygen in its path, consumed by the heat, formed a jagged vacuum cylinder between earth and cloud half a kilometre long and averaging three meters wide.

Time froze.

Then with a deafening roar, the surrounding air molecules crashed together to fill the void. The thunderous implosion detonated and reverberated along the valleys and hills, bouncing to the stratosphere and back. The tall blue gum tree split neatly down the middle, stood poised for a moment before the two halves plunged earthwards in opposite directions. One-half fell towards the pride as they scattered in fright. The other landed directly across the four-meter high double fence surrounding their camp. The immense weight crushed the thick steel mesh of both fences flat onto the ground, short-circuiting the Park's entire electrical system.

Almost immediately another bolt struck a smaller tree nearby searing a scorch mark along the length of its trunk. This was followed by yet another thunderous blast.

The lions were flustered. Their only instinct was to get away as quickly as possible.

Spotting a possible escape route, nKunzi in a calculated move, headed towards it. He mounted the trunk of the fallen tree, gingerly tested his weight then satisfied, crossed over the double fence to the open veld on the other side. His five females obediently followed.

They made their way through the tall grass and began searching for shelter. At last, about a kilometre further on, they came upon a cluster of bushes next to the outer perimeter fence where they lay down, huddled together.

There they waited for the storm to subside.

TWO

Woodlands Private High School situated on the outskirts of suburbia on a huge tract of land bordering the Jukskei River, was scornfully known by the learners of Government schools in the area as 'that larney rich kids' school.' The truth, however, was that parents who could afford it were ensured a solid academic foundation for their children. This almost guaranteed a tertiary follow-up.

The school's policy was to teach life skills along with the sciences, arts, and sport. Of course, discipline was vigorously enforced, and rebelliousness or sloppiness of any nature was met with stern zero tolerance. There were rules and those who would not conform were either politely asked to leave or summarily expelled. This, regardless of how well off, influential or powerful the parents were. There were no exceptions.

On the other hand, leadership and independent thinking were encouraged and nurtured with passionate dedication. Understandably there was an extremely long waiting list. Parents wishing to enrol their children would have to plan years in advance. Of course, a hefty holding deposit was also a prerequisite.

To its many other credits, Woodlands offered grants and scholarships to outstanding academic achievers from schools throughout South Africa. Regardless of the financial status of those bright sparks, every facility apart from certain luxuries was paid for and sponsored by the school. These scholarships, however, were extremely rare.

Rampha Singh was from Durban. His parents ran a highly successful factory manufacturing and distributing throughout the country, children's fashion clothing. Being an only son, it was taken for granted he would one day take over the running of the family business.

But Rampha had other ideas.

His main interest lay in the field of neurobiology and embryology. He was fascinated by the intricate way in which the human body operated; the way complex information was stored in the cells and the composition of the cells themselves. He spent hours pondering the wonders and absolute perfection of the manner in which one task of the body depended on another in order to function properly.

He marvelled at the almost impossible concept of how human memory was stored and recalled in an instant at the whim of its owner. This was really what held Rampha's attention. Memory was his passion.

He conducted endless experiments with his own memory, soaking up volumes of information, some relevant, some not. He would set out deliberately scanning a mundane subject then checking back to see how much of it he remembered. His recall was almost without flaw and instantaneous.

Thus it was that he suggested to his father he should apply for a scholarship to Woodlands Private High School.

'It's my gateway to UCT,' he told his father.

'But you don't need a scholarship,' Mr Annan Singh had objected. 'I can afford to pay for any school in the country. I just can't understand why you want to leave Durban and go to Johannesburg, the biggest crime centre in the world.'

'Come on Dad,' Rampha sighed. 'There's crime everywhere, even here.'

'Your father has worked very hard to give us a good living,' his mother cajoled, 'and who do you think is going to run the business if you leave? Your father will want to retire someday.' Her voice was gentle.

'I want to study medicine Mom, you know that.' Rampha put his slim arms around her ample waist and his head on her breast.

'Yes I know,' she said. She put her arms around him. She was proud of her son and wanted only the best for him. She sighed. Perhaps time had come to let go a little.

The following few months the idea took hold.

He would be allowed to go, provided he obtained a scholarship from Woodlands. Rampha effortlessly sailed through his grade ten exams at the end of that year, obtaining distinctions in all subjects with a ninety-eight percent aggregate. He won the scholarship with flying colours and was hastily and gratefully accepted into Woodlands with open arms.

He arrived with all his belongings and favourite possessions stuffed into his backpack. After the paperwork was dealt with, he hastily took leave of his parents and was shown his dormitory, which he was to share with Paul Patterson. It did not take too long for the two, both only children, to form a strong, bonding friendship. They become inseparable, like the brothers each longed for.

A few weeks later, on Rampha's sixteenth birthday his parents sent him to a motorcycle dealer to select a bike for himself. He chose a metallic blue Suzuki 250. It soon became his most prized possession. He, with Paul as a passenger, often took to the open road whenever a legitimate opportunity presented itself. Sometimes, a clandestine excursion would also be necessary, such as sneaking out for a midnight snack.

WEDNESDAY 16H15

Joseph Dube, the Induna game warden, made the discovery. It was his duty to keep a check on the lions in the southern camp. The tall, muscular Zulu had immediately driven back to the office.

'Boss,' he said a little out of breath. 'There's a tree fallen over the fence in Camp five and n'Kunzi and his females are not there.'

'You sure?' Resnick wanted to know.

'All six are out.'

'Okay, call the rest of the team and get back here fast. I'll have to report it first.' With a sinking feeling, he picked up the phone.

John Faber, the Lion Park's acting CEO answered right away. He was an outsider hired by the owners to put a computerised financial system in place. Since arriving however, he had somehow wrangled his way into positions not even vaguely connected to his brief. At their first meeting, he had insisted Martin Resnick and others report directly to him in all matters, however small. Resnick intended to speak to the owners but to date he had simply never found the time. It was a dilemma.

Resnick told him the situation and assured him the lions would be contained within the outer perimeter fence. 'And, Mr Faber,' Resnick grimly appealed to him, 'no media, please. We'll find them first, and then issue a press release afterwards, *if* necessary, okay?'

John Faber, an ambitious young man with an eye for business, had other ideas. Since he made the decisions, the buck stopped with him. The mileage this publicity would harvest was too good to be discarded. It was an unexpected bonus.

Besides, didn't Resnick say the lions were contained within the confines of the Park? Their capture would be a simple matter and sooner rather than later they would be returned to camp. There did not seem to be any real danger. What possible harm could there be in a little free publicity? He was not too sure which pride had escaped, but he hoped they were not the breeders. He was short of a few cubs for tourist petting even though that goody-two-shoes Resnick was against the practice. Tourists loved getting their pictures taken petting the babies even if it meant separating them from their mothers before they were properly weaned. Often the mothers rejected those cubs, but that was okay. Of course, Resnick was never to know their ultimate destiny once they became full-grown lions.

After banging down the receiver, Martin Resnick instructed his two deputies to throw out some raw bait and search the immediate surroundings.

He called Joseph to one side. 'Fetch the dart guns, some syringes and come with me.'

They drove out in the pouring rain to the southern camp to inspect the broken fence. The two men gazed at the damage as Resnick thought about where to begin. A whole lot was at stake here, including his job.

WEDNESDAY 16H30

The four friends sat together among other students in the prep room. They had to shout to be heard above the heavy clatter and patter on the green Chromadek roof. A general hubbub ensued. Outside small lakes were forming on the level, trimmed lawns between the paved walkways joining the various buildings.

'Should be over in about two hours,' said Rampha. He looked up from his seventh edition of Prescott.

'Think so?' challenged Paul. 'Bet your five bucks back it won't.' He grinned at the girls opposite. They rolled their eyes and sighed in unison.

'Are you two *ever* going to grow up?' Debbie tossed back her blonde ponytail and smiled. When she did that, her face lit up, and Paul's knees became jelly.

'How can you bet on the weather?' She looked at Paul. There was that half smile again. He lifted his hand to hide the bottom of his face.

She was definitely the best looker in school. No, make that the Universe. Also the most sought after prize. She had a no-nonsense head on her shoulders and made it clear she was not available. Paul's heart pumped custard at the thought that she deemed even to talk to him. He could never figure out how she could bear looking at him with those zillions of dreaded blemishes covering his face. But in spite of his looks she seemed to enjoy his company. That he occupied this most envious position did zero for his low self-esteem.

'Boys,' said Ayesha. Her black marble eyes shone beneath long lashes. 'What do they know?'

'Rampha's just lucky, that's all.' Paul glanced at his watch. Four thirty. 'Let's grab the headlines and the weather,' he said. Anything to detain Princess Debbie a little longer.

'Good idea.' She got up and turned on the radio.

TV viewing and radio listening were allowed after supper between six-thirty and eight- thirty except for specified learning channels which were available for revision before any test or exam.

'…and that is the end of the news headlines,' said the announcer.

'Such timing,' smiled Debbie with a flourish and a lilt in her Angel voice. 'We ladies are so perfect, don't you think?'

You have no idea, thought Paul. The others cheered.

'…and now for a look at the weather for the rest of today and tomorrow …'

'Shshshshsh …' said Ayesha.

'…with more dense clouds gathering over Johannesburg and Pretoria, it seems likely that heavy rains are set to continue well into the night spreading throughout the region tomorrow.'

Rampha held out his hand. 'Okay, I will say this only once. It'll be over within two hours. Bet?'

Paul extended his arm for a fist handshake. 'Five bucks says it rains all night.'

He looked at Ayesha. 'Witness?' She rolled her eyes.

'Okay,' said Rampha, tapping his watch. 'Two hours.'

'You're both crazy,' said Debbie. She shut her book with a sharp bang. 'I'm outta here.'

Paul's heart sank. 'Aw, you guys could at least wait till I've won my bet,' he said. It sounded like begging.

'So you can splurge your winnings on us?' Ayesha began packing her books. 'I could do with some decadent dark chocolate.' She took their two umbrellas from the stand. 'Come, Debs, let's make a dash for it.' She tossed one to her friend. They made for the door.

'May I open thine brolly, Lady Ayesha,' said Rampha leaping up. He opened the door with exaggerated gestures. Ayesha fluttered her eyelids. 'Perchance the gallant Sir Galahad wouldst, like brave the elements for poor little me?'

'Gladly, forsooth,' said Rampha. He bowed low. 'Besides, methinks I don't have one of me own.' Ayesha took a swipe at him. He ducked with a laugh.

JUSTICE OF THE WILD   Michael Du Preez

'…and we interrupt this bulletin with an urgent news flash,' declared the radio.

'Wait,' called Paul. Everyone became quiet.

'…Earlier this afternoon,' came the announcement, 'during one of the worst electrical storms to hit the area, six lions were reported missing from their camp at the Lion Park. The animals managed to escape from their enclosure when a tree, struck by lightning, damaged the surrounding fence.

Paul looked at his friend. 'I knew it was there.'

Rampha nodded. They exchanged anxious glances and listened.

'However, officials from the Lion Park have assured the public that the lions are thought to be safely contained within the outside perimeter fence of the Park. A strong warning has been issued that under no circumstances should any person try to approach the lions if sighted near the fence. They are dangerous. Anyone spotting them should immediately contact the nearest police station or phone the Lion Park direct. The number is 011-460 1814.'

Debbie grabbed a pencil and her notebook and jotted it down. Rampha memorized it.

'A spokesperson for the Lion Park,' continued the announcer, 'stated that a hunt is in progress and experts are combing the Park area. They are expected to recover the lions shortly, although heavy rains are said to be hampering operations. That is the end of this news flash, and we turn to …'

Debbie turned off the radio. 'Wow, how about that?' Excitement gushed through the room.

Ayesha linked her slender arm through Rampha's. 'I now *insist* that you walk me to my room.'

'That's rich,' Rampha said. 'Meaning should we meet those man-eaters, I would be the one to like provide their dinner?' The girls giggled.

'You're all skin and bone,' Debbie tucked her notebook into her satchel. 'Not much of a meal there.'

'Just think of it,' said Paul, 'they could easily be lurking around here.'

'Na!' Rampha turned to his friend. 'You heard what he said. There's a perimeter fence around the park. They'll catch them pretty soon.'

'Bet?' Paul's quip fell flat. He could not for the life of him remember anything being said about a perimeter fence. But he knew better than to challenge his friend.

Ayesha hooked the umbrella handle around Rampha's neck. 'Come,' she pulled him to the door. 'Let's go.' They left together.

Debbie fiddled with her umbrella as she turned to Paul.

'What?' he said.

'You haven't been yourself lately Paul, what's wrong?

He looked down. 'It's nothing,' He saw the soft look in her deep, blue, Angel eyes. 'Shall we go?' He got up feeling like a triple-clumsy lummox.

Paul was tall for his age and slim. He wore dark brown hair draped carelessly over his head with a fringe that half-covered his forehead.

She moved gracefully to the door blocking his exit and turned facing him. Also tall for her age, Debbie looked up confronting him, her eyes unflinching.

'You're not leaving till you tell me.'

'What's there to tell?' He felt his colour rising.

'It's your folks, isn't it?'

Paul's shoulders sagged.

'They're probably going to, you know, go their own... er, um ..separate ways.'

'That's terrible,' said Debbie gently.

'Yeah, I really don't know what to do about it.' Paul's gray eyes took on a haunted look. 'And I'm sure I'm partly to blame.' His features reflected the anguish and awkwardness he felt.

'Oh?' Debbie looked alarmed.

'Well, with my Dad being retrenched and our finances not being as they should, I know it's been a bit of a struggle to keep me here. My Mom simply doesn't earn enough.' Suddenly all his frustrations came pouring out. He hated himself for spilling his guts to this marvellous and most beautiful Princess. What an idiotic loser he was.

But Debbie listened sympathetically.

During the next few minutes, she learned that Bernard Patterson had been forced to leave his company as a CFO due to the economic downturn, cost-cutting, and other more sinister issues. He was virtually unemployable. His age was against him, and the only job he had known was the one he lost. Granted, he had been offered a package, but that was hardly enough to see the family through the current year.

Martha Patterson, the only brave remaining breadwinner, was doing typing for a number of small one-man operations. Her income was barely enough to cover household expenses.

Their contented relationship became tarnished a few weeks after Paul arrived at Woodlands when after a row, she moved in with her mother in Cape Town leaving his father alone at the house.

'You mustn't blame yourself,' Debbie tugged gently at Paul's sleeve. 'Perhaps your Dad will snap out of it. Just give him time.'

'That's just it. The longer I'm here, the more it's costing,' said Paul with a stiff smile. He wished the earth would swallow him.

'We all know about that,' said Debbie. After a long silence, she said, 'Things will turn, you'll see.'

He swallowed and sighed deeply. 'We'll see what happens.' She was, without a doubt, a Highly Royal Princess from outer space and not from Planet Earth. 'I'll walk you.'

They strode in silence. At her room, Debbie turned and faced him.

'Are we on for practice on Friday?' she asked.

'Wouldn't miss it for the universe,' said Paul. He was not much of a reader, but his piano playing had improved dramatically since accompanying her on violin. She was right up there with dexterity and reading. Apart from the extreme privilege of sharing her company, practicing together he found the block in his sight-reading melting to newfound freedom. He could now even put some expression into the pieces. Thanks to this Incredible Creature named Debbie White.

THREE

WEDNESDAY 16H45

His shiny bald head flung right back, Brett van Jaarsveld's Adam's apple bobbed up and down as he drained the dregs of his beer. Crushing the can, he tossed it carelessly into the plastic bin on the floor next to him. It clattered noisily against four other empties as he reached for the last one in the pack.

'Six lions,' he said popping open the can and looking hard at the picture of the lion. 'That's worth a couple of grand,' he took a long swig, swallowed and belched. '…in lovely hard cash.'

'Ja, but we've got to catch them first,' came a very high-pitched reply.

'That's your job, Tiny.' Brett's words were beginning to slur. 'Mine's to get the clients. Now shut up and fetch me another six-pack. I wanna watch the rugby.'

'Okay, Okay.' The owner of the vocal tenor clef rose and glided to the kitchen where the beer was kept. He had to stoop as he passed through the doorway, his huge head narrowly missing the top.

Tiny Terblanche was immense, his round baby-face out of proportion to the rest of him. Half as wide as he was tall he carried no fat. He was simply a huge hunk of solid muscle from head to toe. Despite his incredible size, he moved with the smooth grace of a leopard. He was a born hunter with a formidable reputation.

Stories of his exploits circulated reverently amongst the poaching and hunting fraternity. He was once said to have captured a fully-grown warthog with his bare hands and carried it, screeching and struggling, into a caged truck. This story and others like it were debated, retold, embroidered on, enhanced, inflated and deified over many cans of beer, hard tack and shooters around campfires in the bush. Big game addicts on safari with Tiny were humbled by his staggering talent. He was hunting's recognized King. The Boss, the Chairman of the Board, he reigned supreme.

But as he returned like an obedient, snivelling servant with the six-pack he felt once again the familiar, growing prickle of resentment the way Brett spoke to him. Especially of late. Just who the hell did he think he was anyhow?

Tiny slammed the six-pack on the table next to Brett. He tore open the plastic and took one for himself

'We'll have to move quickly if we want to find them before those Park guys,' he said, contemplating whether or not to open the can. He never liked drinking before a hunt. He preferred to keep his wits about him, his instincts sharp.

'In this rain?' Brett sneered, 'Never.' He opened another can and took a gulp as he thought for a moment. 'They could be hiding close to the outer fence. I can feel it in my bones,' he said with alcoholic conviction. 'We'll wait till it gets dark then we'll go get 'em.'

Feel it in his bones, thought Tiny coldly, huh! What garbage. And the Royal We? Who was the hunter around here anyhow? What Brett knew about hunting was dangerous. He was far too sure of himself and everyone knew in the bush such conceit spelled disaster. Whose idea anyhow was it to make an opening in the outer perimeter fence of the Park last year and conceal it with undergrowth?

His. Tiny's.

And hadn't they scored a couple of ostriches and a few buck over the past couple of weeks from his idea and his efforts?

His. Not Brett's.

'I don't think we should wait,' Tiny insisted. 'If they hunt down one of the bucks there, there's no chance if they're not hungry.'

Brett could think of no suitable argument to put down Tiny further. He took another long swig and stood up shakily. 'Okay, okay.'

'I'll go and get some bait ready,' said Tiny. He put down his unopened can and headed for the outside door.

'Yeah,' muttered Brett, 'you do that. I'll call Japie for the forklift.'

Always the last word, Tiny thought. He swallowed his rising anger. One day is one day.

He walked outside towards the sheep pen. The rain stung his face and within seconds the flimsy black T-shirt he was wearing was saturated, as were his jeans. He never minded the rain. It was part of nature. He enjoyed the discomfort. He hated being encumbered with rainwear or any other creature comforts. It made you soft, and the law of the bush was survival of the strongest.

What he did know was exactly how to lure those lions out of the Park into an area where they could be captured. In the process, they would have to sacrifice the last two of six lambs they usually kept in reserve. They needed to restock the sheep pen sometime soon.

WEDNESDAY 17H00

Japie van Rensburg lived on his own on a smallholding a few kilometers from Birdhaven. He had just finished eating leftover stew when the TV in the workshop made the announcement. He sucked his fingers, wiped them on his overall and ducked under the bonnet once more. It was a Toyota, obviously well looked after. Funny, he thought, how ignorant people were when it came to their cars. To him, it was a simple matter of listening then tracing the fault and repairing it. There was no make of car, nor any mechanical problem Japie could not diagnose and fix. He loved cars. He even had all the equipment to do panel beating for insurance companies who paid on the spot.

Brett knew all that. He also knew about Japie's past. Stripping stolen cars for parts was the only way a man could earn a decent living back then. He had given most of that up and gone legitimate. Except for the occasional chop job, he kept on the straight and narrow. But Brett was a dangerous man without loyalty and would not hesitate to bring Japie down.

Of course, he would be calling any moment to borrow the forklift. That meant the operator as well, namely him, Japie van Rensburg. He would be exposed and as much in danger as the two of them.

As it was, when they poached a rhino for its horn a few years back, it was his job to load the animal and cart it to a different location to butcher it. They just managed to avoid the Rangers then, but it was touch and go.

Japie wished he did not have to be involved with them. But Brett paid well, and he could hardly afford to throw away good money.

The phone rang. Japie sighed.

WEDNESDAY 17H15

Although it was still raining buckets, the lightning and thunder had abated slightly. The young lion rose slowly, looked around and headed east along the inside perimeter fence. One by one his five females followed perfectly concealed in the tall grass.

Suddenly his senses became alerted. He assumed a hunting attitude. He put his nose closer to the ground and sniffed.

Fresh blood.

He followed the scent that led him to Tiny's opening under the perimeter fence. It had been carved bigger by the floodwater and was adequate for a grown lion to pass through.

The whole pride was now in hunting mode. They made their way in single file out of the Park's confines and followed the blood trail across the seldom-used tar road into the open veld on the other side. There the thatch grass was taller. About five hundred meters further on, with the fresh scent of wounded prey persistent in his nostrils, the leader slackened his pace.

They now found themselves in ideal grassy terrain. This would provide them with far more cover and space than before. Soon it would be dark. Conditions were ideal for the hunt. Lions hunted best in the dark.

Feeding time was long past, and they were hungry, stimulated by the promise of an exciting chase and a clean kill. They spread out in preparation for the way they hunted best.

They would ambush their prey.

FOUR

WEDNESDAY 17H30

'They can't be too far, Boss,' said Joseph. 'You know what they're like. They'll want to return. This is their territory.'

Martin Resnick doubted that. His eyes searched the ground on the other side of the fence. 'Maybe we can still pick up some tracks.'

Joseph had already stepped onto the fallen tree trunk and had made his way over the flattened fence. It was the most obvious escape route. Bending low he scanned the long grass for any signs.

'No tracks. They're all washed away,' he shouted, getting up. 'What do we do now?'

'I think we should separate and walk around the outside of the camp fence. See if we can find anything.' Resnick started through the long grass. 'After that, we'll take a trip around the outer fence.'

'Okay Boss,' Joseph said. 'Don't worry we'll find them.'

Yeah, we'd better, he thought. 'See you back here in about half an hour. If you see them, dart them right away then come and call me. And for Pete's sake, Joseph be careful.'

They set off in opposite directions. Martin Resnick made his way around the five adjoining inner lion enclosures. He wondered if the animals might stick close to the fence thinking they were still in their camp. That would be luck.

The going was difficult. The uneven terrain was strewn with potholes and rocks. The storm had increased, and he could see no more than a few meters ahead of him. It was an impossible situation. A properly organized search would have to be undertaken later.

It took just under thirty minutes to circumvent his half of the camp. When he reached the halfway point, he found Joseph approaching from the other side.

'Nothing?' he asked. Joseph shook his head.

'Let's get back then. It's getting dark.' They walked back over the broken fence to the van.

'We'll have to put together an organized hunt and scan the perimeter fence,' he said. 'Let's get back to the office.' He started the van and headed back.

As they approached the office buildings, his heart sank. Martin Resnick saw to his dismay that the media had already arrived. Activity was in full swing. Outside it was not yet completely dark, but emergency generators had kicked in, and lights were blazing everywhere. Two TV outside broadcast vans and several police cars were parked next to the restaurant.

Inside, scores of people – cameramen, reporters, police, park officials, game rangers and technical staff were being accommodated at

36

the many tables that had become temporary workstations. Extra staff had been summoned to provide continuous supplies of coffee, tea, and other refreshments.

John Faber's work, no doubt.

His anger rose. He walked into the building to be confronted by two men.

'Mr Resnick?' A big man with a friendly face and a wide mouth stretched out his hand.

'I'm Captain Norvel Peterson from the Security Branch, and this is Sergeant Thomas M'lapha.' The bulky Tswana man his extended hand and gave Resnick the African handshake.

'Mr Faber phoned, and we came as quickly as we could,' Peterson continued. 'Can we discuss this somewhere, please?'

'Yes,' said Resnick. 'And who brought these news vultures here?' he demanded as he led the way to his office.

'Mr Faber and I decided we couldn't put the safety of the public at risk,' said Peterson, taking a seat opposite him. 'So we took the liberty of asking the SABC to broadcast a bulletin, and they kindly agreed.'

I'll bet they did, thought Resnick. They would sell their mothers for a sensational story like this. He was highly annoyed.

John Faber never consulted with him on important issues. He always seemed to be busy at meetings or other time-consuming activities, some of which, Resnick was convinced, were sinister. He could never quite put his finger on it. But the vague answers, Faber gave him when questioned about some of the older lions' relocation, were evasive. But when credits were due, oh boy, Mr John 'Big Deal' Faber would elbow his way to the front of the queue and greedily scoop the kudos.

'This is pretty bad publicity,' Resnick said shaking his head. 'Furthermore, all these nosey reporters out there will only hamper our search.

'Can't be helped.' Peterson's tone was firm. 'Public safety comes first, you know.' He smiled. 'In any case, after this, you'll probably have more visitors that you can cope with. You know what people are like.'

Direct from the mouth of John Faber, no doubt.

'Look,' said Resnick. 'There's no immediate danger. They can't escape from the outer enclosure. The whole place is secure, and we were just about to organize a search.'

'We're here only to help,' said Captain Peterson soothingly. 'Now then,' he said. 'I'm told that lions never stray very far from their own environment or territory. Is this true?'

Great! Suddenly the whole police force and its brother had become wildlife experts, Martin thought savagely. He glared at Peterson but kept his voice even.

'A lion is a clever animal, Captain Peterson, and they have very strong instincts for their own territory, but you can never tell what they'll do next. They're extremely unpredictable.'

'Were they fed before this happened?' sergeant M'lapha asked.

'No, they weren't. They're used to eating once every four to five days and by now they're probably ravenous. So it's likely that they might hunt down one of our buck out there. It's happened before.'

'You mean they've escaped before?'

'No, it was during one of our outings.' Martin Resnick noted with satisfaction the alarm spreading across the men's faces. 'We take them on walks now and again and nKunzi, he's the male who's missing, decided to test his hunting skills on one of our wildebeest.'

The policeman's eyes opened wide. 'Huh?'

'He pulled him down, too.'

'Was he hungry?'

'Not really, just acting on instinct. We couldn't stop him.'

'Hungry lions even …er, sort of tame ones are probably more dangerous then?' ventured Captain Peterson, tentatively.

'Captain Peterson,' Martin Resnick leaned forward towards the policeman. He could hardly contain his rising temper. 'All lions *are* dangerous, hungry or otherwise. Don't think that these animals here at the Park are tame. In fact, our lions are doubly dangerous. They've lost their fear of man. These creatures act only on instinct, and they won't hesitate to attack if they're hungry or riled or simply in a bloody bad mood.' he snapped. 'Which they probably are, right now!'

He got up and moved towards the door. His mind was in turmoil. He was not about to reveal that n'Kunzi's pride were the very ones he was busy training for a possible movie performance. They were invaluable.

'I didn't mean to sound patronizing,' said the Captain.' I'm really not used to chasing lions around the countryside.'

'No, I didn't think you were,' He immediately regretted the sarcasm. He nodded towards the door. 'Sorry. It's those sharks out there.'

'No offence.' The Captain stood up. 'How about putting out some bait to lure them back?'

'I've already instructed my guys to do that,' sighed Resnick. 'But with the rain washing away the scent, unlike a fresh kill, who knows whether they'll ever find it.'

'And live bait?' Captain Peterson asked with raised eyebrows.

Resnick looked hard at the policeman. 'Sure. And have everyone from the Anti-Cruelty League to the SPCA, to every little old lady with a parrot or a dog, breathing down my neck? No way, José. We'll find them with a proper search as soon as I've got my men together and gotten rid of that lot out there.'

'Okay, okay, I'm only a policeman.'

'Let's go face the music, issue a statement and get this debacle over with so that I can do my job and get those lions back where they belong.' He opened the door, and they went through to the restaurant.

The hubbub ceased as everybody looked up expectantly.

Martin Resnick cleared his throat nervously.

'Good afternoon, my name is Resnick,' he addressed them; 'I'm the warden in charge here.' He related the sequence of events and fielded some malicious questions from the reporters.

'The camps are constantly being checked,' concluded Resnick. 'But with the rain, not always at the same time you know. It depends on circumstances.'

'And the outer perimeter fence?' a voice called. 'Is that adequate enough to contain them within the confines of the Park?'

'Yes, it is,' said Resnick. He was worried that at the bottom, by the gully, heavy rains sometimes washed away the soil, leaving an opening underneath the perimeter fence. He needed more time to double-check that possibility from the outside, although it was highly unlikely that the lions would find such an opening by themselves.

Another reporter shouted from the back. 'Have you notified any schools and shopping centres and other public places in the area?'

'All the schools and shopping centres in the area have been notified,' put in Captain Peterson. 'In fact, teachers and students of Woodlands Private School have offered their assistance...'

A scruffy looking individual leaped up accusingly. '...which offer we have gratefully declined,' he added smoothly. The reporter sat down, deflated.

Martin nodded gratefully towards the captain.

The television crew was now ready to start shooting. The 'on the scene' presenter moved closer to Martin Resnick.

'Mr Resnick,' he said politely guiding him to a chair. 'I'm Bonani Pukwa from TV One News and I would like to ask you and Captain Peterson to outline your plan of action to recapture these missing lions.'

'I'll take over from here,' came a voice from the door.

Everyone turned as John Faber strode into the room stamping water from his shoes.

Martin Resnick looked at Captain Peterson and sighed.

It was going to be a long night.

FIVE

WEDNESDAY 17H45

At Woodlands Private High School, the learners and teachers had been urgently summoned to assemble in the gym. The headmaster, Mr Banner, adjusted his spectacles, cleared his throat as a hush settled over the audience. He was a slight man with an oval face framed by a thinning fringe over his forehead and a slim gambler's moustache. He was always immaculately dressed and had the unusual habit of neatly folding up the corner of his jacket before thrusting his hand into his pocket. It was his trademark. He was an avid pipe smoker and in his office was an amazing collection of briars on display, every one of which was well and truly smoked in.

'As you probably have heard by now,' he addressed them with his right hand neatly in his pocket. 'We have an unusual problem facing us.'

Rampha nudged Paul. 'The only unusual problem facing us is the man himself.'

'Ssh!' whispered Paul, grinning. Rampha was sooo full of it.

'As you no doubt have heard,' he repeated. 'Several lions have escaped from their enclosure at the Lion Park.'

He cleared his throat as he paused for effect. No significant response washed back. The news was already old.

'I've been in touch with the emergency sections of the Department of Education, and the Department of Nature Conservation, and of course the Lion Park,' he continued. 'All of whom feel we should carry on with most of our normal everyday activities. However, due to our close proximity the cross-country marathon, due to be run on Saturday past the Lion Park, is cancelled until further notice. In fact, all outdoor activities will terminate forthwith until these animals have been captured.' He paused to clear his throat again and a gratifying murmur spread amongst the students. He had their attention.

'Even though we have been assured by the relevant authorities that there is no immediate danger,' he continued. 'I want to issue the strongest possible warning that these animals are dangerous and because of the nature of our spread out school buildings, you are never, at any time, to walk alone from one building to the next. You should always be in groups of two or more.' He looked around at the two hundred and thirty wide-eyed youngsters. 'Although there is no possibility whatsoever that the lions are lurking anywhere near our school, in the unlikely event of a sighting you are better off in a group, as a precaution. Is that clear?'

There was a chorus of assent.

Paul looked at Rampha. 'We're joined at the hip,' he whispered. Rampha nodded.

'I should like to stress, however,' continued Mr Banner sternly, 'that there is no cause for alarm. Our school is well fenced. At the same time, this is not to be used as an excuse for any out of the ordinary behaviour.'

He cleared his throat twice in quick succession. 'Do I make myself quite clear?'

The silence was broken by shuffling feet.

'Any questions?'

A hand went up. 'Well, Sipho?'

'What if we spot the lions, Sir?'

'Good question. If any of you do happen to see any of these animals even at a distance, you are to report it immediately to the teacher on duty.'

Rampha put up his hand.

'Singh?'

'I have permission to go to the airport, Sir,' he said clearly. 'I'll be travelling on the road right past the Lion Park.'

'On your motorcycle?' asked Mr Banner. 'This late, in this rain?'

'Yes, Sir.'

'Then you'd better take someone with you, hadn't you? And be sure to be on the lookout, Singh.'

'I understand, Sir.'

'Any more questions?'

Another hand went up.

'Well, Cellini?'

Cellini was wearing his naughty face. 'What if the lions attack us in our beds, Sir?'

Mr Banner looked sharply at the boy. 'If you're afraid of that,' he paused long for the most dramatic effect. 'Then I suggest that you come and sleep on the floor in my room where I can keep an eye on you.'

Raucous laughter.

Cellini's face flushed bright scarlet.

'Now,' said the headmaster with a satisfied smirk, 'if there are no more serious questions, I suggest you all put in a few hours of solid study before lights out. You are dismissed.'

Rampha and Paul met the girls outside the gym. Ayesha, dressed in her tracksuit, fell into step beside Rampha. 'Now you'll *have* to walk us to our dorm,' she teased. 'And if we want to go anywhere, you'll have to come and fetch us. So there!'

Debbie laughed. 'We have our own like personal slaves. Just think of the countless possibilities.' The four of them walked towards the girls' dormitory.

'Slaves have got rights too, don't forget,' Paul put in darkly.

'Like being fed and clothed and pampered,' added Rampha with his devastating smile.

'Oh yes,' Ayesha returned his smile sweetly. 'We'll do that alright,' she turned to Debbie who nodded vigorously. 'Won't we?' They laughed excitedly.

They arrived at the girl's dorm in high spirits and paused for a while outside the door.

'Are you coming with me, Paul?' Rampha asked, changing the mood. 'To the airport?'

His friend nodded. He was going to start on math revision, but that would have to wait. 'You can drop me at my aunt's place in Randburg. I'll wait there for you.'

'I can just as easily take you home to your dad if you like. It's not much further.'

Paul looked uncomfortable. 'No, I'll go to my Aunt.'

'Okay,' said Rampha. 'I'm dying to see my folks. Their connection leaves at eight- thirty. I'll drop you off first, and then pick you up again on the way back. But we'll have to leave, like right away.'

'Where are they going?' Ayesha wanted to know.

'New Delhi, via London, replied Rampha. 'Just for a couple of weeks.'

'I wish I'd have known,' said Ayesha. 'We've got family there, and your folks could have taken a gift along and perhaps met them.'

Rampha regarded her for a moment, aware not for the first time, how her long black tresses bounced and settled disturbingly around her slim shoulders. 'Yeah, that could have been great,' he remarked, looking at his watch.

'Okay, so we won't keep you any longer,' said Debbie. 'Come, Ayesha.'

The boys waited politely while Ayesha unlocked the door walked in then came out smiling. 'No wild animals in there,' she declared.

Debbie giggled. 'More's the pity.'

'Okay, girls, we're off,' said Rampha. 'See you later. Goodnight.' He and Ayesha exchanged knowing looks.

'Careful you don't run into any lions on your way,' Ayesha called after them.

'On the main road?' laughed Paul. 'Not likely. 'Night.'

SIX

WEDNESDAY 18H00

Fifteen minutes later they hurried to the carport where Rampha's birthday present stood gleaming and chained to one of the pillars.

The rain had eased momentarily but looked like more was on the way. He opened the pannier on the side and took out two sets of black plastic rain suits and crash helmets. He and Paul pulled the heavy plastic over their clothes. The rain suits felt tight and awkward.

'Make sure you clip the strap under you shoes,' said Rampha.

'Okay, got it,' grunted Paul leaning over.

They pulled the red helmets over their heads and fastened the straps. Rampha mounted and button started the machine. He revved the almost silent engine and pushed the bike backwards out of the carport. He loved his bike and had passed his driver's license first time 'round.

'Hop on.'

Paul climbed on behind him, and he felt a thrill at the surge of power as they pulled off out of the school gate and turned left towards

Randburg. Heavier rain had started up again, stinging their faces as they gathered speed.

The wind whistled past their ears and tugged at their rain suits. The east end of the Lion Park was over to the left. Opposite, on the north side of the tar road lay a vast expanse of unfenced open grassland.

About a kilometre further on Rampha braked suddenly and shouted, 'Hey! Look over there!' he pointed towards the open veld.

'What is it?' Paul's eyes searched the direction where Rampha pointed.

The bike came to a halt, and Rampha put his boots on the tar for balance.

Paul followed suit as they both removed their helmets. It was raining steadily now, and darkness was slowly setting in.

'Over there!' Rampha pointed again.

Paul shifted his gaze. 'All I can see is what looks like a sheep standing near the bottom of the hill. Otherwise, nothing.'

'That's just it,' said Rampha excitedly. 'That sheep is tied to a stake. I saw it reach the end of its tether as the rope jerked it back.'

'So?' Paul was as puzzled, as he was amazed, at his friend's typical observation of the minutest detail. Rampha missed nothing.

'Don't you see?' said Rampha with growing excitement. 'That sheep could be bait for those lions.'

'But aren't they supposed to be in the Park somewhere? How could they have gotten through that fence?' He pointed to his left.

'Yup, it seems quite solid.'

'You mean they'd actually stake out a live sheep to catch them?' Paul was aghast.

'I don't know,' said Rampha. 'But one thing is for sure. That sheep out there is for one purpose only, and that's lion bait.'

He dismounted, leaving Paul to balance the bike. 'I want to take a closer look.'

'Rampha, I don't think we should,' cautioned Paul, as he too dismounted. He kicked down the foot stand and leaned the bike over. 'We might end up as lion bait ourselves. Besides, remember what old Banner said – no outdoor activities and no walking alone. *And* it's getting dark.'

They walked to the opposite side of the road where Rampha stopped and sighed deeply. 'I suppose you're right. In any case, I don't want to be late at the airport.'

'Okay,' said Paul somewhat relieved. 'Let's go.' He found it difficult to believe anyone could be so cruel, as to tie up a sheep for live bait. He felt devastated.

'Wait!' shouted Rampha excitedly, gripping his arm. 'Something's happening.'

They watched in disbelief as the field below suddenly came alive with activity. Paul gaped.

In a blur of movement, a huge tawny coloured shape appeared and charged towards the staked out sheep. The hapless animal, seeing the approach, turned tail and darted off bleating, in the opposite direction.

Neither Rampha nor Paul would ever forget what happened next.

As the sheep reached the end of the rope, it was jerked to a sudden halt. At that precise moment, a charging lioness leapt for the kill. She landed right on top of the sheep, her huge front claws embedding themselves firmly into the victim's soft woolly neck.

The lioness's momentum carried her forward, as her body swung round like the lash of a whip in front of the sheep. The force of the encounter was so great that the sheep's head was severed from its body by the rope in a spray of blood. The bleating stopped abruptly.

The boys swallowed hard.

Seconds later, from their concealment, four other lionesses, and a huge male suddenly appeared out of the surrounding grass. They circled slowly around the kill, keeping their distance from it. Then one by one they moved closer, impatiently waiting for the male to start eating.

Rampha brushed the rain from his brow. 'Amazing!' he gasped. He would not be able to eat lamb again in a hurry.

'I can't believe it,' muttered Paul. He was in a cold sweat and felt nauseous. It was savage in the extreme. A slow burning anger gripped him. It spread from within the deepest recesses of his soul.

Suddenly there was a muffled gunshot, followed by another. The lionesses leapt up looking around warily. The male stopped gorging and also looked up alarmed. His huge mouth was dripping crimson. He looked around for a while before going back to his meal.

'Those two shots,' murmured Rampha. 'Could be a dart gun, by the sound of it.'

'Yeah?' said Paul feeling sick. 'Sounded like some big rifle.'

Another two shots sounded followed by a further two shortly after. Each time the guns went off the lions would rise up, move around a bit then resume their positions once more.

'They're obviously used to gunshots. They don't seem to be too worried.'

'I wonder how long it will be before the drug takes effect,' Paul asked.

'I read somewhere about fifteen minutes.'

They watched in silence for a while. Three of the lionesses rose unsteadily and lay down, disappearing amongst the tall grass.

'They must have given them a double dose.' Rampha said, straining forward. 'They look drugged already.'

'I think you're right,' swallowed Paul. He felt terrible with a numbness that engulfed his whole being. 'To think they could be so cruel.'

'Yeah, it's cruel all right. But I suppose they were desperate to capture them. After all, there *are* plenty of people living around here.' He shook his head slowly. 'Look at that male. The size of him! I'd hate to get on his wrong side. He still seems to be eating as though nothing happened.'

'No – wait! He's stopped.'

The huge lion was beginning to sway. Then shaking his mighty head, he slowly sank to his knees and dropped out of sight.

This had no sooner happened than a large truck with an enclosed metal canopy appeared from behind a clump of bushes and backed up towards the fallen lions. Two men, one of whom was twice the size of the other, emerged from the truck carrying what looked like some kind of a stretcher. Then to their surprise, they saw a small forklift being driven towards the fallen lions. It was almost dark now, and the boys could not make out clearly what was going on. After about ten minutes the rear swing doors of the truck were closed. The delayed bang reached their ears a few seconds later. Shortly after, the vehicle pulled off and disappeared among some bushes.

'Wow, excitement over,' breathed Rampha. 'Captured lions back to their boring life at the Park.'

'And don't forget one sacrificed lamb,' said Paul, pulling on his helmet with trembling hands. He was shocked such tactics were considered necessary by so-called civilized human beings.

'Let's hit the road, you've got a plane to meet,' Paul said in a hoarse whisper. He felt weak and badly shaken.

They were soon heading towards Randburg. The rain started to beat down heavily once more.

WEDNESDAY 18H45

Tiny was satisfied with the four lions they had captured. With Japie van Rensburg's forklift, they should have captured all six. But Brett in his drunken state had spoiled it all. There was not enough time to search for the other two. Chances were they had not been seen, but you don't push your luck. Prison would finish him. Tiny belonged in the bush.

Not so with Brett. He thought about how the man had changed over the years. From a slim, enthusiastic young athlete, he had turned into an alcoholic, fat slob.

Those were the good old days. They had both worked as independent poachers who sold their catches to game farms for cash.

Tiny recalled how they first met at a game farm in the Northern Province where they both arrived on the same day at the same game farm with their catches.

'I don't buy poached animals,' said the game farmer as he regarded the two poachers with suspicion. The charade had to be played out.

'My cheetah is not poached,' said Brett. 'She's from my farm.'

'Oh yeah?' The game farmer said. He turned to Tiny. 'And I suppose you caught your cheetah on your farm too?

Tiny shuffled his feet with embarrassment. He found it difficult to lie. 'I don't have a farm,' he said.

The two cheetahs looked in good condition. 'Okay,' said the game farmer. He could spot an easy target when he saw one. 'Here's what I'm prepared to do,' he pointed to Tiny. 'You come with me.'

Tiny followed to his office in the house. The game farmer opened a drawer on his desk and pulled out a wad of notes. 'I'll give you five hundred for yours.'

'Five hundred?' said Tiny. He would have gladly taken three.

'Okay,' said the game farmer. 'Six hundred not a penny less.'

What??

Later when Tiny and Brett were ready to go their separate ways, Brett called him to one side. He was furious. 'You sold for six hundred? These cheetahs are worth more than double that,' he sneered. 'I'll teach you about prices.'

Thus over the years a loose partnership was formed. They often worked together for mutual benefit.

Brett first came up with the idea of starting a 'canned hunting' game farm.

'Not like the luxury game lodges common to South Africa,' he said. 'But the sort of place where clients could experience raw bush living.'

The problem was it would take an enormous amount of money, which neither of them possessed except for Tiny's meagre life's savings.

Brett approached the Government of Botswana and managed to rent some twenty thousand acres of bush just over the northern border of South Africa. They convinced the authorities that the land would be used as a retreat for tourists wanting to get away from civilization to 'find' themselves. It would also possibly generate revenue for the host country.

The contract was for five years with a renewal of a further ten years upon review. Of course, a small sum unofficially changed hands to secure the deal.

Game that occurred naturally in that region was plentiful, and they set about building their farm. Using up all Tiny's reserves, they built several rondavels of wattle and daub in the true African hut tradition. Some of the rooms had inter-leading passages ideal for larger groups of hunter tourists. The roofs were decked with thatch grass that grew in abundance all around.

The structures were designed to appeal to overseas visitors who wanted to rough it. Their idea of true African bush living.

The operation proved a success from the start. Brett would solicit bookings from numerous overseas hunters' associations. He and Tiny would then poach whatever additional animals they needed for the safari. These were then smuggled back to the farm in their truck, custom built to their specifications by Japie van Rensburg. Once offloaded the poached animals would be placed into several small fenced camps, well out of sight of the living quarters.

When hunting parties arrived in Johannesburg, Brett would travel south to fetch them. Upon their return, while the tourists settled into their rustic accommodation, Tiny would tranquilize the animals to be hunted and herd them to various outlying camps a few kilometres from the base. There they would be released into the bush after being sedated a second time for good measure.

He would then return to base, pick up the hunting party and set off on a long, complicated detour through the bush. He would allow them to 'spot' the game. After a brief period of stalking, the clients would shoot the semi-dazed animals. Tiny would return their customers to camp for a rough bush barbeque and good night's rest before being taken back to Johannesburg.

After being processed and stuffed, trophies of heads and skins would be sent off to customers' overseas residences, paid for, with an upfront cash deposit and balance on delivery.

Canned hunting was a highly profitable business.

Three years later, Brett made enough money to buy a seven-acre smallholding in Birdhaven, an expensive area lying north of Johannesburg five kilometres from the Lion Park.

Tiny could never understand why he had not made the equivalent amount. Maybe it had something to do with the way Brett did the books. Tiny was not an accountant. He could never figure out the expenses and the many other items that had to be paid, according to Brett. He always seemed to be out of pocket. This was also one of the reasons he stuck close to Brett. He had to protect his own interests.

SEVEN

WEDNESDAY 22H15

The boys arrived back at Woodlands. They waved at Thuli, the night watch, as they entered the school grounds. Rampha switched off the engine and coasted the bike to the carport. He was always careful not to make too much noise, especially past the dormitories.

'See you later,' he murmured after they had put away the rain suits, the helmets and secured the motorcycle.

'Ayesha?' Paul asked.

Rampha nodded. 'I told her I'd let her know when we got back.'

'Against the rules, Rampha,' Paul warned him.

'Just a tap on the window, that's all,' laughed Rampha, 'I never go in.'

'No,' said Paul. 'I meant about us going in pairs.'

Rampha looked at him. 'Anyhow, we know that doesn't apply anymore. The lions have been caught. You saw it with your own eyes.'

'I guess.' Paul was tired after all the excitement and was looking forward to a nice hot shower and then to bed. 'See you later.'

Just as he was about to enter the dormitory, a voice called out, 'Patterson!'

Paul's heart flipped a backward summersault. It was Mr Banner with Mr Lister, doing their nightly patrol.

'You're not supposed to be out alone,' said Mr Banner, his voice edgy.

'I know, Sir.'

'Well?'

'We thought that it would be okay now the lions are caught, Sir.'

'Caught? I'm not aware of this,' Mr Banner turned to Mr Lister. 'Are you?'

'Not to my knowledge,' replied Mr Lister. He looked at Paul. 'Where exactly did you obtain this information?'

'We saw it happening, Sir.' Paul looked from one man to the other. They were obviously puzzled but could see he was serious.

'What do you mean, you saw it happen?' Mr Banner wanted to know.

'Earlier, on our way out, Rampha – er, I mean Singh and I saw the lions being drugged and captured,' Paul began.

'What?' Mr Lister was incredulous. 'Where was this? When?'

'Quite close to the Lion Park, Sir. On the opposite side across the road.'

'You mean the lions were outside the Park? What time, Patterson?' demanded Mr Banner

'I'm really not sure, Sir, but I suppose it was about three and a half hours ago, Sir.'

The Principal considered this for a moment. 'Well, as we have not been officially notified,' he said, 'all the rules are to remain in force until further notice. Understand, Patterson?'

'Yes, Sir' said Paul, hoping they were not going to ask where Rampha was. 'Is that all, Sir?'

'For now, Patterson. I'll contact the Lion Park to confirm. And for Pete's sake keep this to yourselves until the whole thing has been officially announced. Goodnight.' The men turned and hurried away.

Paul breathed a sigh of relief as he entered the dorm. He badly needed a shower. He kept on seeing that poor sheep being torn apart by the lion. It was savagely barbaric. That Park officials would resort to such extreme measures was nothing less than criminal. It was a mighty cold-blooded and uncivilized action.

His anger mounted.

He felt mildly better after the shower. As he climbed into bed, he wondered why Rampha was taking so long. He hoped Banner and Lister hadn't confronted him too. The warmth of the blankets slowly relaxed him and his mind wandered back to his aunt in Randburg where Rampha dropped him earlier.

Aunt Hester was a tall, slim blonde woman with short boyish hair and a kind face. Paul told her about their grizzly experience. He related how they saw the lions being captured. She listened sympathetically as he greedily polished off a second generous helping of homemade apple crumble. As any good aunt would do, Hester baked often and kept a ready supply especially for Paul's occasional visits.

He felt predictably sick afterwards. He excused himself and only barely made it to the bathroom. When he returned he felt a whole lot better but his stomach hurt and his acne flared.

After a while, she asked. 'And what have you heard from your Father, Paul?'

Paul swallowed. Bottled up emotions welled up as tears stung his eyes. For a moment he was unable to answer. Aunt Hester got up, put her arms around him and hugged him. 'It's okay,' she said softly. 'I understand what you're going through, Pauly.'

'It's not as if Dad doesn't care for me. I know he does. So does Mom. It's just that I hate the thought of them wanting to … you know …' He could never bring himself to say the dreaded 'divorce' word.

'You know Paul, you mustn't worry about something that may never happen.' She poured more tea. 'Your Dad and Mom are going through a tough time right now. Your father's work was his whole life. I'm sure he feels superfluous right now and vulnerable.'

Vulnerable? Thought Paul. Not his Dad. He was as solid as a rock. Or, had Aunt Hester perhaps touched a nerve? Paul had never looked on his Dad as anything but this strong, invincible superhuman hero. A tough guy was his Dad. One who could handle any trouble that came along? It was a disturbing thought that he might be merely a vulnerable human being. The idea never before occurred to him. But Aunt Hester was positive things would come right.

Just like Princess Debbie.

Now as he drifted into sleep the last image in his mind was of the three of them. He saw his Mom and Dad and himself, splashing each other in their swimming pool at home and having hilarious fun watching Soldier running around the edge, barking hysterically. It was such a warm, fuzzy feeling.

So comforting.

EIGHT

WEDNESDAY 22H30

Martin Resnick paced his office at the Lion Park. His three deputies stood by waiting for further instructions. They were soaking wet and dishevelled but ready for action.

The television crew and reporters had packed up. John Faber announced he had other matters to attend to, and he too had left.

Earlier Martin had called together his two most experienced wardens and the young guest trainee. They had gone out in the rain to search once again. Where the terrain was not suitable for their Jeep, they had proceeded on foot all around the inside of the perimeter fence. The other animals and possible prey, like the buck and the giraffes, seemed to be all there, unharmed and accounted for. After three hours the drenched party returned to base, unsuccessful and mystified.

'I simply don't understand it,' said Resnick, peeling off his soggy raincoat and draping it over the filing cabinet. 'We've been over the entire camp from the inside, and there's no sign of them. They seem to have simply disappeared.' He blew into his hands. He was reasonably sure that one of them at least would have spotted the animals even though a lion could hide quite easily in the long grass.

How many times before had he searched high and low for a lioness in the enclosure, only to find her close by, deliberately hiding in the long grass? They were masters of deception and camouflage. But a gnawing feeling in the pit of his stomach clung to him like honey to bread. It seeped into his tired brain urging him to consider the one remaining possibility.

One that did not bear thinking about.

He finally made the decision and got up. 'Let's go check the fence from the outside. There, by that gully.'

'Do you think…?' Joshua began.

'No time for that, let's go!' He decisively grabbed his raincoat and hurried out.

The four of them sped, in silence, out of the Park's gates; turning right onto the tar road. Arriving at the spot where the culvert was, they got out and approached the fence. The culvert, usually dry where the fence crossed over it, was now a raging torrent. Shining his powerful torch into the culvert, Resnick looked down with a sinking feeling.

The storm water had carved a deep ravine under the fence which was not visible from the inside. Sure enough there, on the far bank in the mud, were distinct, water-filled pugmarks heading out of the camp, towards the road.

He swore as they crossed over the road and tried to follow the faint track remnants into the tall grass on the other side. In the pouring rain, it proved futile.

An hour later they returned empty-handed to the office at the Park.

'It's impossible, in the dark, and we can't wait until it gets light.' Resnick said. 'By then, they could have migrated to heaven knows where.'

'Those tracks we found looked promising,' put in Joseph.

'True,' agreed Resnick, but with the rain, they were fast vanishing.

'And those two pairs of tire tracks coming out of the bush, further up?' Joseph looked at the others. 'They were fresh. What about them?'

Resnick got up and helped himself to a cup of coffee from the flask on his desk. He was reluctant even to go there. But it had to be considered and dealt with. He turned to Joshua.

'Someone else must have found them. Otherwise, what were two vehicles doing, coming out of the veld onto the road in the middle of the night, in this rain? As Joseph said, those tire tracks were very fresh.' He looked from one man to the other, perplexed.

They were silent as they considered the possibilities.

'It would have to be someone who knows what they're doing,' he continued after a while. 'To capture one lion is difficult enough …. but six?' He shook his head. 'No, that would be impossible.'

'So some of them could still be out there hiding somewhere,' said Danny Els, the youngest in the team, speaking for the first time. He was a student at Grahamstown University and was working at the Lion Park during the holidays as part of his practical. He was twenty-one and the least experienced.

Resnick sighed. 'I'm going to call Captain Peterson and set up a search.'

Just then the phone rang.

'Resnick,' he said grabbing the receiver, 'Yes, this is the Lion Park.' He listened, and his jaw tightened. 'What was that? When?'

The three wardens leaned forward and listened intently.

'Are you telling me they saw it happening?' Martin Resnick went pale. 'No, Mr Banner, it was definitely not us.' His knuckles were white as his hand gripped the phone. 'Okay, we'll be there right away … yes, you must wake them … it's very important.'

He jammed down the receiver and turned to his men. He looked grim. 'They've been stolen!'

'Stolen?' they chorused.

'Two kids from Woodlands down the road spotted them being caught.'

'It could be a hoax,' said Joseph Dube.

'Yes, could be,' Resnick hissed angrily, struggling into his wet mackintosh. 'And that's exactly what we're going to find out. Let's go.' He strode outside to the Land Rover followed closely by the others. Eight minutes later they arrived at Woodlands School.

They hurried to the headmaster's office.

NINE

WEDNESDAY 23H30

Rampha and Paul were in their pyjamas, groggy from being woken up after only an hour's sleep. The headmaster's office was thick with heavy blue smoke. With a pipe wedged firmly in his mouth, Mr Banner paced back and forth puffing furiously.

'I wish we could open some windows,' whispered Rampha from the corner of his mouth.

'I wish he'd keep still,' said Paul.

Mr Banner looked at his watch for the umpteenth time. 'I wish they'd hurry up,' he muttered, desperately distributing more billowing clouds.

A knock on the door.

'Come in,' he called. He removed the offensive pipe from his mouth, shook it, wiped the stem with his hanky and jammed it back between his teeth.

The door opened, and the four drenched Lion Park officials filed in.

67

Resnick, hand outstretched, walked towards the headmaster. 'Mr Banner? Martin Resnick.' They shook hands, and he turned to the boys. 'You must be the ones who saw the lions being captured. Now tell us exactly what happened.'

Rampha extended his hand. 'Good evening, Mr Resnick,' he said too politely, 'I'm Rampha Singh, and this is Paul Patterson.'

Rampha *really*, thought Paul. He tried hard to suppress an approving smile.

'I'm sorry,' said Resnick. 'I've had a helluva day. I'm from the Lion Park, and these are my assistants. Joseph Dube, Joshua Phondo and Danny Els.' His smile softened Rampha who smiled back, satisfied.

'Please tell me what you saw?'

Rampha described everything in detail.

'What makes you think the lions were darted?' asked Danny Els.

'Well, first of all, we heard six loud gun shots, then shortly after we saw some of the lions sort of swaying. Then they just lay down in the long grass. One by one.'

'Yup sounds right. They were darted,' Resnick verified. 'What happened then?'

Rampha thought for a moment. 'Well, this truck suddenly appeared. It reversed to where the lions had dropped, and these two men got out.'

'One of them was a very big guy,' Paul added.

'Yes,' said Rampha, nodding towards his friend. 'Then a small forklift came along, and they got busy where the lions had dropped.'

'A forklift? Did you actually see them loading the animals?' Joseph asked.

Rampha hesitated. 'No, not really. It was getting dark by then, and we couldn't make out anything clearly. We just assumed that they were loading them into their strange looking truck.'

'Strange looking truck?' Resnick looked intently at the boy.

'It looked like a Toyota but with a closed body.'

'It had a sort of double roof,' put in Paul.

'Colour?' asked Resnick.

'White,' said Paul. Rampha nodded in agreement.

'After loading the lions, they left?'

'We didn't actually see them being loaded,' replied Rampha. He was being very careful. 'We just assumed they must have. You know, with the forklift working there back and forth in the grass. Anyhow they pulled off shortly afterwards.'

'How long did the whole operation take?' Resnick wanted to know.

Rampha thought for a while and looked at Paul.

'About fifteen minutes' ventured Paul.

'I would say about eighteen,' said Rampha. 'That is from the time we stopped until the time we left.'

Resnick and Joseph exchanged glances. They had seen those tire tracks, and this confirmed it. 'Sounds like they knew what they were doing,' said Resnick. He took out his cell phone. He thought better of it and turned to Mr Banner. 'May I use your landline? I want to call the police.'

'Go right ahead,' the principal pointed then turned to the boys.

'Now,' he removed the pipe and cleared his throat. 'I'm going to have to ask you two to stay here until the police arrive. They're bound to want to question you. I'm firmly convinced that the sooner we have the authorities involved, the sooner we'll find the animals.'

'Anything you say, Sir.' said Rampha. Paul nodded in agreement.

'You'll both be excused if you fall asleep in class tomorrow.' Mr Banner added with a wicked glint.

'In the history class, Sir?' Rampha responded innocently. He never misses a chance, Paul thought with deep pride.

'I'll inform Mr Lister,' retorted the headmaster, getting in the last word and returning to his beloved pipe.

Martin Resnick put down the receiver. 'They're on their way.' He turned to Mr Banner. 'Do I have your permission to ask the boys to come with us? We want to make sure we understand exactly where they saw this happening. By the sound of things, we're about to do some bundu bashing.'

Rampha and Paul exchanged looks.

Mr Banner nodded. He could not think of any danger or any other reason why they should not assist since the lions had apparently now been captured. This plus the fact that both Singh and Patterson were top students and a little lenience would not hurt.

'You heard what Mr Resnick said,' he growled, 'Go to your room and get changed into some old clothes and come back here. On the double! In fact, you are excused from classes altogether tomorrow.'

'Yes, Sir,' they chorused excitedly and hurried out. 'What a bonus!' laughed Rampha as they ran.

'Mr Banner,' Martin Resnick said when the boys had left. 'Is it at all possible they could have made up this story? You know what schoolboys are like. They start something, then when it gets out of hand, it's too late to retract.'

Mr Banner turned to him.

'Not them, never!' he said sharply, shaking his head. Then his face relaxed a little. 'I am more than willing to stake my reputation on the integrity of those two.' He paused. 'What they told you is what they saw.'

Resnick felt better. 'Then I'll take your word for it.'

A car's headlights sliced through the office window and crawled along the wall opposite. Martin Resnick went to the door.

Captain Peterson, dressed in jeans and a regulation police raincoat, entered with two uniformed policemen. He greeted Resnick with a nod and introduced himself to Mr Banner.

'Sergeant Gobi and constable Bambha, my assistants from the station.' He waved his hand in their direction. 'I've also instructed our Chief Liaison Officer to contact you concerning the media publicity angle.'

A step in the right direction, at last, thought Resnick. 'I'm very relieved to hear that,' he said. He then brought the policeman up-to-date with the latest discoveries and informed him that the boys would be coming with them to point out the exact location.

'Good. As soon as we've been out there and taken a look, we can discuss what MO to adopt and how to proceed.' Captain Peterson rubbed his hands together and looked around the room. 'Right,' he said. 'Now, where are the boys?'

Right on cue the door opened and in walked Rampha and Paul, both wearing tracksuits and takkies and carrying macs.

'Ah!' said the policeman, greeting them, 'I'm Captain Peterson from the Security Branch, and you must be our two amateur detectives.'

The boys introduced themselves and once again had to relate what they had seen. Captain Peterson listened in silence, thought for a moment then turned and made for the door. 'Okay,' he said. 'You two come with me.' They made a dash through the rain, for the police car. 'The rest of you, follow us,' he called over his shoulder.

Excitedly Rampha and Paul clambered into the back seat with constable Bambha as the two cars set off.

TEN

THURSDAY 00H15

It was the first time either of them had ever been on a police investigation, and the excitement was overwhelming. Every trace of tiredness had evaporated. Adrenalin was pumping.

Rampha grinned at Paul. 'Wait till we tell the girls,' he said, his eyes shining in the dim interior.

'You'll have to keep very quiet about this, I'm afraid,' commented Captain Peterson; having overheard. He wiped inside of the windscreen with the back of his hand. 'Things easily get out of hand,' he went on. 'The fewer people know about it, the better.'

The boys remained silent.

'For the time being anyhow.' He glanced into the rearview mirror. 'Make sense?'

'Sure,' said Rampha looking at Paul who nodded.

Captain Peterson observed the exchange. Smart kids, he thought. His two daughters, Tammy and Sara, were equally smart, and he wondered if he ever would have been able to handle all the pressures modern kids had to put up with these days. His daughters went to a government school, and the amount of homework they received was daunting. Nevertheless, their grades were good even though he and his wife Emily were dissatisfied with the new Outcome Based Educational system in place in post-Apartheid South Africa. It was not ideal but hopefully, would improve in the future.

They drove in silence. The tyres hissed on the wet road, and the windscreen wipers beat out a steady rhythm.

Captain Peterson broke the silence. 'Okay,' he said. 'Where to now my young friends?'

'Straight across the next intersection,' said Rampha. 'Then we can start slowing down.'

Paul took a deep breath and wiped his moist hands on his trousers as the car slowed. He did not feel nearly as confident as the rest of them. The thought of messing around in the long wet grass, in the dark, held little appeal for him. Most of all he was not looking forward to seeing the grizzly remains of that poor sheep.

The car idled along slowly wipers click-clacking at top speed. Behind them followed Resnick's Jeep. Its headlights carved through the heavy rain like two lasers.

'There,' shouted Rampha. 'We stopped right next to that milestone over there.' He pointed to the left. How did his friend remember all these details, thought Paul? He could hardly recall leaving the scene and going to his aunt.

Captain Peterson steered off the road, onto the verge and stopped. The Jeep behind followed suit. They clambered out, and the boys hurriedly donned their raincoats. Powerful flashlights beamed and guns gleamed as the men gathered around the boys.

'It was here,' said Rampha, pointing past Captain Peterson into the darkness beyond. 'Over there in the open veld. There are trees and bushes scattered about.'

Flashlights swung around trying to penetrate the murky night, but rain simply refracted the beams.

Visibility was zero.

'Let's take a closer look,' said the policeman decisively. 'I want to see that sheep you told me about.' He addressed his men. 'Don't forget the phones. And check your weapons.' He turned to Rampha as they set off across the road. 'You guys stick with me, okay?'

Resnick and his men followed close behind.

The long grass was saturated and very soon all were soaked to the skin. Paul wondered how they would ever find anything in this rain. He was scared.

With Rampha in the lead and Captain Peterson following closely behind, they waded through the wet grass to the spot where they had seen the lions. It was impossible to see anything outside the rings of light shed by the torches. Darkness oozed around them.

'Scary, isn't it?' Paul whispered to Rampha. He was a little out of breath. They lifted their feet high to avoid tripping over thick tangled grass.

'You can say that again,' muttered Rampha. He turned to Captain Peterson. 'What are we actually looking for Sir, apart from the sheep's remains?'

The police Captain swung his light around. 'That, and any other clues or evidence.' He beamed his flashlight in a wider arc.

'But first, let's see if we can find any trace of that sheep.' He held his light up high, moving the powerful beam slowly back and forth.

'I'm reasonably sure this is the spot,' said Rampha. He sounded unsure. Paul didn't blame him. He too felt disoriented in the dark. A foreboding presence lurked.

'Let's spread out a bit,' Captain Peterson said to Resnick. His men searched right and left.

They trampled the area in widening circles.

'Over here!' Constable Bambha called out suddenly. His light shone down. 'I've found something.'

Captain Peterson pointed his torch onto the flattened grass. The rest of the lights quickly followed his beam, focusing.

There, lying on the ground was the corpse. White bones with scarlet cords of torn flesh clung to tufts of blood-soaked sheepskin. They gazed at the bleak remains of the hapless young ruminant.

Almost the entire carcass was gone.

'Here's the head,' shouted a voice a little further away. It was Martin Resnick. Everyone trudged over to him. In amongst the grass and mud lay the grotesquely bloodied head of the unfortunate lamb. It was still attached to the rope.

'Just like the boys told us,' said Danny Els. 'I'm surprised we never saw this earlier.'

Paul turned away. It was a gruesome sight. He could not bear to look. A briefly edited image of the massacre replayed and flashed around his brain before settling like a stone in his stomach.

'We were way off course,' commented Joseph Dube. 'We were searching near some trees much further up there where we found those tire tracks.'

'At least the lions will have a little food in their bellies,' Martin Resnick stated. His first priority was his concern for the lions. He would hate anything bad to have happened to them.

All except Paul bent over for a closer inspection.

Rampha nudged his friend pulling him to one side. 'One thing worries me,' he whispered

'What's that?' asked Paul.

'The remains of the carcass…'

'What d'yuh mean?'

'Remember when that lion pounced on the sheep …?'

'Yes…?

'If you think about it, none of them had much time to finish off their meal.

'You mean before they went down?'

'Exactly.'

'What are you saying Rampha?' His scalp prickled.

'Well, something finished off that sheep.'

Paul thought for a moment. 'That means those poachers might not have captured all the lions.' He swallowed hard as a feeling of terror clutched at his chest. It overshadowed his nausea.

'Genius!' Rampha was apparently unconcerned. Did he have no fear?

'We'd better tell Captain Peterson, like right away,' Paul urged.

Rampha had already moved over to the policeman who was still examining the remains of the sheep's head.

'Excuse me, Sir.'

Captain Peterson looked up.

'My friend and I have just had a thought, Sir.'

The rest of the company fell silent as they listened in.

'Yes?' The police captain really liked these two outspoken lads. They were bright and helpful without being too forward.

'When we heard the six gunshots and the lions were darted, we assumed all of them had been hit.' Rampha pointed to the sheep's head. 'But if you think about it, none of them had a chance to finish their meal.'

The policeman's face hardened as he absorbed the information. He looked hard at Resnick in the reflected light. He did not like the implications.

'You mean ...?'

'There could be one of them still on the loose, Sir.'

There was a moment of tense silence, then, in a loud voice, Captain Peterson addressed the others. 'Okay, everyone pay attention!' Torch beams swung around and focused on him.

'There could be a lion still on the loose around here!' he echoed Rampha. He drew his Vector SP 1 service pistol. The other two policemen followed suit.

'The carcass has been eaten by something,' he told them. 'So it's possible the poachers left one of them behind.' He silently cursed himself for not considering that possibility in the first place. He should never have brought these kids along.

'We must stick close together! Especially you guys. If you see anything,' he barked to his men, 'shoot to kill.'

'No!' Martin Resnick objected loudly. 'We have dart guns here. If anyone spots it, we'll dart it, besides…'

'Listen to me, Resnick!' Captain Peterson turned on him irately. 'Lives are in danger here.' He turned to his men. 'We shoot first and ask questions later. Is that understood?'

His deputies nodded.

'No, you listen.' Resnick's temper rose. 'If you think you are going to kill a fully grown lion with those toy pistols, you're living in cloud cuckoo land. There's nothing more dangerous that a wounded lion. Trust me.'

He glared at Captain Peterson.

A tense power struggle flashed between them.

The policeman's features relaxed a little. 'I suppose you know best,' he conceded. He was out of his depth and big enough to acknowledge it.

Resnick appreciated his frankness. 'And besides,' he said in a calmer tone. 'A lion is a pretty valuable item, as you know.' Particularly these, he thought to himself. He was convinced that if they encountered anyone of this pride, he would be able to pacify them just by talking. They would recognize his voice. There was no need for any rash behaviour.

'I'm only concerned how valuable human lives are.' Captain Peterson retorted, blowing a drop of rain from the tip of his nose. 'But if there's a lion out there we must get it. Tonight! Think about the people living in this area.' He turned to his deputies. 'Okay men, give the Lion Park boys the first chance, but if they mess up, then blast it with everything you've got.' He shone his flashlight onto Rampha and Paul. 'You two. Stick with me. We're Siamese twins okay, is that very, very clear?'

'Yes, sir,' they chorused. Neither of them had any intention of doing otherwise. He turned to Sergeant Gobi. 'Gimme that phone.'

The man handed over the instrument and Captain Peterson got through to headquarters and explained their whereabouts and the situation. 'We still have a lion on the loose here. I'd like you to send some reinforcements immediately. Do you understand me?'

'We read you,' came the reply. 'There's a patrol car in the vicinity, and it's on its way.'

'Roger that. But we also need some tracker dogs and some marksmen with hunting rifles.'

'That'll take a little while,' crackled the voice. 'But we'll get to it right away.'

'I'm sending a man to meet your patrol.' Captain Peterson beckoned Gobi. 'He'll be up at the road in about five minutes.' He turned to the sergeant. 'I want you to take Constable Bambha with you and go and fetch those guys from patrol. They should be there by the time you reach the road. Have your guns out and ready and be careful.'

The two policemen set off retracing the flattened grass tracks they had made. The lights from their torches bobbed up and down as they melted into the darkness over the rough, wet terrain. The rest of them remained huddled together with torches blazing. In the rain, the beams danced like ghostly apparitions auditioning for a macabre, midnight ritual.

'I'm scared,' said Rampha.

At last, thought Paul and moved a little closer to Captain Peterson. The policeman took out his handkerchief and wiped his face.

'Now, everybody,' he said. 'We'll stay close together with our lights on and wait until reinforcements arrive.' He was reassuringly in command. 'When they get here,' he continued, 'we're going on a lion hunt.' He looked down at Rampha and Paul. 'Except you two. I'm taking you guys back to the car.'

'We really don't mind staying, Sir' Rampha said. He looked to Paul for support.

'Speak for yourself, Ram,' said Paul. What? Was he psychologically challenged or crazy or something?

'Certainly not,' said the Captain. His tone was firm.

Paul's reaction was pure relief. Thank you, Captain, he prayed silently. He really was in no mood to become some hungry lion's midnight snack.

Suddenly a loud, hoarse shout penetrated the dark stormy night. This was followed by a pistol shot and more frenzied screeches.

For a moment everyone froze, rooted to the spot. Rampha and Paul were petrified. The dreadful screams pierced the dark. Shrieks mingled with the steady hiss of the downpour created a ghoulish, distorted concerto of chilling sounds.

Captain Peterson sprang into action. 'Come on!' he shouted, hurrying towards the agonized shrieks. He completely forgot about his two charges, leaving them behind in the soggy, sinister dark.

'Let's go!' yelled Martin Resnick to his men. They thrashed and crashed after the policeman.

Rampha's voice was now thick with fear. 'Come on,' he hollered. 'I'm not staying here in the dark.'

'Me neither,' cried Paul. 'I'm right behind you.' They scrambled in convoy.

The closer they got, more desperate and guttural the throaty cries became. Minutes later they arrived at the scene of the commotion.

In the torchlight, the boys looked aghast at the shocking scene before them.

Sergeant Gobi was lying on his back in the long grass. Astride him, with vicious teeth barred, was a huge growling lioness.

The Zulu's arm was in front of his face in a feeble attempt at protection. The lioness was clawing him with both huge front paws trying to reach his throat. Deep scratch marks like crimson knife wounds covered his arms and face. His flashlight was lying on the trampled blood-soaked grass with its fading beam pointing upwards at a grotesque angle.

It was a terrifying spectacle.

Constable Bambha, his gun raised, tried to get in a shot.

'Don't shoot!' shouted Captain Peterson. 'You'll hit Gobi.' He ran towards the lioness.

'Get away,' yelled Resnick. You'll get hurt!'

'Shut up and shine the lights.' Peterson responded as he sprinted right up to the lioness and heaved his regulation boot with a solid thump into her flank.

Snarling, the lioness turned on Captain Peterson and with a swift, mighty swipe of her huge paw, razor claws extended, knocked him flat into the grass. He lay there stunned, blood oozing from a deep scratch in his shoulder. The animal turned back to her first victim.

'Dart it, damn you,' ordered Resnick desperately.

'I'm trying to,' countered Dube who had the dart gun. 'But I can't get a clear shot.'

Resnick grabbed the dart gun from his young assistant but before he could get a clear shot, Rampha, with his raincoat in his hands, rushed past him towards the lioness. 'Shoot it,' he yelled as he ran.

'Hey! Are you crazy!' screamed Paul desperately. 'Come back!' But Rampha was already there.

He tossed his raincoat over the head of the lioness. She tried to reverse from under the covering, moving away slightly from her victim.

Rampha dashed out of range as the huge animal shook off the raincoat and turned towards her puny assailant.

Captain Peterson, who had recovered a little, saw what he had done and registered the boy's predicament. He got up and ran once more, shouting, towards the lioness to distract her. She swung her massive head from the boy to the policeman, undecided.

Seizing the advantage, Resnick shouted, 'Now!'

There was a volley of shots as both he, with the dart gun and Constable Bambha with his service pistol, opened fire.

The lioness with several bullets in her neck and body stood for a moment, then with a loud bellow charged towards the light of the torches.

The men scattered.

Paul turned to run but tripped and plunged headlong into the wet grass. Seconds later Rampha landed right next to him. With the speed and roar of an express train, the charging lioness pounded close by them. They both held their breath as the crashing sounds faded into the dark, rainy mist.

'After her,' screamed Resnick. He and the rest of the men chased after the wounded animal, their lights receding into the gloom. With any luck, the tranquilizer would soon kick in.

As the two boys lay in the thick tangled grass, Paul reached out for Rampha. 'Are you okay?' He whispered. He was almost paralyzed by the events and overawed by what his friend had done.

'Yes,' returned Rampha in a whisper. 'I'm fine, but that poor cop.'

The chilling, eerie sounds of Sergeant Gobi's whimpering groans were pervading the night air.

'D'yuh think they got her?' Paul wanted to know.

'Dunno, maybe just wounded it.'

'I'm really scared Rampha.'

'Yeah, me too,' Rampha brushed a tuft of grass from his face. 'I can't believe I just did what I did.'

'Me neither. It was crazy! Why?'

'I don't know. When I saw that poor guy being eaten up, I just lost my head.' His teeth chattered, and his whole body shook.

In the darkness, Captain Peterson's voice called out. 'Can someone help me!'

Just then another shot rang out, and someone shouted in the distance. 'It's okay, we've got her.' The voice of Martin Resnick.

'Danger over,' said Paul breathing a huge sigh of relief. He helped Rampha to his feet. 'Let's see if we can help.'

They tramped their way towards the direction of the Captain's voice.

'Where are you,' called Paul in the darkness. 'Keep talking.'

'Over here,' came the reply, a little to their right.

They reached the clearing where the wet grass was trampled flat.

'Who is that?' asked Captain Peterson as the sound of their approach reached his ears.

'It's us,' called Rampha, having regained a little of his composure.

'My torch has died, and I've got Gobi here. I think he's lost consciousness. I need a light and some help.'

'There's someone coming,' said Rampha. 'What can we do in the meantime?'

'See if you can make him more comfortable. He's lying in an awkward position. If you can just straighten his legs under him, it'll help.'

In the heavy darkness, Rampha groped his way to the stricken man and gently moved his legs to a more comfortable position.

'Thanks,' said Captain Peterson. 'Did they get the lioness?'

'We think so,' Paul raised his voice and called out. 'Over here!'

'Coming!' The lights got closer.

'Hurry!'

Martin Resnick and one of his men arrived with constable Bambha. They flashed their lights on the scene and gasped.

Sergeant Gobi was half sitting, half lying in the arms of Captain Peterson. His head lolled loosely on his chest. It was torn and covered in blood, and his eyes were closed. Captain Peterson's tee shirt was soaked crimson as he gently held his comrade.

'Oh my gosh!' exclaimed the game warden. 'Is he still alive?' He shone his torch on the man's disfigured face.

'Only just,' said the Captain looking up. He spotted his constable. 'Bambha, give me a hand, and we'll carry him to the car.'

The constable obeyed immediately. He manoeuvred himself into position, gripped his superior's arms and, forming a chair, they set off through the grass, carrying the unconscious Zulu between them.

'Here,' said Resnick. He handed a torch to Rampha. 'You two come with me, and we'll walk ahead and light the way for them.'

Rampha took the flashlight. 'What happened to the lioness?' he asked as he and Paul stepped into the lead.

'She fell eventually,' said Resnick. 'After we gave her another dart.'

'Yes, we heard it,' said Paul.

'She's badly wounded as well,' Resnick went on. 'But Danny and Joseph will stay with her and take care of her in the meantime.'

At last, they reached the road where the cars were parked. The reinforcements had arrived and were milling about. There were floodlights everywhere. Eager hands helped lift the wounded Sergeant Gobi into the squad car, and minutes later it sped off to the nearest hospital ten minutes away.

Martin Resnick walked across to the boys. 'I'll take the two of you back to get some sleep.' He led the way to his Jeep.

Rampha looked at his watch. 'Gee, look at the time.' It was after three in the morning.

All at once they felt totally drained. It would be great to climb into a nice warm shower then bed.

THURSDAY 03H25.

Danny Els and Joseph Dube who stayed behind to attend to the wounded and dazed lioness looked at each other. The animal was in a bad way.

'I don't think she's going to make it,' said Joseph as he examined the pistol wounds the lioness had received. One bullet had caught her jugular vein, and she was bleeding profusely. 'We gonna have to put her down.'

'I think you're right.' said Danny and swallowed hard. He had seen many large animals put down, and it always affected him badly. 'Anyhow I don't think she's feeling any pain,' he said. 'Looks like the drug has taken effect.' He shone his light into the animal's staring eyes.

'Tell you what,' said Joseph with a catch to his voice. 'Why don't you run back to the road and fetch the boss. Tell him to bring his rifle. I'll wait here with Gwala. Take the light with you.'

'No, it's okay, you keep it,' said Danny getting up. 'It's starting to get light, and the rain is easing off a little. I'll just head straight for the road.' He ran off with a heavy heart.

Neither of them noticed two yellow eyes and the tawny shape of the other lioness. She had been silently and furtively stalking the two men. With the help of the mascara strip on the underside of her eyes, her excellent night vision was enhanced by the reflected light into her pupils. She was a supreme nocturnal hunter. Moreover, it is irresistible for any cat, domestic or otherwise, not to chase a fleeing prey. It was in the genes. Any hunter will tell you that when a lion charges, remain standing. If you dare!

The jogging Danny Els did not know what struck him. One moment he was hurrying towards the road less than a hundred meters away, the next he was lying on the wet ground with an immense weight on top of him and a huge jaw encircling his throat suffocating the life out of him.

THURSDAY 03H40

Having dropped off Rampha and Paul at the entrance gate of the school Martin Resnick, returned fifteen minutes later to where he had left his two men with the lioness. He carried with him his Winchester .375. He suspected he might have to put down the wounded animal. He hated the thought. It just added to his already frazzled nerves.

The powerful lights of the Jeep penetrated the misty dawn as he carefully drove into the long grass towards the spot where he had left his men.

Suddenly he braked, and his heart sank. There before him, was a lioness astride a man, dragging him along by the shoulder. In the bright lights, she dropped her victim and gazed at the Jeep. Her mouth dripped red. It was Tembi, one of his absolute favourites.

Realizing with shock what had happened; Martin Resnick raised his rifle and with a heavy heart and an audible sob, put a bullet into her forehead. The animal collapsed next to the body of Danny Els.

With eyes streaming with tears, he made his way to Joseph nursing a badly wounded lioness.

Shortly after, another deadly shot rang out, shattering the tranquil air and silencing the chattering, early morning, birdsongs.

THURSDAY 03H50

After waking Mr Banner, and awkwardly explained everything to the bleary-eyed headmaster, the two friends took a quick shower and finally crawled into their beds.

'Thanks for your support, Paul,' Rampha said wearily.

'Not much support, but you're welcome,' yawned Paul. 'You're the hero.' Crazy as a circus full of clowns, he thought, but still a hero.

As they drifted off to sleep, Rampha suddenly had an alarming notion. 'Paul,' he said, sitting bolt upright in bed. 'What if there's still another lion on the loose?'

There was no reply.

'Paul!' he repeated urgently. 'There could be more lions on the loose!'

But Paul Patterson was fast asleep.

The more Rampha considered it, the more convinced he was that he could be right. He flopped back onto the bed with images of torn faces and bloodied clothes whirling around his brain. He shivered as delayed reaction took hold. Exhaustion induced a dull state of confusion, and he spiralled into semi-consciousness. At last, fatigue overcame, and he submerged into a restless sleep interspersed with nightmares of huge monsters with yellow eyes and jagged teeth coming at him.

THURSDAY 08H15

Later that morning, Rampha woke up to Paul roughly shaking him by the shoulder.

'Wha…what is it?' he muttered in a daze. 'What's the time? We're late for class!'

'Rampha,' he said. 'Another man was attacked last night!'

The boy sat erect, suddenly wide-awake. His premonition had been correct.

'There was another lion.'

Rampha felt ill. 'How serious?'

'Dead, I'm afraid.'

'Who?'

'Danny Els,' Paul was in tears, shaking. 'That young guy, the ranger from the Lion Park.'

'Oh shit!' Rampha leaned over his bed and was sick all over the floor.

There was a knock at the door.

Paul climbed over the mess and opened the door a crack. Mrs Austin, the school secretary, stood outside.

'Mrs Austin,' said Paul as politely as he could.

'There's a Captain Peterson in Mr Banner's office waiting to speak to the two of you.'

'Okay, we'll be there as soon as we can.'

So much for their free day.

They learned later from Captain Peterson what had transpired.

THURSDAY 08H30

Banner headlines in the early morning newspapers blazed the night's events. 'ESCAPED LIONS MAUL TWO, ONE DEAD,' declared one. 'LIONS ON THE LOOSE IN JOHANNESBURG,' shouted another. 'PANIC AS LIONS ESCAPE,' proclaimed yet another. On every morning television and radio station, newscasts were being broadcast every hour, on the hour.

The Lion Park was besieged by newscasters, outside broadcast units and reporters with beta cams, video recorders, and audio recorders. Milling about were policemen, firemen and hundreds of onlookers and curious motorists who spilled out onto the main road adjacent to the Lion Park causing a major traffic jam.

People throughout the northern suburbs of Johannesburg and the surrounding areas could talk of nothing else. Bogus sightings and hoax calls came pouring in from every direction. Every missing person and domestic pet were presumed to have been attacked and eaten by the predators.

Bedlam reigned supreme as Martin Resnick, and Captain Peterson found themselves embroiled in the midst of their worst nightmare.

ELEVEN

THURSDAY MORNING, 08H30.

Brett van Jaarsveld and Tiny Terblanche were headed north in their four-ton, custom-built Toyota van. The rough, gravel road was wet, slippery and very bumpy, and they were heavily laden. Tiny was driving. Brett, sitting next to him took another swig from his half-empty beer can. He drained it in two large gulps, crushed it and flung it out of the window.

Litterbug, Tiny thought.

'I'm still upset about losing the other two,' he nagged for the umpteenth time.

Tiny sighed. 'Those,' he jerked his thumb towards the rear, 'are *my* four.' He was sure about that. His partner had been too plastered to hit an elephant at point blank. Never mind a lion under those conditions.

'I'm sure I got two of them,' slurred Brett, sliding further down into his seat. He propped his head against the back of the headrest and closed his eyes. Lulled by the steady drone of the engine, he finally sunk into an alcoholic slumber.

They had been driving non-stop for almost five and a half hours, and there was yet another two to go before reaching their destination. The weather had cleared, and the sun was out. The rains had not yet reached this part of the country, and although the surrounding bushveld looked lush, it was dry.

As he negotiated the many obstacles in the road, including many early morning donkey-drawn vehicles used by the rural inhabitants of that area, Tiny's mind went over the events of the previous evening.

He slaughtered a young ram and butchered it for its offal. It was a bit of a waste, he thought. But those parts which had the most appealing scent, lions went for first. There was not sufficient time to cut up the rest of the meat properly so he threw the carcass into a plastic bag and hoped it would not go off during the long journey ahead.

The warm entrails he slid into a separate bag. This he had used to lay the scent trail along the inside of the Lion Park's perimeter leading to the gap in the fence. The rain had helped substantially by gouging out the soil beneath. Plenty space for a lion to crawl under. Tiny knew that a fresh kill, especially the soft belly of the prey, would attract the lions and lead them to where he wanted them.

After they had staked out their last live young sheep with a long rope, he and Brett had hidden in the long grass and waited.

Japie van Rensburg was at the wheel of the van, concealed amongst the bushes a little way behind them. In it was his battery operated forklift that he had brought along.

It had been raining heavily, and the grass was wet where they sat waiting with their dart guns. Tiny had seldom experienced such a storm, and he hoped the trail he had laid would not dissipate in the rain. He had also loaded an extra strong dose of Zoletil into his own custom-made darts. He wanted them to succumb more rapidly. Next to them on the grass was a strong stretcher that Tiny had devised and built sometime before. It helped them tremendously with loading drugged animals into their van. You simply put the stretcher next to the catch, grabbed the victim by the legs and rolled it on. The fork-lift did the rest. Easy, quick and ready to go.

That was the way Tiny liked to operate.

Just then the hapless sheep had begun bleating, and Tiny sent up a silent prayer of thanks. Things were going so very right. If anything, lions are irresistibly drawn to prey in distress. He waited for them to carry out their ambush.

With all his years in the bush and his hunting instincts in sharp focus, Tiny still experienced the expected tingling rapture as a large lioness suddenly appeared and charged towards the sheep. The rest of the pride including the huge male also came into sight, exactly as anticipated. It was the way they hunted. Perfect tactics.

Tiny thrilled as he gazed in wonder at the sheer skill these predators employed in a kill. It was so professional, so focused, so natural. He raised his rifle and waited. The kill was quick, assisted greatly by the rope around the sheep's neck. The females rallied around impatiently allowing the male to first select his delicacies.

Then suddenly without warning Brett prematurely fired off his first shot.

'I got the male,' he stage-whispered.

Tiny cursed! The fool, he thought. He wanted to stalk a little closer. He shifted his aim from the male and darted the furthermost lioness. A good shot. He reloaded and fired at the next one. Perfect. Twice more he repeated this smooth action, first at another female then directing his second shot at the male Brett had supposedly darted.

Just to make sure.

Another shot from Brett followed.

Tiny's four shots had all found their marks in the neck of each animal. Brett, however, his vision blurred by alcohol and rain, had been less accurate. His shots had ineffectively grazed his targets.

As they waited for the heavy anaesthetic to take effect, the male continued to tear at the carcass as the females settled down following the disturbance.

Seven or eight minutes later the animals went down one by one. Tiny beckoned Japie who drove the forklift to where the dazed lions lay and they began their task of loading.

'Where the hell are the other two?' Brett shouted after they had loaded four of the animals into the back of the van.

'You tell me,' sneered Tiny. He made a mental vow never again to go on a hunt with Brett. The man was brain dead.

'Never mind, leave them. We got no time to look for them now.' Tiny climbed into the driver's seat. 'Get in, let's go.' Someone was bound to have heard the shots.

'Yes, sir, boss,' said Brett sarcastically. 'Anything you say, boss.' He was in a foul temper because he suspected that he might have missed his targets. But he would never admit it.

They returned to Brett's smallholding. There they spent the next couple of hours preparing for the trip. Tiny shuttled in and out of the house attending to the truck, while Brett sat on the phone, speaking in undertones and making notes. In the early hours of the next morning, they set off. The four captured lions remained sedated and imprisoned in the closed van.

Now, as they headed towards the north-western border of South Africa, Tiny's thoughts returned to the present.

He glanced at the man sleeping next to him. The only thing Brett was good at was to bring in clients. Yes, he was very good at that. But when *this* hunt was all over, Tiny was going solo. He did not need Brett. He would find his own farm and start up his own canned hunting business. He might even start a legal game farm. Yes, that's what he would do. He pictured himself as a valued member of society. That would be really something, he thought. He might even find himself a woman and settle down in some small farming community where he would be needed and accepted.

It would make up for all the years he was rejected by his parents who kicked him out of the house when he was fifteen for turning on his father. Jackals Terblanche was a man even larger than Tiny. His only interests were drinking and gambling. When he became sufficiently inebriated, he would go home and beat up his wife and their only son.

Tiny would never forget that fifteenth birthday when his father gave him a backhander for daring to ask for a party. His face stung, but his pride hurt more.

'Don't you look at me like that,' his father had rasped as he shoved his foul smelling unshaven face close to Tiny's defiant eyes. 'I'm your father, do you understand? And if I wanna give you a little smack to discipline you, I'll do so. No party, d'yuh hear me?'

'If you hit me again, I'll hit you back,' said Tiny quietly. A strange, unfamiliar resolve took hold, and his eyes never wavered. They glared at each other for a long while. His father turned to go but suddenly without warning swung around again. His huge fist hurtled in an arc towards his son.

Tiny ducked the blow with lightning speed and sent his own left fist crashing into his father's face knocking him to the ground. When his father struggled to his feet and faced his son, there was blood all over his face and fear written in his eyes.

'Get out of my house,' he croaked and staggered towards the bathroom.

Tiny's mother, a large woman, stood by impassively. She watched from the door. She too had been drinking. 'You should never have done that, Tiny,' she said simply. 'God will punish you.'

She followed her husband to the bathroom and closed the door.

When they emerged half-an-hour later, Tiny had packed his meagre belongings and was gone.

Over the ensuing years, he worked as a hired hand on many game farms throughout the country slowly developing his hunting skills. He soon learned that poaching animals was far more lucrative than the subsistence pay he earned as a farm worker. So he became a poacher for hire. Thus he met up with Brett and formed their partnership.

He glanced over at Brett who was deeply comatose. His head rode the backrest of the seat, and his mouth hung open loosely. Things could have been different if only this man had been more honest and treated him with a little more respect.

Tiny turned his attention back to his driving.

The road led towards a small border post between Botswana and the Northern Province of South Africa. About twelve kilometres before the border, a well-concealed track branched off to the left. At the entrance was a signpost that read 'Wessel's Ranch.'

Any traveller wanting to stop off at this so-called ranch was in for a disappointment. The narrow dirt track was nothing more than an illegal route across the border.

Tiny slowed down. He swung the van into the turnoff and reduced speed even further. About a kilometre along the rough winding road, another track branched off. This little-used road was almost completely overgrown with grass and small bushes. They slowed to walking speed.

At last, they arrived at a dry riverbed. It was about a hundred meters in width and filled with sand and boulders of varying sizes. Tiny was pleased that rains had not yet arrived. When it did rain, this dry sand river became a raging torrent.

They were fortunate.

He expertly picked his way across and up the bank on the other side, the engine whining comfortably in the lowest gear. Now, it was only a matter of another twenty minutes through the bushy terrain before they arrived at the farmstead.

Many animals, such as a large variety of buck, baboons, and smaller predators, occurred naturally in this area. In the distance, Tiny spotted the slow, deliberate movement of a small herd of elephant. He smiled. He had successfully poached this pachyderm family from a very well-stocked game farm that lay two hundred kilometres east from here, two bulls, three cows, and two calves. It was a prize indeed, and it greatly enhanced their operation.

Customers could not help being impressed with encountering the largest of all land animals there. Shooting these elephants, however, was not allowed, nor was it part of their canned hunting program. They were merely there for the hype and to provide authenticity.

As he drove, Tiny breathed in the pungent aroma of the bushveld. He loved it dearly and felt at home in these surroundings. This was where a man could be in contact with his real inner self.

His very soul.

TWELVE

THURSDAY 09H00

Rampha and Paul arrived at Mr Banner's outer office having showered, dressed and tidied up. Considering their lack of sleep, they looked as best they could, but still in a state of shock at the news of Danny Els's misfortune.

This was made worse when Captain Peterson related in detail what had happened. But that was not the reason he summoned them. He wanted to be absolutely sure there was nothing else, no tiny detail the police might have missed.

He read the exasperation on the boys' faces and sighed heavily. 'Rampha, you and Paul saw all the lions drop after you heard the shots?'

Rampha turned to Paul and shook his head. How many times did they have to go over this?

'No, Sir. It was raining and getting dark, and as I told you before, we only saw four of them go down.'

'That's right,' agreed Paul wearily.

Captain Peterson was reasonably sure four lions were hijacked. With the other two dead, they all seemed accounted for. But he had to be absolutely sure. They were sitting in the staff room, facing the captain. The events of the previous night were repeatedly analyzed in detail from every possible angle.

'Please think carefully,' the older man went on. 'If there is anything else you might have missed.'

'Sir,' Rampha was losing patience. 'I can't think of anything else. We've told you everything.'

'I understand you're something of a memory buff,' said Captain Peterson, changing the subject. Rampha lowered his eyes. 'I'm interested in it, Sir.'

'It follows that you would play a mean game of chess?'

'Well, er, Sir.' He shuffled his feet.

'When all this is over, I'd like to have a game with you.'

'I'd like that very much, Sir.' Rampha said modestly, his eyes lighting up.

Paul suppressed a smile. If the policeman fancied himself as a chess player, he was in for a surprise. Rampha was the Province's unbeaten junior chess champion for three years running. To say nothing of the esteem he held at school chess.

'In the meantime,' Captain Peterson rose. His fingers combed restlessly through his thinning hair. 'If you remember anything more, or if you see anything you think I should know I'd like you to contact me, okay?' He handed over a card. 'All my details are there.'

'Thank you, Sir,' said Rampha, glancing over at Paul. 'My friend and I would just like to say how sorry we are for what happened last night.'

'Yes,' the captain's shoulders sagged a little. 'Tragic. Poor Danny Els that youngster. The funeral is next week Tuesday. My sergeant Gobi is still on the danger list, although not critical. He was lucky.' He made for the door. 'He might have to undergo some serious reconstructive surgery.' He reached the door and turned as an idea occurred to him.

'Listen, guys, how would you like to come on patrol with me this afternoon? Perhaps we can spot that truck. I'm convinced it's from this area.'

The friends looked excitedly at one another. 'Yes, we'd like that.' They said almost in unison. 'If we see it, I'm sure we'll recognize it.' Rampha added.

'Right then. I'll get permission from your headmaster and pick you up later this afternoon after school.'

When the boys had left, Captain Peterson lifted the phone on the desk and punched in a number. 'Mr Banner, may I come through and see you?'

Later as the boys hurried to the science class, Paul asked, 'Have you seen the girls this morning?'

'I passed them in the quad. They were so inquisitive.' Rampha laughed. 'Even more so when I gave them our 'sworn to secrecy' bit.' He gestured inverted commas.

'I'm sure they've guessed it has everything to do with us and the cops,' Paul puffed beside his friend. He always had trouble keeping up. In spite of his slim build, Rampha had the energy and speed of a hyperactive roadrunner. 'Are you feeling a little better?'

'Tired and a bit stressed after last night,' replied Rampha. 'And you?'

'Same.' Paul could not get over the attacks. Last night was a terrible recurring nightmare that refused to go away. It repeatedly played in his head.

They entered the classroom, and the science teacher Corrine Bevan paused in her lecture and waited until they were seated. The rest of the class turned and stared, but Miss Bevan hurriedly and firmly brought their attention back to the task at hand. She and the other teachers had all been instructed to put up with any unusual non-attendance or late arrivals. They were told the boys would be working with the police.

Be that as it may, she was going to approach Mr Banner this afternoon and insist that Singh and Patterson underwent some counselling.

When the bell sounded the ten-thirty break, Paul and Rampha were surrounded by the rest of their classmates. However, when they discovered the two were not prepared to talk they slowly lost interest and dispersed.

'Well, if it isn't the hero of the day.' Debbie teased, as she and Ayesha approached.

'Heroes, plural,' laughed Ayesha.

'I'm rich,' Debbie announced waving a note. 'Anyone for a coke?' She was greeted by a chorus of yeses and the four set off towards the tuck shop.

'Rob a bank?' Asked Paul, falling in step with Princess Debbie. He noticed how her blonde hair glistened in the bright sunlight. It choked him up.

'Guess what,' she laughed with a voice tinkling like silver glass bells. 'I peddled some secret information about the two of you.'

'Oh yeah, any buyers?'

'Plenty.'

The Jukskei river flowed northwards through the school grounds, its banks lined with sweeping kikuyu lawns and lush green weeping willow trees. The riverbank bordering the school grounds was known as the Left Bank. This was where most students or groups would gather during breaks to discuss issues, gossip or simply soak up the tranquil setting.

The four friends made their way there.

'Okay,' said Ayesha, when they had settled on the grass. 'Now you can tell us everything, starting at the top.'

The boys exchanged glances.

'You heard what we told the others,' began Rampha. 'You know the secrecy deal.'

'Hey! It's me you're talking to,' Ayesha retorted, gazing challengingly at him.

Rampha's look softened. 'I know.' He took a sip. 'But we really have been asked to keep quiet about the whole thing.'

'What whole thing?' demanded Debbie. 'Who asked you to keep quiet?'

'The cops.'

'So now you're some big game lion hunters?' Ayesha smiled winningly at Rampha. 'Debbie and I know that you guys actually saw them being caught.'

Surprised, Paul raised his eyebrows and looked at his friend. News travelled.

Rampha shrugged. 'I just sort of mentioned it when we got back from the airport last night.'

'Oh yes, last night.' Was it only last night, thought Paul? Such a lot had happened since then.

'We also heard on the news one of the wardens at the Lion Park was killed by a lion early this morning.' Ayesha added.

Rampha's face clouded. 'Terrible.'

Paul turned to him. 'Maybe we should tell them, just a little.'

Rampha was silent as he thought for a while. 'Okay,' he said, looking from the one girl to the other. 'Look, it's nothing really. Paul and I are involved because we just happened to be there from the beginning.' He took another sip. 'We've also been asked to go out this afternoon.'

'With the police?' Debbie asked. She looked anxiously at Paul.

Rampha nodded. 'But until we can tell you more, you guys must simply trust us. And please, they don't want the media to get hold of anything.'

'The media? Excuse me,' said Debbie, eyes sparkling. The girls looked at each other. 'What are you, celeb idols or something?'

Paul grinned at her. He looked at his watch. 'Hey, we're gonna to be late. Come on, let's get back.'

THURSDAY 15H30

The afternoon classes dragged on like a neverending rap song. When the bell finally went, the excitement of the prospect of going on patrol with Captain Peterson had worn off a little. The boys were desperately beginning to feel the strain.

'My bed's calling me,' said Rampha wearily, as they made their way to the dormitory. 'I could sleep forever.'

'You and me both.' Paul tried unsuccessfully to stifle an enormous yawn. 'If I sat down right now, I'd be a goner. I hope Captain Peterson doesn't keep us too long.'

'Duty first,' sighed Rampha.

Typical, thought Paul.

They brushed quick greetings past Debbie and Ayesha on their way and promised to catch up afterwards.

'We've got a heavy scrabble game on this afternoon,' Ayesha told them. 'So we may be a bit late for supper.'

'Okay,' said Rampha. 'Make that a loose arrangement.'

'Done,' she said. 'Cheers!'

They walked on.

Paul turned and took a last quick look at Debbie who also turned. Their eyes locked for an instant then both looked away quickly. Paul felt needle pricks of embarrassment.

They put their things away and made for the main gate. Captain Peterson was waiting in the driver's seat of a Nissan four by four. Next to him sat Martin Resnick.

'Right on time,' the captain greeted them opening the rear door. 'Hop in.'

The boys climbed into the back and sank into the luxurious soft linen seats.

'What we're going to do,' the policeman informed them, as the car eased silently onto the main road, 'is to patrol this area to see if you can spot that truck. If we're not successful, we'll send in some heavy infantry to question all the residents around here.'

They headed in the direction of Birdhaven, an urban residential area where each property was about seven acres in size. These agricultural holdings adjoined the Lion Park on the southern side. The area was very affluent, and most residences consisted of opulent main dwellings with cottages, stables and other outbuildings that could be seen from the road. Domestic livestock was allowed and most of the wealthy families owned horses, sheep, and a few milking cows, along with ducks, geese, chickens and other livestock.

'Unless that truck is hidden away in a closed garage, it shouldn't be too difficult to see,' Martin Resnick said.

'I agree,' said Captain Peterson. He looked into the rearview mirror at Rampha. 'And by what you told us, the high canopy would not fit easily into a conventional garage.'

'But how do you know it might be around here?' Rampha wanted to know. 'It could be anywhere, kilometres away.'

'True,' smiled the Captain. 'But common sense tells us that anyone poaching lions would hardly take them to their house in the suburbs. They'd need a farm or at least a smallholding,'

Martin Resnick turned around to the boys. His face was drawn, and he looked very tired. 'What Captain is saying everything points to the poachers living in this area. Particularly considering the time they took to find the lions.' His eyes held Paul's face for a moment. His stillborn son would have been about the same age. How unkind life could be.

'Correct,' said Captain Peterson. 'Anyone using a sheep as bait, firstly would have to be nearby and secondly, available livestock would have to be close at hand. Time simply did not allow a poacher to learn of the lions' escape, and go out and beg, borrow or steal a convenient sheep for bait, as quickly as they did.' He turned into a side road. 'So everything points to the fact that these poachers either have connections or live here somewhere.' He drove on in silence for a while as they all scanned each smallholding from the road.

They patrolled for the next few hours with no success. Finally, they had to give up, and Captain Peterson headed back to the school. Rampha was pleased. They both really needed a good rest. He glanced over at Paul. His nodding head betrayed his gallant battle to overcome drowsiness.

Martin Resnick, too, had been quiet for a while now. He was devastated about Danny and losing two lions. He was not in the mood for social niceties. He just wanted this whole nasty thing to go away, to disappear and to be settled. With the media pressuring him from one side, the police from the other, he felt he was in the coils of a giant anaconda from the Amazon.

After dropping the boys, the police car sped away. Rampha and Paul arrived at the canteen as throngs of people streamed in for supper.

'We going in?' asked Paul with no great enthusiasm.

'If we spot the girls, you could twist my arm.' Rampha looked despairingly at the queue.

'Haven't they got Scrabble or something?'

Here it was first come first served. Hungry bodies with hungry mouths milled around ready to scramble for the first available table. Ayesha and Debbie were nowhere to be seen.

'Yeah. Let's rather wait till after the rush,' he suggested. 'We can avoid the questions too.'

'Suits me,' Paul readily agreed. 'We'll put our heads down for a few minutes and come back in half-an-hour.' He yawned widely. 'The food will keep.'

Once inside the dormitory they flopped fully clothed on their beds and within minutes were both dead to the world.

THIRTEEN

THURSDAY REWIND TO 12H30

When they arrived at the farm, Tiny reversed the truck towards the open gates of the small enclosed camp. This was where the lions would be kept until Brett secured a customer. The enclosure was about an acre in size surrounded by a three-meter high chicken mesh fence.

Brett opened his eyes, yawned and stretched lazily. He looked round. 'We're here,' he declared unnecessarily. Following their usual routine, he climbed out the van, walked around to the driver's side and stood by the open gate. 'Okay, back up a bit more,' he shouted, beckoning.

Tiny, with his arm out the cab window, looked backwards as he guided the vehicle into the gates. 'Before we let them out I think we should check for any holes. You never know.'

'Naw,' scoffed Brett. 'No one's been here since we left last time. I'll check later. Besides, these lions are not going to be here very long. Our clients are already in Johannesburg. I'm fetching them tomorrow.'

Tiny was surprised. This was news to him. He seethed with suppressed fury. Why was he not told of this earlier? Why did Brett have to undermine him all the time? Was he not an equal partner in this venture? When this hunt was over, after he collected his share of the money, Tiny was going to dump his underhanded partner.

The back of the van fitted neatly between the gateposts, leaving just enough room on either side to walk through.

'Whoa!' shouted Brett. 'That's far enough.'

Tiny climbed out. 'Right, open up.'

He squeezed past the gatepost, entered the enclosure and unlatched the rear doors of the van. He grabbed the rope fixed to the door on his side and moved out of the camp. Brett did the same on the other side.

'Ready?' asked Brett.

'Okay.'

'Right, let's go.' They both pulled their ropes, and the two heavy doors parted and swung wide-open closing the gaps on either side.

They waited.

For a moment the four lions were blinded by the sudden bright sunlight streaming into the back of the vehicle. They sniffed the air and grimaced, analyzing the smells of their new environment. Looking around cautiously, the male lion loped to the edge of the van and without further ado, jumped out. The three females followed without hesitation.

Once inside the camp, they paced around the perimeter then moved slowly towards the centre where they grouped together and waited. They looked almost fully recovered from their ordeal.

'Okay. Take her out now,' instructed Brett. 'I'll close the gate.'

There it is again, thought Tiny. Never a civil word, always an order.

Brett walked along the side of the gate, and as the van pulled forward, he closed it. A chain and padlock were dangling from the fence. All that now remained was to secure it.

'I'll put the van away. Be back shortly,' Tiny announced. He was still angry as he drove to the carport, a simple structure with four poles and shade cloth stretched over the top. He parked next to Brett's new but rather dusty looking open Jeep. There he switched off the engine, pulled up the handbrake and closed the windows.

He looked around at the rondavels to the right of the carport. All the doors and windows were closed. Everything seemed just as they had left it two months before.

He got out, heaved their luggage onto his shoulder and walked over to the largest rondavel closest to the carport. He unlocked the front door and pushed it open. Everything was still there, dusty, but in place and untouched.

In the meantime, at the camp, Brett was struggling with the chain and the rusty padlock that had jammed. The more he tried to dislodge it, the more it resisted his attempts.

The four lions stood by silently watching. Camps, such as this one, trucks, and people were familiar to them. Unlike their wild counterparts, they were used to human activity in and around any confined habitat they occupied.

One lioness, however, smarting from the indignities of the rough journey, fixed her yellow eyes on the unfamiliar human at the fence.

She moved stealthily and silently in his direction.

Brett, cursing under his breath and sweating profusely, jerked hard at the stubborn chain, leaning his head against the mesh fence to gain more leverage. Impatiently he bent lower to get a closer look at the problem.

Gathering momentum, the lioness charged towards the man and with a mighty leap flung herself at him. The rapier sharp claws of both front paws, extended to their limit, embedded themselves through the flimsy mesh, firmly into the scalp of her unfortunate victim. There they lodged, deep in his brain.

Brett died instantly.

The mesh between them, absorbing the impact, arched outwards then stopped the lioness in mid-flight. For a brief moment, Brett's body hung grotesquely from the fence. Then sheathing her claws, the lioness fell back. Brett's corpse sank to the ground outside the enclosure.

Having deposited their belongings in the combined lounge and kitchen area of the rondavel, Tiny did a cursory review around all the rooms. Satisfied, he stretched, yawned and walked slowly back to the lion enclosure. He loved the remoteness of this place and would be devastated to abandon it.

From a distance, he saw Brett lying on the ground near the fence.

At first, nothing registered. He had seen his partner sprawled in a similar drunken fashion many times before. With a start, he realized Brett had been more or less sober when they arrived. Puzzled, he increased his pace. Seconds later, he was standing over the body. For a moment he stared down trying to make sense of the awkward position in which his partner lay.

He leaned forward for a closer examination and his perplexed look changed to horror. Brett was dead.

Tiny was dumbfounded. His brain became numb and unable to function. He stared for a long time at Brett's head. It was gashed open. What could have happened?

Just then, the same lioness charged once more, taking a swipe at Tiny through the mesh. He automatically jumped back.

It slowly dawned on him. Brett must have been fiddling with the lock and chain when this happened. He glanced towards the gate. It was closed but still unlocked. Tiny tried to work the chain loose from the fence, but it was rusted solid. He would have to find another means to secure the gate.

But first things first. He looked down once more at the body of his partner lying there. With mixed feelings, he wondered what to do.

He knew Brett's circle of friends was limited to Japie van Rensburg and himself. So who should he inform of his partner's untimely death? What if he told Japie and he went to the police? Then they would want to come here, to the farm and investigate. There would be a lot of questions. But would Japie do such a thing? No, Japie himself also had a criminal record. Tiny thought about it for a moment and decided against telling Japie.

Did he have to report it? Surely someone had to be notified?

But who?

Tiny was in a dilemma. He looked again at the distorted face lying on the ground as he pondered the situation. What was he to do with the body? He could not leave it out here. He would have to bury it somewhere. But where?

What about all their hunting clients? Who were they? How could he get hold of them? What was he going to do about this particular hunt?

His mind was in turmoil.

Two of the lionesses were pacing backwards and forwards. They were hungry, and the smell of fresh blood was getting to them. Their soft growls were becoming more and more insistent.

Tiny looked at them. He would soon have to go out and shoot a buck or something for them to eat. The few intestinal remains of the sheep they had brought with them would certainly not be sufficient for the four of them.

But first, he would have to do something about Brett lying there. He looked down once again at the crumpled body and a thought crossed his mind. He dismissed it immediately. It was too depraved even to consider.

But the thought persisted, invading his brain like a dreaded disease. It played like a horror scene from some Steven Spielberg movie.

He looked again at the restless lions and back to Brett's body. He thought for a little while longer then made his decision.

It was the perfect solution.

He bent down and began to remove the clothing from the dead man's body. It took less than five minutes. He then lifted the corpse, booted open the gate to the enclosure and heaved the naked Brett inside.

The body hit the ground with a dull thud, and Tiny slammed the gate shut. With one accord amidst clouds of dust swirling, the four lions pounced and started to tear at the soft flesh.

Tiny turned his back on the gruesome spectacle. He gathered up the clothing and with sounds of satisfied grunts ringing in his ears, he made his way back to the rondavel whistling softly under his breath. At least now, he would not have to feed them.

When he returned later with a length of thick wire to secure the gate, there was not much left of Brett van Jaarsveld. Tiny would bury the remains later.

FOURTEEN

The girls were last to finish the tasty lasagne supper and were leaving the dining room.

'I could have kicked myself when I challenged Shyria on her last word,' said Debbie. 'I mean who's ever heard of a 'hafiz'?'

'That was really a bummer,' Ayesha agreed.

'It threw me for the rest of the game.'

'You can't win 'em all.'

'I guess you're right.' Debbie sighed. 'I wonder if our hunters are back?'

'Let's take a peek,' Ayesha said. 'Maybe we should have saved them some supper. I'm sure they'll be starved.'

They made their way to the dorm and Debbie tried the door. It was open. She peeped in and withdrew quietly closing the door softly.

'They're both on their beds, out like the proverbial,' she whispered smiling. 'And still fully clothed, shoes and all.'

Ayesha had a wicked glint in her eye. 'Suppose we slam the door and disappear.'

Debbie gave her a sharp look.

'Only kidding,' said Ayesha. 'I guess the only other thing to do is catch up with some Facebook.'

'Good idea,' said Debbie. 'I've also got a bunch of e-mails to answer.'

The two friends ambled to their dorm breathing in the early evening jasmine fragrances.

Later Debbie sat on her bed. Ayesha stood over her brushing her hair.

'One of these days I'm going to shave my head and become Amber Rose,' said Debbie. 'It takes a zillion hours to keep this straight hair neat.'

'You've still got some curl in yours,' Ayesha said. 'You want straight? Try mine.' She gave the hair one more brush. 'I'm going to show you a lovely style that'll make the guys drool.'

Ayesha was so ultra artistic. She took a bunch of Debbie's blonde hair from the left side of her face, divided it into three and began braiding.

'Wait a minute Ayesha, I hate plaits.'

'Quiet and bite the pillow. I wanna show you something.' With each completed plait Ayesha dropped one of the braids and selected a third cluster of strands from the side, braiding towards the back of the head. There she completed the plait and inserted a clip. Starting at the fringe in front, she shaped a similar braid on the right finishing at the back, then clipping it. She then brushed the remaining hair straight down.

'Okay, now look at that.' She passed the hand mirror.

'Wow,' said Debbie. 'A plaited crown right around my head? I'm a queen. You're a genius.'

'And that's not all,' Ayesha smiled. 'You can put the rest in a pony like this.' She swept the remaining hair towards the back and secured it with a hair band.

The effect was electrifying.

'I can go to any debutante's ball with this style,' Debbie said, admiring her hair. 'I wonder what Mrs Norris will say about it.'

'Music tomorrow?'

'I haven't even practiced,' Debbie said. 'I'll have to busk it.'

'I'm sure you'll sparkle. Rampha told me that you and Paul are playing up a storm.'

'I love playing with him. He's a bit avant-garde and improvises when the reading gets tough. But he's improved a lot since we've been playing together.' Debbie's colour elevated a few notches.

'I wish I'd taken up an instrument. I really love music,' said Ayesha.

'But you've got your poetry,' Debbie said. 'Now there's something I wish I could do. I loved your one about the owl. How's the writing getting on anyhow?'

Ayesha looked away shyly. 'I've started on my first novel.'

Debbie jumped up and hugged her friend. 'Ayesha, you never told me,' she said. 'You're real deep, you know. I'm so ultra-impressed.' She stepped back and stared deep into Ayesha's shining eyes. 'Does Rampha know?'

'If you tell anybody, I'll have to kill you.' Ayesha smiled at her friend.

'I won't, I swear.' Debbie glanced at her watch. 'Wow, look at the time! I've got to shower. My bed's calling. Promise you'll tell me the plot sometime, okay?'

'I guess,' said Ayesha. 'But not yet. It's still too new.'

'Okay, but I won't stop nagging. Pass the towel.' Debbie got up and went to the bathroom then turned. 'Are you still coming to my place for the weekend?'

'And miss going to the mall? Are you kidding?' Ayesha laughed.

Debbie went in then popped her head around the door. 'I wonder if our heroes will sleep through the night?'

'Probably, I guess we'll catch them at breakfast.' Ayesha said.

'That's if they haven't been summoned for more police work.' She closed the door. If Paul was out in the morning, Debbie thought, it meant they might have to miss another lesson. Mrs Norris won't be too pleased, that's for sure.

FIFTEEN

FRIDAY 01H45

Six hours later, from of a deep sleep, Paul woke with a start. He looked at his luminous watch. It was one forty-five in the morning. Feeling a little disoriented he sat up on the edge of the bed. Gradually everything came back to him.

Supper!

They had intended to go, but now it was too late. They had missed it.

He was famished. He could not remember when last he had eaten. Besides his raging hunger, he felt a great thirst.

He peered through the darkness. Rampha was still fast asleep. He was lying on his back, still fully clothed. Without a sound, Paul made his way in the dark to the bathroom for some water. Returning, he sat quietly on the bed contemplating whether or not, to get undressed and go back to sleep.

'Is that you?' asked Rampha sleepily.

'Did I wake you?'

'No, not really. What's the time?'

'Almost two.'

'Two o'clock?' Rampha sat up suddenly. 'We missed supper. I'm starving.'

'Me too,' said Paul. 'I could do with a nice juicy burger right now.'

'Stop!' groaned Rampha. He lay down again and gazed in the dark at the ceiling. Paul lay back and closed his eyes.

Minutes passed.

After a while, Rampha murmured. 'Are you asleep yet?'

'No,' his friend replied. 'I keep thinking about that lovely juicy burger.'

Rampha groaned again. 'Now you've done it!' he said. 'I'm so hungry I could eat a truckload of horses.'

They fell silent once more.

'Paul,' a hungry voice whispered from the dark.

'Are you thinking what I'm thinking?'

'How much have we got?' Rampha got out of bed and went to his locker. With his cell phone, he beamed the light to where he kept his money. 'Three twenties.'

'I've only got about fifteen.' Paul apologized.

'Don't worry, it's enough,' said Rampha. He replaced his cell phone in the drawer. His excitement was taking hold. 'Let's go.'

'Sloppy Joe's?'

'Where else?'

'If we get caught?' Paul said, suddenly anxious.

'It's either that or starve to death,' said Rampha recklessly.

'That's not even an option. Okay, let's do it.' Paul matched Rampha's enthusiasm and discarded his concern to file thirteen. 'Sloppy Joe's, here we come.'

Slipping into their jerseys, they crept quietly out of the dark room gently closing the door. Outside, the streetlights in the school grounds competed with the bright moonlight above.

'Do you think there might still be a lion on the loose?' asked Paul. 'We'd better be on the lookout.'

'No, I don't think so,' said Rampha. He felt an involuntary shiver down his spine. 'I really believe they've all been accounted for, just like the Captain said.'

They stayed in the shadows as they made their way to the carport.

'We'll have to push,' Rampha whispered as he unlocked his motorcycle. They donned their crash helmets then pushed the machine towards the gates.

Thuli, the night watchman, grinned and wagged his finger at them as he opened for them. He knew what they were up to was illegal. He also knew he was in for a treat when they returned.

They had done this a few times before. He shook his head. School was never like this for him. The rural area where he came from boasted the only elementary school for miles around. Attending classes those days was never compulsory. It was more like a casual meeting place for the local kids. He and his buddies would go to school at least twice a week, or whenever their subsistence farming chores allowed.

Today, however, in the New South Africa, it was different and better in a whole lot of ways, he thought.

At least now everyone had the vote, and the Government had generally improved the lot of most people in the country, even though much had still to be done. In any event, anything was better than the old days.

He smiled widely as he waved them through.

Once outside they mounted in the moonlight. With legs wide, they coasted all the way down to the bridge that crossed the Jukskei river. They freewheeled as far as they could up the other side before coming to a stop.

Rampha started the engine. 'I'm always scared we might wake up the entire neighbourhood,' he said, carefully revving the silent engine.

'We've never been caught yet,' said Paul.

'Don't push the stats.'

'Yup,' said Paul. He kicked out the footrests and leaned close up against his friend. 'I'm on.'

'Excellent,' cried Rampha joyfully. 'Let's go.'

They pulled off, and the cool air swept past their faces as they gathered momentum. Both were wide-awake now, as they headed excitedly for their destination.

Paul remembered suddenly that he had left his cell phone behind. It was too late now to go back.

Besides which, they would be back in no time at all.

Sloppy Joe's was a very successful twenty-four seven, fast food roadhouse that catered for the needs of those who did not, could not or would not sleep. Truck drivers, railway shift-workers, musicians, waiters, reporters and late night party-goers, all gravitated there throughout the night. The venue was situated just off the junction of several major roads, making it an ideal rendezvous for the ravenous. It was a favourite haunt for the motorcycle fraternity, so the boys knew that they would attract little or no attention. They had been there several times before but never this late, or rather early in the morning.

Rampha pressed the flash indicator, and they swung left into the entrance of Sloppy Joe's. The place was buzzing like a disco gig.

Cars, motorcycles, trucks and vans were parked, one behind the other in several queues facing the many serving hatches. Waiters and waitresses with red striped aprons and peaked caps were hurrying about, taking orders and serving customers on trays that hooked on their half-open windows. Other cars, engines idling, were bonnet to bumper in line in the drive-thru lane.

They pulled up close to the serving hatch reserved for motorcyclists. Seated on the several wooden benches provided, were a number of leather-jacketed hippies, mostly young men, laughing and enjoying their late night carousing.

'What are you having?' asked Rampha, dismounting and leaving his friend on the bike.

'Make mine a burger with plenty of tomato sauce and chips,' replied Paul, digging in his pocket for his contribution.

'And to drink?'

'Don't bother,' said Paul. His stomach was growling.

Rampha knew Paul was a little short. He decided he would get him a coke anyhow, plus one for Thuli. He walked to the hatch and placed the order. As he waited his gaze swept across the many other vehicles parked there.

It was then he spotted the truck. It was parked under a tree away from the queues.

Rampha went cold.

He was certain it was the same one they had seen in the rain, loading the lions. It had the same unusual roof. There seemed to be an extra section moulded on top. This gave it more height than the average, similar model, closed van.

He was in a dilemma. What should they do now?

He looked over to Paul, caught his eye and beckoned to him.

Paul put out the footrest, left the bike and approached his friend. 'Don't tell me,' he said smiling. 'No tomato sauce.'

Rampha was serious. 'Look over there.'

Paul followed his gaze and froze. 'It's that same truck!'

'Yes, it is. What are we going to do about it?'

'Dunno. What do you think?'

'There doesn't seem to be anyone inside and the windows are closed.'

'You're right. But what is it doing here?'

'Maybe it's been abandoned.' Rampha looked at his friend. 'I think Captain Peterson should know about this.'

'Yes,' Paul said, looking a little concerned. 'But how are we going to explain this?'

'You mean, us, here?'

Paul nodded.

Rampha thought for a while then shrugged. 'We'll just have to face the music.'

'Did you bring your cell?'

'No,' said Rampha. 'And you?'

Paul shook his head. 'Same.'

Just then the cashier at the hatch shouted, 'Three hamburgers with chips.' He dumped the packages on the counter and bent down to the refrigerator. 'And three cokes,' he grunted, standing up again.

Rampha put down the money. The cashier punched the till and slapped the change on the counter. They grabbed the packets, the cold drinks, and the change and walked back to the bike.

Rampha clipped open the pannier and stashed the three cokes and one packet for Thuli then opened his and took a huge bite. 'I think we should have a closer look at that truck,' he said with his mouth full.

'…And take the number,' added Paul as he grabbed a handful of soft potato fries and stuffed them into his mouth.

They were oily, hot and delicious.

With their packets in their hands, the two of them walked slowly towards the truck.

Tiny Terblanche was sitting on a bench close by. He gazed idly at the two boys approaching his truck. They looked very young to be wandering about so late at night. It was none of his business. He felt tired after the long journey back from the farm. He had eaten two double hamburgers and was in no hurry to get going again. For the moment, he was very much in relax mode.

So much had happened in the past twenty-four hours.

After Brett's corpse had been devoured by the four hungry lions leaving only a bloodied skeleton remaining, Tiny had gone back to the main rondavel to search for Brett's papers and the keys to the Jeep.

He had found nothing. This puzzled him.

He knew that there had to be papers. How otherwise had Brett kept track of all his dealings? There simply had to be lists of his clients' names and addresses, bank statements and lease agreements for the farm. Even his personal letters, where were they kept? More importantly, however, where were the contact numbers of the clients for this hunt?

He had gone through Brett's rucksack, but when he opened it, all he found was a few American hunting magazines. There were also two brandy flasks, one empty and the other half full.

He then went on to search through all the dead man's clothing. There too, he found very little. A bunch of house keys, a few loose coins and about two hundred rand in notes. He removed the money and the keys and burned the clothing after soaking them in petrol. The ashes he buried under a tree a little way from the house. He then spent the rest of the afternoon combing the premises, going through each and every rondavel.

He found nothing.

At last, he was satisfied that any papers Brett might have kept, had to be back at the smallholding in Birdhaven.

That meant only one thing. He would have to return. Four lions could not go to waste. He could not afford to lose a hundred thousand rand or whatever price Brett would have asked for them. Pity he could not take the Jeep, it would have been so much quicker. But he was in no mood to break the gear lock or try to hotwire the ignition or damage the car in any way. He might have a use for the vehicle later, and the keys and the electronic remote were probably also at the smallholding with the rest of Brett's stuff.

No, he would have to take the heavy truck.

He filled it with gasoline from the storage tank they kept there and set off on the long journey back to the smallholding.

It was about one-thirty in the morning when he drove past Sloppy Joe's. As he saw the neon sign flashing a picture of a large hamburger, Tiny realized just how hungry he was. He eased the van to a stop, made a u-turn and headed back to the roadhouse.

Now, as he sat on the bench having finished eating, he felt a lot better. The two kids were looking at the rear end of his truck. Why should they be doing that?

Suddenly the hairs prickled on Tiny's arms and the nape of his neck. His hunter's instincts became aroused, and his brain suddenly became alerted. His huge body tensed. Those two were snooping.

Why?

Rising casually, he walked away from the truck. Then very slowly and smoothly he melted into the shadows surrounding the roadhouse. There, in the semi-dark, concealed by trees and bushes he silently made his way round to the far side of the truck. His fluid movements were impossible to detect. He moved like a panther in the night. His stalking ability was unsurpassed. He simply drifted silently and unseen from one shadow to the next like a ghostly vapour. Soon he was within earshot.

The boys were examining the back of the truck.

Tiny listened carefully.

'Look at those scratch marks and those tufts of hair,' said one of them.

'I think we should take some of it back, as evidence,' said the other boy, the Indian. He picked a few strands of fur off the metal and folded them into his handkerchief.

Tiny was now fully alerted. They must have seen something.

His first reaction was to confront them, but he realized that in this public place, such action was bound to attract attention. He would bide his time. Patience was a hunter's best ally.

'Let's get back and phone Captain Peterson right away,' said the first boy.

'I think we should wait a little and see who owns this truck,' replied the other one.

'Maybe we'd recognize them again.'

'That'd be difficult,' said the Indian. 'Except for the big guy.'

That would be me, thought Tiny.

Hidden in the darkness behind the bushes, he held his breath. These kids must have seen everything. How was that possible at night and in that rain? He thought about what they said. Could the police also know? How about Brett's smallholding? Maybe they had set a trap there and were waiting for him to return.

He listened again intently.

'…and I think we should follow them to find out where they live,' the Indian was saying.

'Captain Peterson would be really pleased about that,' agreed the other.

Tiny let out his breath slowly. So, they did not know about Brett's smallholding.

But he had a problem.

His truck was not the fastest thing on wheels, and they had just said they would follow him. He saw no point in leading them on a wild goose chase with no prospect of losing them. His most important task was to go to the house and search through all Brett's things and secure those customers his partner had mentioned. He had to secure the hunt and get rid of those lions. That was his first priority. His future depended on it. But he would also have to get rid of these boys somehow and prevent them from spoiling his chances of making any real money.

Perhaps he could capture them and take them to the farm. There, he could keep them locked up in one of the rondavels, at least until he had contacted the clients. On the farm, he could keep an eye on them until he had the money for those lions safely in his pocket. He would then decide what to do with them. Right now, however, he would have to think how to capture them without too much fuss.

A thought occurred to him. It was easy, and he liked easy solutions. He would simply let them follow him and then he would ambush them like lions do. It was easy, neat and tidy.

Yes, that was the best plan.

Tiny silently made his way back to the bench where he had been sitting earlier. Once there, he made a big show of stretching, yawning and coughing before he walked noisily, but slowly back to the truck.

Seeing him approach, the two boys moved back to their motorcycle and made such an exaggerated show of not looking at him that he almost laughed. They were such amateurs.

He climbed into his cab, started the engine and reversed the truck. Driving slowly, he pulled into the main road. He adjusted his rear view mirror and noted with satisfaction the single light following at a safe distance.

He drove the remaining eight kilometres very slowly, always keeping the bike's lights squarely in the centre of the side mirror.

At last, he swung into the dirt road leading to Brett's smallholding. The light followed. Satisfied, Tiny turned into the short driveway. The light behind him had disappeared. They must have parked and were approaching on foot. Sly little beggars, he thought, but not clever enough.

He drove to the front of the house, switched off the engine and walked to the front door. Whistling tunelessly, he entered. He turned on all the lights and made his way to the back door where he noiselessly slipped outside. He circled the house in the shadows and in a wide arc headed across the dark lawns to the driveway entrance. Two thick wild olive trees stood on either side of the open gates.

Tiny smiled.

Sure enough, there propped up against one of the trees was the bike. The boys were probably halfway up the drive.

He went to the machine and bending down, ripped off the single cable leading from the distributor to the spark plug. He left the motorcycle standing where it was, tossed the cable into the bushes and turning towards the house, began stalking his prey.

The boys were huddled at the back of the truck, peering around the side into the house. Tiny soundlessly crept up behind them and pounced.

They both struggled fiercely, but Tiny's hands were as big as spades with fingers like steel springs. He bundled them through the house and into a large guest bathroom where he callously banged their heads together and flung them onto the tiled floor.

Without saying a word, he went out, locked the door and removed the key.

SIXTEEN

For a moment they lay there stunned.

Paul was first to recover. His head was pounding, and in his mouth he tasted the salty texture of blood. Rolling over onto his hands and knees, he crawled over to his friend sprawled face down on the floor tiles, lying in a very awkward position.

'Rampha,' Paul could hardly speak. His tongue was numb and felt thick. He must have bitten it. 'Rampha,' he whispered again and gently shook his friend.

Rampha stirred slightly.

'Rampha,' Paul repeated. 'Are you okay?'

'What happened?' Rampha's eyes opened, and as he tried to lift his head, the room spun, and he slumped back to the floor.

Paul lifted him into a sitting position and cradled his head and shoulders in his arms. Rampha's eyes rolled back uncontrollably as he tried desperately to regain consciousness.

'Rampha, wake up,' said Paul urgently. His friend stirred again.

'I'm awake,' he said. His speech was slurred as he tried to focus his eyes once more.

'Just take it easy,' said Paul, as relief washed over him. Rampha seemed okay.

They sat huddled together for a few minutes. They were in a fix. The seriousness of their situation slowly began to sink in.

'Where's the big guy?' asked Rampha, gingerly sitting up by himself.

'I don't know. I think he went out.' Paul said. He struggled to his feet. 'Do you think you can get up?'

'I'll try,' said Rampha. 'Give me a hand.'

Paul helped him gently to his feet.

'I've got a funny taste in my mouth,' he said, standing up shakily.

Paul looked closer at Rampha's mouth. 'It's blood.'

'I thought so,' said Rampha. He licked his swollen lips wincing as he did so. 'Ow!'

'I'm also is a bit damaged, said Paul. He stuck out his thick tongue.

Rampha examined it. 'Yes, you've got a nasty gash there on the side. Looks like it's still bleeding.'

Paul spotted the basin. 'I think we ought to get cleaned up,' he said.

'That can wait,' said Rampha. 'We've first got to get out of here.' He was beginning to feel himself again. He looked around.

'How can we manage that?' Paul wanted to know. He looked up at the only window in the bathroom. It was securely burglar-proofed with heavy iron bars on the outside.

'So much for that bright idea,' said Rampha, following his gaze. 'Unless one of us can squeeze through that, we'll have to stay right here.' They looked helplessly at each other.

'You know something?' Rampha ventured.

'What?' Paul said expectantly.

'You've got one helluva hard head.'

'And so have you,' Rampha's attempt at humour made Paul suddenly feel a whole lot better. 'I wonder what he intends doing. Do you think he spotted us following him?'

'He must have,' said Rampha. 'He'll probably come back and torture us. We must pretend to know nothing.'

Paul crossed to the basin opened the tap He rinsed his mouth took a drink then splashed cold water onto his face. 'Yes, the less he thinks we know, the better.'

Rampha nodded as he followed Paul's example. The cold water refreshed them. They looked around again. It was a very ordinary bathroom with a bath, a basin with the usual cabinet beneath and a toilet.

Rampha rattled the cabinet door. It was locked.

Above the toilet was the one small window with bars. Apart from the door, which was locked from the outside, there was no other way out. They would simply have to wait and see what happened next.

'As soon as we get a chance, we must phone Captain Peterson,' said Paul. 'Do you still have those numbers he gave you?'

Rampha tapped his head. 'They're all in here,' he said. 'I still can't think why I didn't bring my cell phone. That was really stupid of me.'

'And me.'

Just then they heard the rattling of a key in the lock.

'Let's jump him!' whispered Rampha his eyes wide. He hastily stepped back.

The key turned, and the door opened. Tiny entered.

One of Paul's blows caught the man on the side of his head. It felt like punching a brick wall. Rampha fared no better. He could hardly lift his arm for a second strike.

Tiny had been expecting just such an attack. He brushed both boys off like insects. His strength was immense.

Once more they both landed on the floor with a painful bump.

'Now you listen to me,' Tiny commanded in his high-pitched voice. 'I've had enough from the two of you. If you try anything more, I'm really going to hurt you.' He looked down coldly into two pairs of defiant eyes. 'D'you understand?'

The boys said nothing.

'Now get up. We're going for a little drive.' The big man folded his arms and waited.

They reluctantly got up off the floor. Tiny kept his eyes on them alert for any tricks.

'You can take your pick,' he said. 'You can either walk out of here on your own two feet, or I carry you out. It's entirely up to you.' He stood to one side. 'Stay close together, I'll be right behind you. Now move!'

He waited until they had squeezed past him. He followed close behind.

'Straight through that door over there.' He pointed to the front door that led out of the lounge. 'And don't try anything!'

They made their way out onto the veranda towards the steps that led outside onto the lawn.

Rampha thought quickly. If ever there was going to be a chance to get away, this was it! He made a dash towards the darkness.

He was rewarded with a stunning blow to the back of his head.

'I warned you,' growled Tiny. He pushed them ahead of him. 'Now just get into the back of the truck. Hurry!'

Paul and Rampha approached it with fear. Where would they be taken?

Tiny opened the back door of the truck.

'It's dark in there,' complained Rampha, stalling for time.

'How would you like another clip on your ear?' shouted their captor. 'Get in!'

They climbed onto the rear bumper and into the back of the truck. It was like a huge empty room inside. Their nostrils were assailed by a heavy stench. The smell of lions.

They were really scared.

As they entered Rampha caught a glimpse of his motorcycle propped up and secured with thick wire to a metal stay against the far wall. Then the heavy doors clanged shut.

The darkness was total.

'Looks like we're going for a long ride,' Rampha said. 'He's got my bike. Did you see it?'

'Yes,' said Paul. 'Let's turn the lights on.'

They cautiously felt their way to the front of the truck. Rampha's hand touched metal. 'I've got it,' he said and switched on the lights.

As their eyes adjusted to the sudden brightness, they looked around and saw that four solid steel walls and a very high roof surrounded them. Apart from a pile of sacks and a handmade stretcher in the one corner and his bike, the truck was empty. The strong odour was almost overpowering. It clung to them like a thick fog.

Paul gazed in amazement at the sheer size of the interior.

Rampha swung the light towards the pile of dirty sacks in the one corner. 'Tell you what,' he said. 'Let's make ourselves a mattress to sit on.'

'Good idea,' agreed Paul. He welcomed the chance of doing something constructive. They put the bike on its stand and guided the light towards the heap of sacks. They toiled for about five minutes, piling one sack upon the other. Finally, the rough mattress was complete. Rampha, in a sweat, flopped backwards onto it amidst a billow of dust. Paul followed his example 'Perfect,' he said. There was ample room for the two of them.

'We must save the battery,' said Rampha getting up to switch off the light.

'Wait,' said Paul.

Rampha paused. 'What is it?'

Paul went over to the bike and reaching into the one carrier he pulled out two unopened cans of coke. 'Look,' he announced with a flourish. 'The other one is Thuli's.'

Rampha smiled approvingly. 'Well done. At least we won't die of hunger or thirst,' he said. His hand moved towards the light switch. 'Are you ready?'

Paul nodded as he switched off the light.

Total darkness engulfed them once more. An oppressive silence that followed stifled them. Paul wondered desperately what would happen next.

They were trapped.

SEVENTEEN

Tiny's future meanwhile had brightened considerably. Quite by accident, he stumbled across all Brett's documents. They were neatly packed in a brown leather briefcase, along with the keys and remote for the Jeep back on the farm.

The case was concealed in the bathroom cupboard beneath the basin. Tiny never used that bathroom. He preferred the separate shower situated at the far end of the house. He noticed this cabinet for the first time when he had locked the boys in there.

What luck!

He would never have thought to look there. After hunting in vain through the whole house that was the last place he would have searched.

He forced open the flimsy lock and there it was.

Everything.

Brett had been ever so cunning.

He took the briefcase to the table, opened it and laboriously began studying the many papers inside. He discovered that Brett had lost no time in securing two American trophy hunters or agents, for these lions.

In fact, they were already in Africa and were due to return to the States on the eighth of March. Everything, including their contact numbers, was meticulously recorded in a hard-covered notebook. They were due to be picked up at six in the morning of the fifth at the Michelangelo hotel in Sandton. They had also been quoted a figure of seventy-five thousand rand for each lion shot.

Seventy-five thousand?

That would make a total of ... He found a pencil in the case and using a blank page of the notebook worked out the total using his own quick method of multiplication.

Three hundred thousand? The thief! The bloody friggin lying cheating thief! Tiny stared blankly at the wall opposite as he digested this information. The sheer magnitude of how he was to have been ripped off took his breath away.

He would have to formulate a plan of action. But brain exercises never came easy. Give him a hunting situation in the bush anytime. But all these papers? All that hard thinking and planning was definitely not his best.

He sighed. But what had to be done, had to be done. He would have to meet them at six-fifteen on the fifth. Now, when exactly was the fifth? He went to the open plan dining room and examined the fancy clock on the wall above the fireplace. The time showed three forty-five a.m. The date was Friday, the fifth of March.

The fifth? That was now, today!

Brett's clients were to be met in a few hours' time, at six. His two captives were still in the back of the truck. Tiny faced a dilemma.

What was he to do?

He was reasonably sure if they rode in front with him they would never suspect anyone was imprisoned in the back of the truck. But it could become an issue if they had any baggage they might want to take along.

He spent long minutes mulling over this problem. He sifted through the pile of papers with a sinking feeling. This whole lot would have to be read sooner or later. That was a mission and a half.

Shit.

But first, the customers had to be dealt with. Think, think.

At last, he decided he would persuade them if necessary, to leave behind any luggage that would not fit into the front cab. He would tell them that the back doors were jammed. Yes, that was a good excuse.

Okay, now some more reading.

He focused again on Brett's documents and notes. He discovered that over the years Brett had robbed him of hundreds of thousands of rands. Maybe even millions. The bloody dog. He deserved what he got, Tiny thought with satisfaction. He sighed heavily as he poured over the many transactions Brett had made and meticulously recorded in his book.

He turned his attention back to the names and contact numbers of the two clients they were supposed to meet today. He discovered they had requested a five-forty-five a.m. wake up call from Brett. It was a cell phone number. He got up again and studied the clock on the wall. That was about half an hour from now.

Again he read the fax. They explained they were not the usual American trophy hunters. The one wanted an opportunity to experience first hand what their clients' needs were and what could be expected on a safari. He was taking a whole lot of video equipment along to shoot the event. This way they could sell more hunts at bigger profits.

Tiny's heart sank. He would have to convince him about the truck's defective back doors.

At ten to six Tiny picked up the phone and dialed the contact number.

'Er … Mr Kentridge?' he enquired tentatively. His nervous voice ascended a minor third.

'Yes,' came a Texan drawl. 'Is that you Van? You sound terrible. Got a cold or somethin?'

Tiny cleared his throat, he told him Brett was not available but would be joining them later. Instead he, Tiny, Brett's partner, would be taking them to the farm.

'Okay,' drawled the voice at the other end. 'Say, Mr Tiny, we're no longer at the hotel. Would you meet us instead at our friend's house in Bryanston in about thirty minutes? That'll be six-thirty. Would you mind very much if we followed you to the farm? You see, we've picked up some video equipment here that we'd like to use, and it's all packed up. We've hired our own beach buggy. Besides, we'd really prefer to be independent.

'You'll follow …?' Tiny could hardly believe his ears.

'Sure,' came the reply. 'If that don't set you back none.'

'No, no,' Tiny assured them hastily. He swallowed several times. 'I don't mind at all.'

'Great. See yuh then. Don't be late.' Kentridge gave him the address and repeated it. The phone clicked, and the line went dead. In a daze Tiny slowly cradled the receiver. What amazing luck! All his problems were solved.

Now the only problem remaining was how to deal with those two prying, snot-nosed kids in the back of the truck. He would have to think of something along the way.

He marched through the house one more time to make sure he had missed nothing. He switched off the lights, locked the front door, then strode over to the truck. Tossing Brett's briefcase onto the passenger's seat Tiny climbed in and started the engine. His mood, his circumstances and his future had improved considerably. Now, all he had to do was to meet his clients

His clients.

EIGHTEEN

FRIDAY 05H30

As the truck jerked forward, Rampha got up from the mattress and felt his way to the back. A thin line of grey light appeared through the crack between double doors and at the hinges on both sides. He peeped through. He could only just make out the dirt road below, unfolding beneath him. Soon they turned right and bounced onto tar.

The truck picked up speed. He peered out. Apart from the road unwinding beneath them, he saw nothing else of value.

A half hour passed. Rampha could recognize outlines of rows of suburban houses as they flashed by on either side. Daylight approached.

'Paul,' he called out. 'Come and join me.'

Paul got up and made his way to his friend. He put his one eye to the crack. 'I can't see much out there.'

'Me neither,' said Rampha. 'If only we could pick up some clues. He's bound to stop sooner or later. There has to be traffic lights somewhere along the way. Maybe even some street names.'

'I suppose so,' said Paul. He felt despondent.

After a while he said. 'I'm just wondering what the girls are going to say when we don't pitch at the flagpole this morning.' Meeting at the flagpole before class was a ritual for the four of them.

'Yeah, I was thinking the same. They'll probably think we're still sleeping.'

'And old Banner. What will he say if we're not in class?'

Just then, without warning, the truck braked and lurched to the left taking a sharp turn. The boys were flung to the floor.

Tiny swore under his breath as he swung the truck to the left. He had almost missed the road sign that was concealed behind a bus shelter. He forgot the number of the house where he was to meet his clients, but he was confident he would spot their beach buggy. Sure enough, it was parked on the side of the street facing him. He slowed down as he drove straight towards it.

As the truck drew to a standstill, Paul and Rampha picked themselves up and ran to the back doors. They peered through the cracks to see if they could catch a glimpse of a street name or any other landmark. It was now almost light, and the street outside could be seen quite clearly.

Suddenly the truck swayed to the left and made half a u-turn. It reversed a little then moved forward again, completing the turn.

'Will you look at that,' said Paul peeping through the crack again. 'There's a beach buggy right here next to us.'

Rampha strained to get a better look. They could see two men dressed in safari outfits, sitting in the front seat of the open buggy. Rampha was just about to shout for help when he heard footsteps crunching next to the truck.

'What took you so long?' demanded the man in the passenger seat. 'And where's Van?' He had an American accent.

'Er, he's up at the farm,' came the high-pitched reply.

'So what are we waiting for?' said the American 'Let's get outta here.'

Moments later the front door of the truck slammed shut, and they set off once more. The beach buggy followed a short distance behind.

'I bet they're going to hunt those lions,' exclaimed Paul.

'Captain Peterson was right,' said Rampha. 'These people poach them and then sell them to big game hunters.'

'Canned hunting,' said Paul. 'Wonder where the farm is?'

It was now light enough for them to see one another quite clearly. Paul took another peek. The buggy was maintaining a steady distance behind them.

'Maybe they'll send a search party for us,' said Paul.

'Hope so,' said Rampha. 'But we were given Thursday off, remember. So they might think it applied to today as well.'

'Crap, that's a real bummer.'

Paul looked at his watch. It was eight minutes past six. 'By ten this morning maybe the girls will be worried and start looking for us.'

'Let's trust it's earlier than that,' said Rampha.

The two friends looked hopefully at each other. There was no need to panic.

They were wrong.

NINETEEN

A t ten to eight, the girls were waiting at the flagpole. Debbie looked at her watch.

'Those two are becoming slack, you know,' she said in exasperation. 'I hate being kept waiting.' She looked at her friend. 'I think we've been stood up.'

'Debbie,' Ayesha chided. 'They're probably still recovering. Or maybe they had an early appointment with the police like you said.'

Debbie laughed. 'I know. It's just that I'm absolutely *obsessed* with curiosity. I mean, I simply hate not knowing everything.' She sighed deeply. 'It kills me, it positively *kills* me!' She flicked her ponytail and said with a naughty smile. 'Besides, I wanted to savour their expressions when they feast their eyes on the new me.'

'We certainly did a better job this morning,' said Ayesha proudly. 'You look gorgeous.'

'We? I had nothing to do with it.' She laughed. 'But now it's all going to waste.'

'I'm sure they must be off on some secret mission somewhere,' smiled Ayesha. She was ever so proud of Rampha.

She remembered the first time they met. He had arrived at Woodlands only the year before, not like the rest of them who had been there since grade eight. His arrival was heralded by all the teachers as a coup for the school and was even publicly announced at assembly.

She, along with the rest of the kids, was expecting a right spoiled, rich brat, but Rampha had charmed the pants off her, (so to speak, she reminded herself hurriedly) and the rest of the school.

She had been in the prep room struggling with some biology problem when in walked Mister Rampha Know-It-All Singh. He greeted her with a huge smile designed to melt the most stubborn of hearts. He invited her to approach him, if she, or anyone else for that matter, needed help with any subject.

The absolute gall of the creature, she thought at the time. To test him, or more truthfully to catch him out, she had asked him to explain one of the most difficult biology questions in the book, namely cell division or mitosis. Not only had he answered in a way that made it simple to understand and grasp, but the rest of the learners in the prep room had slowly gathered around to listen in open-mouthed amazement to the *way* in which he explained it.

After that, she was his slave.

'I can't see what on earth could be so secret about a couple of lions on the loose. It's all over the news and the whole world knows about it anyhow.' Debbie interrupted her thoughts, looking at her watch for the umpteenth time. One whole minute had passed. She sighed again. 'We can't wait any longer, let's go.'

Ayesha glanced hopefully towards the boy's dormitory to see it there was any sign of them returning. But the girls had looked in before. The two of them had left without as much as a 'see you later'.

'Okay,' said Ayesha. 'Come on.'

They strolled along the walkway towards the classroom. First period was math, and the teacher was Miss Chadwick. Along with the rest of the teaching staff, Miss Chadwick had been summoned to a special staff meeting earlier on Thursday. There, Mr Banner had informed them that Rampha Singh and Paul Patterson were assisting the police in that dreadful escaped Lion Park saga that was earning the school such a lot of unwanted publicity due to its close proximity.

When Miss Chadwick walked into the classroom and boys were not there, she was not unduly perturbed. She assumed their absence yesterday applied to today as well. She proceeded to the front of the class and started the lesson.

By lunchtime, five lessons had come and gone.

Five different teachers had thought as Miss Chadwick had. It never for a moment crossed their minds to report the boys' absence.

The rest of the day progressed normally.

FRIDAY 08H30

Sam Kentridge was at the wheel of the Volkswagen buggy. He wished he had not been so hasty in procuring this ridiculous little car. It was the only vehicle available that had a top that opened. There was barely enough room to contain all the video equipment they had bought. He wanted to make a movie to show their prospective clients.

How was he to know that the roads here in South Africa were so bad? Why back home in Dallas the going would have been so much smoother. He jerked the steering for the millionth time to avoid another pothole.

'How much longer do we have to put up with this?' he complained.

'Yeah,' said Hank Bass. 'And all this rain! Ain't this sunny South Africa?' He shifted in his seat for more comfort.

They were both dressed in what they thought was typical African hunting gear. Khaki shirts and shorts with all the bells and whistles. The only non-African items were the Stetsons on their heads.

'When I was a'huntin' in Kenya with Brett van Jaarsveld,' said Hank, picking up their conversation. 'My guides told me they ain't never seen a better shot with a rifle.'

'Well I'm the novice here,' said Sam Kentridge. 'Done a bit of clay shootin' back at the ranch. But never shot no live animal.'

'I've done plenty. I'll teach you,' said Hank modestly.

Sam's real interest in this trip was to explore canned hunting. This was a big thing in specialized tourism. His medium size business in downtown Dallas had done well over the years. It had made him very wealthy.

Lately, however with the global recession biting deeper, the travel business was in a slump. Trophy hunters, on the other hand, seemed to have plenty of money to throw around.

So when Hank Bass strolled into his office and asked him to book a trip to Johannesburg South Africa, Sam Kentridge wanted to know more. Thus a loose partnership was formed.

He swerved again narrowly missing a deep gash in the road.

TWENTY

In the back of the truck, the trip was harrowing. The road seemed endless. After a while, they lost interest in the car behind them. It was simply always there attached like an invisible umbilical chord.

'It's no use,' said Paul in despair. It was his turn to keep a lookout. 'The road just goes on and on. No landmarks, nothing. Just open country. And that stupid friggin beach buggy following as if their lives depended on it.'

Rampha sighed deeply. 'This is such a waste of time. I think we should rather be making plans to escape.'

'Yeah,' said Paul. 'And I suppose you could just force open the doors and jump out.'

'No,' said Rampha. The sarcasm brushed past him. 'I'm thinking that we should be prepared, if and when the doors are opened.'

'I don't understand.' Paul looked at him. His friend was serious. Was there no end to his craziness?

155

'Think about it,' said Rampha. 'Are we just going to stand there like two idiots and let that big guy do what he likes with us? Or are we going to be pro-active?'

'Pro-active?' said Paul in exasperation. 'You mean like jumping out and running in opposite directions so that only one of us might be caught?'

Rampha looked at him with that deep contemplative, faraway look he sometimes got when an idea was forming.

'What?' Paul prompted, impatiently.

'Excellent! Genius!' exclaimed Rampha. 'Now that's *really* a good idea.'

'Cut the crap, I was being sarky.'

'No seriously. If one of us can get away, it makes our chances of survival so much better.'

'And if he shoots us? Not much chance of survival then.'

'Paul,' Rampha burst out in frustration. 'We have to be positive about our situation. We can't be negative. Don't you think that I'm as scared as you are, *and* as irritated? Do you think I live in cloud cuckoo land and have no fears of my own? Well, let me tell you that I *am* scared shitless. But I'm not going to let it take over my life.' He looked hard at his friend. 'While we're alive, we'll fight.'

Paul was silent for a moment. His eyes stung, and he felt ashamed.

Of course, Rampha was right. He had guts. No wonder he did so well at school. Nothing was impossible for him. Paul wished he had just one percent of the courage his friend possessed.

'Okay,' he said, quietly. 'Let's make that a ruling. When the doors open, we rush out at the same time. He can't run in two directions at once.'

'Correct.' Rampha's face relaxed into a half-grin. 'But it does mean one of us might get caught.'

'Yup, that's possible,' Paul nodded. 'But, like you said, it's better that both of us are not prisoners. At least, if one of us is free, the other should be able to get help or something.'

Rampha lay back on the mattress, his hands behind his head. 'I'm glad we have a plan of sorts,' he said yawning widely, suddenly feeling tired. 'I'm going to close my eyes for a bit.'

'I'll take one last look,' said Paul.

Rampha was often an enigma to him. His brain power was enormous, and Paul knew for certain his friend was destined for greatness in life.

He got up and peeped through the crack. In the morning light, he saw the road flashing by like a movie in reverse and the beach buggy flapping tenaciously like the tail of a kite.

He made a silent vow never again to be negative. Or try, at least.

His thoughts wandered back to the rift between his parents. What would happen to him if they parted for keeps? He knew some friends whose parents had separated. He saw the trauma they had suffered as a result. Taffy Long, for instance, had gone completely off the rails and had taken to drugs. That was a few years ago. Today he was in rehab, out of school doing menial jobs. Paul had spotted him a few weeks back.

Taffy was a car park attendant at the Fourways shopping mall working for tips. His life was a shambles. Paul was shocked at his friend's unkempt appearance.

The light had faded from his eyes.

He seriously did not want that to happen to him. But the relationship between his Mom and Dad had worsened visibly over the past few months. It was not pleasant. In all probability, it would deteriorate even further.

Paul turned his attention back to the road, peering through the slit in the door.

'It's raining,' he reported, after a long while. 'We must have travelled at least a hundred km's by now.'

'Probably more,' said Rampha. His voice was sleepy.

Paul stretched and yawned. 'I think I'll turn in as well,' he said flopping down on the dusty mattress. The hum of the tyres on the road and the monotonous drone of the engine had a hypnotic effect, and they soon drifted off again.

FRIDAY 11H45

In the buggy behind, hypnotized by the boring journey Hank Bass cast his mind back to the month before. He had a large cattle spread in Texas, fifty miles outside Dallas. After he and Sam Kentridge had hammered out a deal, Sam drove to his ranch to finalize everything.

Hank glowed with pride as he showed his new partner around. When they entered his den downstairs, he tried gallantly, but failed miserably, to hide his euphoria as Sam wandered around gawking at the stuffed trophies decorating his wall. Each head was illuminated with cleverly concealed lighting that gave each animal a lifelike appearance. The place was like a national museum and almost as big.

'Shot everyone myself,' he boasted. The only stuffed head missing was that of the king of the beasts. Hank coveted the animal that would fill that space.

At the fully equipped bar in the corner, they finally agreed on percentages each partner would cough up to clinch the South Africa deal.

Sam was more than willing to pay the lion's share. He was looking to boost his tourism business, and canned hunting seemed to be the most lucrative option.

That was a little more than a month ago.

The plan had materialized, the trips booked, the planes caught, and now here they were in South Africa almost at their destination.

'Looks like we're here,' said Sam. He longed to get out and stretch his legs.

The van in front of them swung left onto a dirt road. The rain had increased.

TWENTY-ONE

FRIDAY 12H00

Asleep for almost two hours the boys were rudely awakened by bumping and swaying as the truck made a left turn and hit a rough dirt road.

'I'm thirsty,' hinted Rampha. 'Where's that remaining coke?'

'Excellent suggestion,' said Paul, producing the remaining can. 'We'll have to share, you first.'

He tossed it over. Rampha caught it deftly.

He popped it open and sucked gratifying draughts of the sweet liquid.

'Nectar of the Gods,' proclaimed Rampha, emitting a long, loud and satisfying burp before passing the can. Paul drank deeply and tried to match Rampha's effort but failed miserably. They laughed spontaneously.

Their situation hit the dregs, but their spirits topped the brim.

Three meters from where they lay, Tiny sat behind the wheel in the cab. He was scheming how to stall his clients.

He had to deal with two issues. The first and lesser of the two was what to do with his stupid captives. If he tied them up and left them in the one outside rondavel, he would be able to deal with them after the hunt. They were a minor irritation. His main problem was he needed time to prepare the lions and this he could not do with his clients hanging around. He had to find a means of stalling them somehow. But how would he do it?

He had a thought.

With the rain beating down as it had been for the past two hours, with any luck the dry riverbed could have enough flow to make it impassable for any low-slung vehicle.

The beach buggy was a low-slung vehicle.

He had to persuade his clients somehow to wait at the riverbank. He would then go on ahead prepare for the hunt and take care of his prisoners at the same time. He would then return with Brett's Jeep to fetch them. He was glad he had the keys.

He smiled to himself as he whistled Sarie Marais his favourite tune. Nothing beats a simple plan.

He rounded the corner overgrown with bushes and trees and held his breath. What would the river be like? Would it be flowing; would it be full?

Indeed, it was. Flowing and full. Che Sera Sera.

Tiny changed down to first gear and entered the river carefully. The swiftly flowing water lapped the top of the truck's tyres. It was almost a meter deep. He slowly made his way across. In his rear view mirror, Tiny noted with satisfaction that the beach buggy, with its nose at the waterline, had come to a standstill. The two Americans were waving madly and shouting for him to slow down. He ignored them and kept going till he reached the other side. There he stopped.

He climbed out of the cab, walked to the water's edge and waved.

His clients waved back.

'Hey!' Tiny shouted in his high-pitched voice. 'You wait there. I'll come back in a couple of hours and fetch you with the Jeep.'

'No! You come back right now. We can go in your truck,' shouted Kentridge.

Tiny pretended not to hear and waved again. 'You just wait here,' he shouted. 'I'll be right back.' With that, he swung himself into the cab, slammed the door and set off. In the mirror, he could see the men gesticulating wildly. He smiled as he gathered speed. Another twenty minutes and he would be at the farm.

His plan was working.

In the back, Rampha and Paul were standing up. Their shoes and socks were soaking wet. The water that had seeped through the bottom and sides of the doors was sloshing back and forth across the floor. The mattress was floating about like some hairy science fiction movie monster.

The truck climbed the bank on the other side, and the water surged to the rear like a tsunami and gushed out through the bottom of the metal doors.

'I hope this will wash away some of the awful smell,' said Rampha.

'Imagine some stray lion picking up this scent and not being able to follow it.' Paul said. They giggled at the thought. He peered through the crack. 'Now, why is he leaving those two behind?'

They were puzzled by the deliberate way in which the big guy had left the beach buggy stranded on the riverbank opposite.

'He's up to something,' said Rampha looking worriedly at his friend. 'And I think it has to do with us.'

'He's got to get rid of us first.' Paul felt a knot in his stomach. 'I'm really scared.'

'We must stick to our plan.' Rampha said. 'As soon as he opens the door, we rush out and go in opposite directions.'

Paul nodded. 'I'll go left; you can go right.'

'Fine.' Then Rampha had another idea. 'Tell you what. Let's each take a few of these wet bags and throw them at him before we jump.'

'Great,' agreed Paul. 'That way, we may both get away.'

The two of them set about piling the soggy, evil-smelling bags close to the door.

When they had completed their task, Paul heaved a sigh. 'Now all we have to do is wait.'

'Hello, we're very good at that already,' laughed Rampha, hollowly. 'It can't be much further now. Remember, if either of us gets away, we must simply go the nearest house or farm, and phone for help. I'll give you Captain Sharp's cell number.'

'But I've got no pen or paper.'

'Then you're just going to have to remember it, aren't you?'

'I'm the world's worst number rememberer on this entire planet, maybe even the whole galaxy.'

'So, I'm going to have to teach you, and you're going to have to learn, simple.'

'My dear Rampha, I can remember most things. But don't ask me to remember numbers. It's my worst. You know what my math marks are like.'

164

'Well, that's about to change forever.'

Paul grimaced and sighed deeply as he shook his head slowly.

'Right,' said Rampha enthusiastically. 'Let's begin.'

The instruction took less than five minutes for Paul to fix the number firmly in his head.

'You never cease to amaze me, Rampha,' he said afterwards, regarding his friend with a mixture of wonder and disbelief. 'Where do you *get* all that stuff?'

'It's very simple,' Rampha smiled indulgently. 'You're walking around with the most sophisticated computer in the world. It's right there on your head in your brain. All you have to do is know how to use it. Simple'

'Ah, but therein lies the rub,' quoted Paul.

'Everything in life has a key to it,' Rampha went on patiently. 'Think of it as a board in front of you. The board contains thousands of keys hanging up. Each key is clearly marked. Next to this board is another panel with thousands of little drawers or compartments, *also* clearly marked. It's simple to select the right key. We use that key to unlock the drawer to the knowledge and power contained *in* that drawer. You insert the key, unlock the drawer, pull it open and voila, there it is! As I said, simple.'

'To *you* maybe. But to mere mortals like me…'

'Nonsense,' Rampha interrupted him. 'If you want a pair of socks, you don't go to the drawer where your shirts are. Or if you're looking for your trousers, you don't search in your shoebox. Of course, if all your clothes are stuffed randomly into a cluttered up drawer, you're not going to find anything in a hurry, are you? The same with your mind.'

Paul contemplated him thoughtfully. 'You're seriously sick, do you know that? You belong in an institution.'

Rampha laughed delightedly. 'Hey, it's your turn in the barrel.'

'Okay.' Paul peered once more through his crack. Shortly after Rampha followed suit, then looked at his watch. It was past one in the afternoon and still raining very hard. They had covered hundreds of kilometres.

Just then the truck began to slow down.

Rampha swallowed and spoke softly. 'I think we're here.'

Paul took a deep breath. 'Yes, I think we are.'

They both moved to their positions and waited. The truck came to a halt and then reversed slowly. It stopped again, engine running. They heard footsteps.

'He's coming,' whispered Paul. 'Ready?'

Rampha nodded.

They waited, tensed, for the huge doors to swing open. Nothing happened. They then heard the sound of a gate scraping open.

'What's happening?' whispered Rampha, perplexed.

'I wish I knew.'

The footsteps crunched past them to the front of the truck once more. Then the truck reversed again, just a little, then stopped.

'He's coming now,' whispered Rampha urgently. 'Get ready.'

Paul nodded. They picked up their sacks and stood poised.

The doors were being unlocked. One of the doors swung open. No one was in sight!

For a brief moment, Rampha looked at Paul, then made a decision.

'Jump and run for it.' He shouted, putting action to words. He leaped out. His feet hit the ground with a thump. Looking around, he noticed that Paul had also landed safely. He was dashing off to the left. Paul veered to the right, just as they had agreed.

They had taken no more than a dozen steps when Rampha skidded to a halt. He looked over at Paul who was still running.

'Lions,' he screamed hysterically. 'Back in the truck.'

Paul stopped dead and looked up. He was no more than ten meters away from four lions watching the unfolding drama with interest.

They swung around on their heels and charged to the back of the truck and scrambled into their former prison. The lions all leaped up poised for action. Their black tufted tails swayed slowly back and forth.

Leaning nonchalantly against the gate of the camp, stood Tiny. A smile played on his lips.

He had predicted exactly their every move. His hunter's instincts told him they would not sit idly by, waiting to be taken.

Uncanny.

The lions wanted nothing more to do with the truck that had caused them so much misery. They moved back to the centre on the enclosure. There they huddled and looked on with great curiosity.

Tiny stood and watched with a satisfied expression. He was enjoying the drama of it.

'Okay,' he said, his high voice echoed into the back of the truck. 'Now that I have your attention, you know what will happen if you try anything funny.'

He reached for some rope hanging over the gate. 'Right, one at a time now, with your hands behind your back.' He looked at Paul. 'You first.'

Dejected, Paul glanced at Rampha who shrugged and nodded. They could not possibly escape now.

He walked slowly towards his captor. Rampha followed.

Tiny pulled them out of the van and thrust both under the open doors of the truck. He bound and gagged them firmly and marched them to one of the free standing rondavels away from the main cluster.

There he tied them securely to the centre pole that supported the thatched roof.

Rampha wanted to puke as the cloth filled his mouth. It was tied securely 'round the back of his head. He could hardly breathe. His eyes rolled wildly. He thought he would choke or go into a spasm. Paul fared no better. He managed to breathe through his nose.

'You two are going to be quiet until after the hunt. That's tomorrow. Then we'll decide what happens to you,' Tiny threatened. 'Nobody's gonna spoil this chance of mine.'

He closed the door with a bang and shot the bolt on the outside. He was not a killer at heart, but nothing was going to spoil this opportunity.

The boys looked around their prison. Apart from the door, there were no windows at all. The rondavel was some kind of storeroom.

Satisfied there was no chance of their escape, Tiny went back to the truck. He drove it out of the enclosure and closed the gates. He parked it next to the Jeep under the shade cloth. He climbed out, slammed the door shut then strode purposefully into the house to prepare the next step.

TWENTY-TWO

He reached for the Boito 12-gauge capture gun that hung over the fireplace and prepared eight darts. He then opened the gun safe and brought out his Ruger .375. He checked the magazine; four in one up. Satisfied, he headed back to the lion enclosure two rifles gripped firmly in one huge hand. The black bag of syringes hung around his neck.

Opening the gates and leaving them wide, he cautiously made his way towards the four lions. Four huge heads followed his every move as he walked slowly but surely around to their rear. Suddenly, with one accord, they turned and swung around to face him, their tails swishing slowly from side to side, muscles taut and senses alert.

Tiny slipped off the safety catch on his rifle and with one hand, fired a shot into the air.

The lions jumped with fright and trotted towards the entrance of the enclosure, out of the gate and into the open bush. As he anticipated, they headed instinctively away from the domestic surroundings.

The rain had now settled into a steady, heavy drizzle. The animals moved towards the bush. Tiny followed them. He moved through the

169

thicket without a sound, his huge frame gliding along behind his quarry like a phantom.

He was awesome in the bush. With nostrils flared to pick up any scent and his whole body vigilant and rapt with concentration, he followed the lions' trail. They may just as well have painted a bold white line through the bush.

His ever-watchful eyes darted from side to side, observing a pug mark here, a flattened piece of grass there, or a broken twig on the side of a bush. As he picked up every possible clue, his mind computed and translated the data into the language only an expert tracker would understand. He kept moving upwind of his quarry, knowing their senses too, were needle sharp.

Although he could not actually see them, he knew the predators were no more than a hundred meters ahead of him, keeping a steady pace. They could travel many kilometres a day in this way, but Tiny knew that they would soon stop for a rest and to acquaint themselves with their new surroundings.

He increased his pace and, within a few short minutes, he caught up with them. His biggest advantage was that these four lions were not unduly worried by the presence of man.

Just as he expected, they had stopped in a small clearing to take stock of their whereabouts. It was the perfect place.

He loaded the dart and taking careful aim, he fired the first shot. It found its mark on the flank of the male. The huge animal merely flinched as he turned his head towards the sound. The rest of the pack looked on but remained where they stood. He loaded again and connected the lioness furthest away. She leaped around and attempted to bite the syringe that dangled from her right buttock. The rest of the pride disdainfully ignored the crack of the gun with no more than a casual reaction.

Two down, two to go.

Tiny was amazed that they had not yet taken off. He accurately darted the third lioness with a chest shot and still they remained standing. To get a clearer view of the remaining lioness, Tiny had to move to his right which was downwind of them, and it was then that they spotted his movement for they started walking off. He kept his focus on the target and fired his last shot. This time, at the sound of the gun, the four lions increased their pace. Tiny was not too sure whether he had successfully managed to dart that last lioness. But time was against him, and he had to get back.

He was reasonably sure, even if she had not been hit, she would not stray too far from the rest of her pride.

Taking a quick bearing, he picked up his gear and set off back to the house. A short while later he was in Brett's Jeep and speeding on the dirt road towards the river where he had left his clients. It took twenty minutes to get there.

He reached the brow of the riverbank. The beach buggy was still berthed on the bank opposite. The two Americans huddled on the back seat were sharing the only umbrella they had. Tiny drove slowly through the river and pulled up alongside them.

'Where the hell have you been?' Whined Mr Kentridge. He was getting mighty fed up with this whole sorry, trophy hunting business. Give him the luxuries of a decent hotel or his palatial home in the States, any day.

'Yeah,' chimed Mr Bass, 'What took you so long?'

'As you can see,' explained Tiny. 'I had to fetch the Jeep.'

'Well, let's get going then,' said his client, climbing out of the beach buggy. 'Do you think this buggy is safe here? It's a hired car, and I'm responsible.'

'Of course it is,' Tiny assured him. 'No one ever comes here. Take the keys out anyhow.'

They removed all their bags and their video equipment and bundled them onto the floor in the back of the Jeep. The two men then flopped onto the back seat and slammed the door shut. 'Okay,' said Hank Bass, making his dark mood felt. 'Let's get outta here and get us some lions.'

Tiny was annoyed and felt slighted that his clients had not sat in the front seat with him. It made him feel like a paid chauffeur. He could never understand why people treated him so badly. He turned the Jeep around and entered the river once more.

Back at the farm, Tiny showed his clients to the guest rondavel and helped them to transfer their belongings.

'As soon as you're ready,' Tiny said. 'We can go out and see if we can find anything.'

'Yeah? Well, we've been ready since early this morning,' Mr Kentridge retorted. 'After this disastrous day, the least you can do is find us some lions.'

'We'll find them alright.' Tiny assured him. These foreigners were all the same, he thought. They presumed lion hunting to be an afternoon picnic in the park.

But he had a difficult first task ahead of him. He had to somehow get the money out of them. He was at a total loss how to broach the subject. Part payment up front was what Brett had written in his notebook.

Tiny was, therefore, dumbfounded when Mr Kentridge confronted him with a fat envelope. 'Here's the up-front payment, one hundred K in cash, just as Brett arranged. The balance when we've got our lions.'

One hundred thousand, and more to come! Tiny could hardly believe his ears.

Brett was one helluva operator.

'I'll see you back here in five minutes.' Tiny said He gingerly took the envelope and hurried back to the main rondavel. En route, he stopped to check on his prisoners. Approaching the door silently, he listened. There was no sound from within. Probably sleeping, he thought. They were becoming a big headache. But they were worth every ounce of the trouble he had taken to buy himself time. He needed to conclude this hunting deal.

He would then attend to the two boys after he got rid of his clients.

One hundred thousand! It was his ticket to an independent life. He deposited the money in a duffle bag in his room and quietly made his way back to the kitchen where he fetched his rifle off the wall, loading an extra cartridge into the breech. He went to meet them.

'Okay, we're ready,' said Sam Kentridge as Tiny approached.

The man was wearing a bright green mackintosh over his safari suit. Stetsons on their heads, both he and Bass wore binoculars, video cameras, compasses, haversacks and a whole assortment of gimmicky hunting paraphernalia hanging from their necks and shoulders. Tiny sighed but made no comment. They looked like a pair of circus clowns and would be visible for kilometres around.

'Please follow me,' Tiny said. He turned and set the pace towards the bush. The two behind him followed, chatting excitedly.

'When I was in Kenya I remember going with clients on a hunt like this,' rambled Bass. 'There, the grass was so high it could hide an elephant. I said to my guide ….'

'Please keep quiet!' Tiny snapped in annoyance, and then added hastily, 'Mr Bass, please.'

'Say, what's the matter with you, friend?' He glared at Tiny. 'The lions are far from here. They can't hear us, can they?'

'Well.' said Tiny, his voice rising a little, 'sound travels in the bush, you know.' He kept walking.

The rain had wiped out most of the tracks, but Tiny could still follow all other signs and landmarks quite easily. The two Americans trailed behind through the bush as the rain started falling heavily once more.

There was a constant jabbering from the two men behind him. They were really no-nonsense, up-front novices, Tiny thought, and making it very difficult for him to concentrate on his job. Twice he had almost lost the tracks.

A short while later they approached the clearing where he had left the lions earlier. They were nowhere to be seen. Tiny realized they would have to hurry before it got dark. He picked up some faint tracks and followed them. They led to the edge of a shallow gully overgrown with thick bushes and tall grass. A stream about three meters wide flowed at the bottom. The rookies stopped beside him, firing questions.

'What is it?'

'Have you spotted them?'

'Here, let me take a look.'

Tiny turned on them. 'Shut up!' He commanded in a stage whisper. They obeyed immediately, and Tiny turned back to his task.

From the top, he searched for pugmarks near the water's edge on the opposite side of the creek. There were none. This meant that the animals were still on the side where they stood. They had to be very close.

He was now on full alert as he sniffed the air around him. He was usually able to smell them if they were close by. He listened for any sound that did not fit the pattern of falling rain, sighing wind, bush insects and rustling leaves. He knew that the dose of Zolitil he had administered could not have worn off already. But he had seen many animals recovering from a dart. They did some very unpredictable things in their confusion.

Then, almost imperceptibly, a different sound invaded his subconscious. It was out of place with the rhythm of the other noses. A stealthy sound!

Tiny's eyes darted around trying to detect a shape or a shadow in the falling dusk.

The lions were close – he could sense it.

'This is such a waste of time,' Bass's rasping voice shattered the silence.

Then suddenly the scene changed.

About eight meters to the right, a huge dark shape, emerged from the tall grass, and there stood one of the lionesses, looking directly towards them. Tiny could see that she was still slightly groggy.

But aroused enough she could turn dangerous.

Sam Kentridge gazed at the animal in wonder. She was unquestionably the most beautiful creature he had ever seen. As she stood there in all her regal majesty, he felt profoundly humbled in a way that left his heart pounding. If it was not for money, that went with deals like this, who in their right mind would want to destroy such a magnificent animal?

Bass fumbled to unsling his rifle. 'This one is mine,' he whispered hoarsely. 'This is mine. Please!' He was shaking with nervous excitement. Sam Kentridge in the meantime had taken out the video camera and was ready to roll. Bass gestured for him to be quiet and to make no move.

Tiny held his own gun at the ready in case the other animals were nearby and were waiting in ambush. Although judging from the appearance and condition of this female it was unlikely.

'Just leave this one to me,' the American kept muttering as he put the rifle to his shoulder. He took careful aim.

At such point-blank range, the man could hardly miss thought Tiny with disdain. He watched as the man squeezed the trigger.

Nothing happened!

'What's the matter with this gun?' Bass demanded.

Sam Kentridge was quite relieved the gun had not gone off. Looking at the splendid lioness through the camera lens and from such a close range gave him a sudden deep feeling of remorse. He suddenly realized he did not want to go through with this. He wanted no part of such a cruel event.

It was murder plain and simple.

He did not want to destroy this lovely creature, but he could neither back down nor say anything at this point.

'Your safety is still on,' Tiny told him sarcastically. Shaking his head in disbelief, he put his own rifle to his shoulder.

'No, no!' shouted Bass. He released the catch and took aim once more. 'This one is mine.'

Tiny lowered his rifle.

The shot rang out followed by a thud and a roar of pain from the lioness as she disappeared wounded, into the bush.

Kentridge winced.

'Now look what you've done,' said Tiny. His voice quivered with anger. 'You've gone and wounded it.'

'You're supposed to be the guide,' the angry man flung back at him. 'If you had told me sooner my safety was on, I would've had more time to prepare.' He slung his rifle over his shoulder, furious that he had made a fool of himself.

Sam Kentridge felt sick. He hoped against hope the lioness was not in too much pain.

'You can take us back to camp now,' said Hank Bass 'We'll go out tomorrow.' He turned to go, and then muttered under his breath. 'I've had enough incompetence for one day.'

You're telling me, thought Tiny, overhearing the remark.

'But we can't just leave a wounded animal,' protested Sam Kentridge. 'It's cruel.'

Hank Bass turned to him. 'Tomorrow we'll go on a proper hunt,' he said smarting with embarrassment.

Yeah thanks a lot, that helps, thought Kentridge. He would feel a whole lot better if he had the courage to switch this job description. He would love to save these creatures instead of promoting their destruction. Heck, he would much sooner pump his money and his energies into some sort of conservation effort.

Canned hunting was a shoddy excuse for a career, and he would be damned if he was going to promote it further. He had enough money to ride the economic storm.

'We'll find her tomorrow,' said Tiny, not reading the undercurrents, but not wanting to upset his clients any further. At least not until he had secured all his money out of them.

Hank Bass shrugged his shoulders indifferently.

Sam Kentridge was deeply upset. He would try later to persuade the big guy to go out and finish off the wounded lioness. It was the humane thing to do. He really did not savour all this unnecessary barbarism. Not for the sake of some stuffed predator's head decorating some wall. No Sir!

It was fast becoming dark. They made their way back to the rondavels. Sam Kentridge's footsteps dragged through the long grass. With each step, the guilt he felt gripped like giant jaws crushing him. He had no idea the hunting packages he contemplated selling, could result in anything like this.

To tell the truth, he had never even considered that the realities of this so-called lucrative money-spinner would be anything as inhumane as this. His visit to South Africa was to serve two purposes. One was to secure more discounted destinations for his legitimate tourist operation. The second was to meet van Jaarsveld and see for himself what canned hunting was all about.

But this?

This gave new meaning to the word depraved. It plumbed the greatest depth of cruelty.

His disgust leaked all over him like an Iceland volcanic ash cloud covering him with cloying stickiness and filth. Hank Bass walking behind was immune to the consequences of their actions.

Tiny also appeared unconcerned.

Sam Kentridge had embraced this venture with too little forward investigation. Hank Bass had swept him away with the promise of adventure and easy money. It was painful in the extreme. He was determined to remedy his mistake as soon as he was able.

Yes, he would resist any further involvement in this little excursion. He would become an activist and strive to prevent other such so-called hunting practices. Hell, canned hunting was an accepted norm. He resolved to put thoughts into action as soon as he got back home. He would start with his company.

TWENTY-THREE

FRIDAY 18H30

The girls headed to their dorm. The boys were neither to be seen on campus nor in their room.

Ayesha voiced the question. 'It very strange they should be called away for the whole day, Debs,' she said worriedly.

'I know,' said Debbie. 'And Mrs Norris wasn't too happy either. He's never missed music lessons before.'

'Weren't they supposed to be picked up by the cops?' Ayesha chewed on her lip. 'I think we should go to Mr Banner.'

'We could risk serious humiliation.' countered Debbie. 'Everyone knows they're helping the police.' She wondered if any teachers knew that she was soft on Paul. If she openly expressed anything more than just passing concern, what would they think?

'I know that,' persisted Ayesha. 'But we should have heard from them by now.' She looked at her friend with an expression of anguish. 'I'm *really* worried, Debs. I honestly think we should see Mr Banner.'

'But it's so late. What if he tells us to mind our own business?'

'Too bad, it's a chance we'll have to take.'

Debbie thought for a moment. To be truthful, she also felt more than a little anxious. She thought for a moment then made up her mind 'Okay, I'm with you. Let's go.'

A deluge of relief washed over Ayesha as they hurried to Mr Banner's office. They were in luck. The lights were on.

Knocking tentatively, they waited.

'Come in!'

They went in.

'What a pleasant surprise,' the headmaster beamed benevolently. He rose from behind his desk and cradled his warm pipe in the rack on his desk. 'What can I do for the two of you?'

'We're worried about Paul and Rampha, Sir,' Ayesha burst out.

'What about them?' Mr Banner gazed over the top of his glasses.

'They haven't been in school all day.' Debbie felt awkward and flushed as she held her breath. If he fobbed them off with some vague explanation, she would simply *die*.

Here it comes.

'You are probably aware the police have asked for their assistance in this Lion Park case. I have told the staff that the boys should be excused from time to time,' said Mr Banner.

'For the whole day?' persisted Ayesha.

Debbie suffered rising embarrassment as she looked across at Mr Banner.

A frown creased the headmaster's forehead. He picked up the phone. 'We'll soon find out won't we?' he said, dialling a number.

'Captain Peterson, please,' he waited.

Minutes later, but what seemed like hours, Mr Banner spoke again.

'Hello?' he said, as he selected a fresh pipe. 'Hello, Captain Peterson? Banner here, Woodlands School.' He jammed the pipe into his mouth. 'Yes, yes. I'm fine, thank you. Sorry to trouble you, but may I have a word with either of my lads.' He listened in silence then removed the pipe. 'You haven't? No, no according to two classmates they haven't been seen in school today.' He listened again. 'Right, we'll expect you shortly.' Mr Banner replaced the receiver slowly.

His face was like stone.

'They're not with him,' he said gravely. 'They haven't been with the Captain since yesterday afternoon.'

Ayesha paled. Debbie shuffled uneasily as her colour drained.

Mr Banner leaned over, scraped the dregs from his pipe into the dustbin and filled it from the bowl on his desk. 'Look,' he said. 'I really don't think there should be any cause for alarm. We'll wait for Captain Peterson to see what he suggests.'

He lit the pipe, and great billows of smoke filled the air. 'Tell you what,' he went on, pressing the hot tobacco firmly down with his thumb, 'Why don't you take a quick look in their dormitory.' He waved the pipe around. 'I know it's against rules, but I'm giving you special permission.'

Debbie and Ayesha hurried towards the door.

'I presume you do know which room is theirs?' He added pointedly. 'See if you can find anything at all, then report back to me, on the double.'

The girls opened the door and fled. They dared not tell him they had already looked.

'How can he be so flippant at a time like this?' puffed Ayesha.

'I think he's like really so ultra-bugged, but won't show it,' said Debbie breathing heavily as they approached the boys' dormitory. 'I'm scared. What do you think might have happened?'

'I *wish* I knew,' said Ayesha. 'It's so unlike them. I'm really afraid something might have happened.' She then voiced the fears that had been assailing both of them. 'You don't think that one of the lions could have …?'

'That's impossible,' Debbi almost shouted, not wanting to hear any more. 'If only one of them was missing….'

She reached out and touched Ayesha's arm. 'We mustn't go upsetting ourselves. It won't do any good. We have to be positive about the whole thing.'

They reached the dorm a little out of breath.

'I know you're right,' Ayesha agreed. Using their legitimate excuse, she entered the room boldly and lifted the pillows off both beds, began searching. The boys' pyjama shorts were folded neatly at the head of their beds. 'They were still dressed when we saw them last. This means they must have got up sometime in the night,' she said.

Debbie opened the top drawer of one of the cupboards. There she spotted a cell phone lying on top of some folded items of clothing. It looked like Paul's.

'I can't imagine Paul going too far without this,' she said holding it up.

'You're right,' repeated Ayesha.

She rummaged in the drawer of the other cupboard. She recognized Rampha's Blackberry right away. 'They couldn't have gone too far,' she said moving towards the door, ready to leave.

'Hey!' She stopped and turned around. 'What about Rampha's bike?'

'Good idea, let's check if it is still there?'

'Yes. Come on.'

They hurried to where Rampha's motorcycle was usually chained to a strut in the carport area.

The vehicle was not there.

'Sloppy Joe's!' they said simultaneously.

'But surely they wouldn't have stayed out the whole evening, and the next day, without calling or something?'

'You're right.' A feeling of dread engulfed Ayesha for the second time. 'Let's go back to the office.'

They ran back to Mr Banner's office and tapped on the door. The response was quicker this time. 'Come in.'

The headmaster was on the line to the Lion Park 'Yes, certainly,' he was saying. 'I'll let you know as soon as we hear anything, Mr Resnick.' He replaced the telephone and resumed his furious puffing.

'Sit down. We seem to have a problem,' he said. 'Did you find anything?'

'They are not in their room, Sir, and they didn't sleep there last night,' said Ayesha taking a seat.

'And their motorcycle is missing,' added Debbie sitting down.

Mr Banner paced the floor lost in thought.

'So! They must have gone somewhere – without permission of course – and either decided they did not wish to return or, they are unable to return for whatever reason.' A few heavy puffs of blue smoke obscured his face for a moment. 'I rather think it might be the latter.'

He stopped pacing and looked at the girls. 'I think you two should wait to see Captain Peterson when he arrives. He might wish to ask you a few questions.' He went behind his desk and replaced his pipe in the rack and began shuffling some papers.

The girls looked silently at each other. To say they were very worried was the understatement of the century. The boys' fates hung in the balance. The truth could possibly see them being disciplined, or even worse, expelled. Mr Banner's stony silence did not help either.

The huge clock on the wall noisily ticked the minutes by.

A knock on the door broke the silence. With a start, Ayesha turned in her chair.

'Come in.' called Mr Banner.

The door opened and in walked Captain Peterson. He was alone and looked grim as he faced the three of them. Mr Banner rose and stepped to the front of the desk where he perched himself on the one corner.

'Captain Peterson, this is Ayesha Surtee and Debbie White.'

The man nodded to the girls. 'Pleasure to meet you,' he said politely. 'Now tell me everything you know.' He found a chair in the corner and dragging it closer, sat down and waited.

'There's nothing to tell really,' said Ayesha. 'It's just that we noticed the boys were not at school the whole day.' She looked appealingly at Debbie for support.

JUSTICE OF THE WILD   Michael Du Preez

'And neither were they in their room,' added Debbie. 'Nor had they slept there last night.' She glanced at the headmaster who maintained his uncompromising expression.

'Are you sure about that?' asked the policeman.

Ayesha told him about the neatly folded shorts under the pillows and the cell phones.

'Well, I know when I dropped them off yesterday afternoon, they were both very tired. So I can't think why they should want to go out again at all.' Captain Peterson was puzzled.

'Well ...' Debbie was unsure of how to put it. Mr Banner looked at her sharply.

'Yes ...?' he prompted icily.

Debbie's eyes fell.

'I'm fully aware of what goes on here, Miss White, including illegal nocturnal jaunts that compromise our school's reputation,' the headmaster said evenly.

'It's in the boys' best interests to tell everything you know,' urged Captain Peterson. 'It may help us find them.'

'I'll tell them,' put in Ayesha defiantly.

'No! I will,' cried Debbie quickly. She looked at Captain Peterson avoiding Mr Banner's eyes.

'Sometimes, very seldom,' she added hastily. 'When we, er I mean they, have been hungry at night, they would go out to Sloppy Joe's for a take out.'

'How often?' Enquired Mr Banner, drawing himself backwards. His voice had a frosty edge.

'Not often, I swear,' replied Debbie, tears of embarrassment stinging her eyes. She felt such a traitor.

Captain Peterson rose and went over to her, offering her his handkerchief. 'You've done the right thing,' he said quietly. 'Did either of you ever go with them?'

'Never,' sobbed Debbie, blowing her nose. 'I swear!'

'So, it's possible that they went out for a snack and perhaps saw something on the way.' The policeman had a sudden thought. 'Did they have supper here?'

'We didn't see them in the canteen,' ventured Ayesha looking straight ahead.

'Do you usually?'

'Yes. We always sit together.'

'You'd have noticed if they had been there, but hadn't sat with you?'

'Of course, we would,' said Debbie. 'If they'd have been there in the canteen we most definitely would have seen them. Besides, we had a music lesson later.'

'Okay,' continued Captain Peterson patiently. 'That means possibly that they were tired, lay down for a while before supper, fell asleep, woke up in the middle of the night, felt hungry …' He turned to Ayesha. 'Did they have any money?'

'Rampha always has money,' she replied.

The Captain went on. 'So, they got up, took some money and went to Sloppy Joe's.'

There was a long pause as they all considered his theory.

'But then,' wondered Mr Banner, 'Why haven't they returned?'

'That's precisely what I intend to find out,' said Captain Peterson. He then proceeded to tell the girls the whole story. When he described Rampha's bravery, Ayesha had to fight back the tears. She was so *absolutely* totally proud of him.

'Now, now,' said Mr Banner with no hint of compassion in his voice, 'No need for histrionics. The fact is they returned safely after that episode, none the worse for wear. The school is, um, proud of them both.'

Captain Peterson went on to tell them the poacher's part in the drama and that the stolen lions would probably pay the supreme price.

'Now you know everything, I'll have to insist you say nothing of this to anyone.' Mr Banner cleared his throat. 'Is that absolutely clearly understood?'

The girls nodded.

'Another thing,' he added. 'As much as this particular episode may not yet reflect badly on the two of them,' he stood up. 'The two of you and the rest of our nocturnal deviants are going to have to pull up your collective socks. Is that abundantly clear?'

'Yes, Sir, Mr Banner. We understand perfectly.' Both the girls spoke simultaneously through their tear-stained tissues.

'In the meantime, I'll check with the night watchman and see what he has to say.' Mr Banner returned to his desk and sat down. His face was stern. 'I suppose he too is complicit in these moonlight jaunts.' He cleared his throat. 'We are going to see about enforcing stricter rules in future.'

He turned his attention to Captain Peterson, and after several other details had been discussed, he said. 'We shall have to inform their parents and mount a search immediately.'

'Yes,' nodded the policeman in agreement. 'We'll do that as soon as we have established that they are, in fact, missing.' He reached for his cell phone and dialled a number. 'Find the manager who was on night-shift duty at Sloppy Joe's last night,' he instructed. 'Get all the details of very single staff member. I want that information ASAP. You can get me on my cell.' He ended the call and slipped the phone into his pocket. Turning to the girls he said. 'You two are now as involved as the boys are.' He fished for a card. 'If there's anything I should know, even the slightest thing, I want you to please phone me.' He handed his card to Debbie and smiled. 'Don't hesitate. Any one of these numbers will find me.' He stood up, extending his hand. 'Thank you both for your cooperation.'

The girls stood about uncertain what to do next.

'You may go,' said Banner avoiding their eyes.

They opened the door and left quietly. They were both relieved to be out of Mr Banner's angry presence and his smoky, foul smelling office. Hurriedly they made their way across to the dormitory.

'Wow!' murmured Ayesha, breaking the silence. 'He's a real piece of work, ol' Banner.'

'Telling me,' responded Debbie. 'Anyhow, now we know the whole story, don't we?'

'No wonder the guys were so edgy about the whole thing.'

'I just hope they haven't been kidnapped or something worse,' said Ayesha.

'You mean they might have stumbled on something?'

'I really hope not.'

'The only thing to do is wait,' sighed Ayesha.

Debbie looked at her worried friend. What else was there to do?

'I'm glad he didn't find out about Rampha sometimes tapping on our window, with goodies from Sloppy Joe's,' said Ayesha. 'Then we'd really be in trouble.'

'We mustn't get caught, that's all.' Debbie wished Paul would visit as often as Rampha did. But she knew he felt awkward. Also, he never had enough money to spoil her. She wished she knew where they were right now. She desperately regretted not being more open with him about her feelings. She really was crazy about him if the truth be told.

She wondered where they could be.

TWENTY-FOUR

FRIDAY 19H30

It was seven-thirty in the evening. Rampha and Paul awoke still trussed up in the rondavel. They had fallen asleep from sheer trauma and exhaustion. The aching in their joints and the cold oozing into their bones had finally woken them up.

They were stiff and sore from their ordeal. Rampha suffered particularly badly from claustrophobia with the gag still jammed in his mouth.

He wriggled closer to Paul and laid his face next to Paul's bound hands. In the semi-dark, Paul got the message and gripped Rampha's gag tightly.

Rampha then squirmed and twisted his head until he felt the gag working loose.

Finally, it slipped from his mouth and fell loosely around his neck. He could breathe at last.

'Phew, What a relief! I'll try to get yours off with my teeth,' he whispered thickly. His tongue was sluggish, and his jaw ached on both sides. 'Turn over.'

Rampha lay face down as Paul moved towards him. He gripped the knot with his teeth and began working it loose. It was a difficult job, but at last, he managed to loosen it.

Paul spat out the wet gag. He gulped down deep lungs full of sweet, fresh air.

They sat up and peered at each other. Rampha's mouth was bleeding a little. 'I thought we were goners,' he whispered, flexing his jaw. 'We've got to get out of here.'

'You're right,' said Paul looking around. 'But our first priority is to untie or cut these ropes somehow.'

'If only we could free ourselves from this pole, we could manage.'

'Just a minute!' Paul had an idea. He remembered something he had once read about the way these rondavels were constructed. With his fingers, he searched the bottom of the pole supporting the roof. Sure enough, it was not actually planted, but merely rested on the surface of the ground. It was typical of this rural method of building.

'If we can somehow dislodge this pole we can slide the rope to the bottom and slip it off.'

'Genius. It's worth a try,' said Rampha. There was a lilt of hope in his voice. 'Let's put our backs against the pole and push together.'

They gave the pole a hefty shove, and it came away quite easily, as did a small portion of the thatch roof. Some debris fell to the ground, narrowly missing them. It left a gaping black hole up above.

The rain poured in.

'Right,' Rampha said. 'Now let's get this rope from underneath the pole.'

This they achieved without too much difficulty. But, it still left them tied to each other.

'What now?' Paul asked, despondently.

Rampha thought for a while then crouching, he forced his bottom through his bound hands until they were under his knees. Then, one at a time he eased each leg through until, at last, his hands were in front of him. In the semi-darkness, Paul watched the contortions with interest.

'Okay now you,' said Rampha.

Paul tried but was unable to twist his body as Rampha had. 'You must be double-jointed or something,' he said. 'Anyhow, maybe you can untie me now.'

'Turn around,' said Rampha. It was far easier to work with his hands in front of him. The knots were very tight, but gradually he managed to loosen them until finally, the rope came away.

'Wow! That feels good,' said Paul, rubbing his wrists. He then set about untying his friend.

'Thanks,' said Rampha. His wrists too were swollen and painful, but he was free. 'What now?'

Paul gazed up at the opening in the roof and pointed. 'We'll have to try and get out of there?'

Rampha looked up. 'It shouldn't be too difficult. We need something to stand on.'

'How about each other?' Paul's spirits had lifted considerably. He was smiling. 'But I'll have to go first.'

'Bet?'

'There's no ways you could pull me up. So I'll climb on your shoulder then once I'm up there, I can pull you up.'

A slow grin spread itself over Rampha's face. 'I'm losing my touch.'

Just then they heard footsteps outside crunching towards them.

'Wait!' whispered Paul. 'Someone's coming.'

They held their breath whilst the footsteps hesitated for a second then passed by.

'Let's get out of here,' Paul urged.

'No,' whispered Rampha. 'What if he comes back?'

'I don't know. What should we do?' asked Paul with a sinking heart.

'Let's not be too clever. I think we should tie ourselves up again. Pretend to, anyhow.'

'But if we climb through the roof now we can both be out of here in a few minutes,' argued Paul desperately.

'I have a feeling he's going to look in,' persisted Rampha. 'And if he does and finds us gone we're done for.'

'He'll have to catch us first.' Paul was defiant. Freedom was too close at hand to let it slip away now. 'Come on, it's our only chance.'

'No!' Rampha was firm. 'If he comes back now and sees us tied up, he'll probably leave us alone for the rest of the night.'

The more he thought about it, the more convinced he was right. 'That would then give us a good head start.'

Paul considered this. He was torn between his almost overwhelming need to leave this prison and the good common sense of his friend. He sighed deeply. 'I suppose you're right.' He gazed longingly at the inviting hole in the roof.

'Let's hurry,' urged Rampha.

They found the pieces of cloth and gagged each other again.

'Not too tight!' cautioned Rampha. 'Yeugh!' he almost gagged as the soggy cloth jammed into his mouth. When they had finished, they appeared to be trussed up as before.

They were just in time.

Outside the bolt rattled and the door creaked open. The big man leaned in. The weak beam from his flashlight swept the inside of the rondavel resting on the boys. The light settled on their faces, then moved slowly from one to the other. They appeared to be sound asleep.

Eventually, their captor withdrew and dragged the door shut. He closed it behind him and locked it once more. His footsteps faded.

Paul immediately slipped his hands out of the rope behind him and removed his gag.

'That was close,' he whispered. '*Now*, let's get out of here.'

'Yes, let's.' Rampha voice had an, 'I told you so' tone, as he removed his ropes.

'Okay, so you were right. Don't let it go to your head.' Paul gave him a friendly punch. 'Now come and stand here in the middle and give me a lift up.'

'Right,' said Rampha. He positioned himself in the centre of the room directly beneath the gap in the roof and cupped his hands for Paul's foot.

Paul climbed onto his friend and standing on his shoulders he could only just reach the supporting roof poles. Grabbing a pole on either side of the gap, he swung his legs upwards through the opening and onto the sloping grass roof. It gave a little but held firm. He pulled himself through the hole and rolling over, found himself on top of the wet thatch. The cold rain was pelting down, penetrating his thin clothes. Paul reached headfirst downwards through the gap and stretched his hand towards Rampha. 'Jump and grab my hand,' he whispered. After a few attempts, Rampha succeeded, and he felt his friend's grip. They held on tightly like trapeze artists, and Paul pulled him upwards through the opening. Once on the roof, they slid down easily to the eaves and dropped to the ground below.

'We're free, Rampha,' Paul had a lump in his throat. 'Do you realize it, we're free!' They hugged each other, overcome with emotion.

'For the moment,' cautioned Rampha, his voice low as he peered around at the cluster of rondavels a little way off. Light seeped through the bottom door gaps of two of them.

It was lighter outside. And as their eyes adjusted, they made a detour around all the buildings and eventually found the twin tracks of the dirt road leading into the bush.

'Let's get as far away from here as possible,' whispered Rampha.

In the eerie, misty, wet, semi-darkness, with rain still coming down hard, they followed the road, away from the buildings, towards freedom. When they were out of sight of the farmyard, they increased their pace to an easy jog.

'I hope we don't come across any dangerous animals along the way,' remarked Paul between breaths, as the rhythm of their shoes on the wet tracks crunched and splashed out a steady pattern.

'Especially the lions,' agreed Rampha.

'Freedom doesn't come cheaply,' Paul observed philosophically. 'But this is worth any sacrifice.'

Genius, thought Rampha, as they ran on.

TWENTY-FIVE

FRIDAY 19H30

Captain Peterson tracked down the man at Sloppy Joe's who served the boys. He was the owner.

Yes, he remembered them well.

'How come?' the policeman wanted to know. 'You see hundreds of customers.'

'That's easy,' said Pompy Jackson. 'We hardly ever get kids that age coming here so late. Those school kids are playing hooky, I says to myself. That same Suzuki 250's been here before, you know, but never so late. Then I says to myself, Pompy, I says, why are they acting so, you know, like strange.'

'Strange?' asked Captain Peterson.

'Very strange! They takes their three burgers and three cokes I gives them, and they pay wif two brand new twenties. I says to myself, Pompy, I says, where do these kids get those clean twenties from? So I watches them careful-like. Very strange! They eat, then they goes over to this truck over there,' he points. 'For a long time, they stand checking this truck over there.' He points again.

'Was it a closed truck?' Captain Peterson felt very tempted to shake this man, but he knew if he adopted any strong arm tactics he would obtain much less information.

'Yes, it was. Like a funny looking one.' He scratched his head then adjusted his cap back on. He was enjoying this interview. 'Not the usual kind, you know. It had a sort of a double top if you know what I mean.'

Captain Peterson had been right. The two of them had gone out for a snack and had spotted the truck.

'What happened then?' he asked.

'Well like I says. These kids are eyeballing this truck big-time when the owner spots them.'

'The owner?' The policeman leaned forward. 'Go on.'

'Yes,' Jackson was warming to his subject. 'He comes in wif this truck about half an hour before the kids arrive and like he sommer orders two double hammies. Pompy, I says to myself, I wouldn't like to tangle wif this oke. He's like big, man, you know. The biggest oke I've seen for a long time. Bigger than those okes on Smackdown.' Jackson paused dramatically for effect.

Captain Peterson was now convinced the boys had somehow brushed with this man.

'Go on,' he encouraged patiently.

'Well, like I says. This big oke take his two double hammies and sits over there on the bench. Two minutes flat and boaf hammies have disappeared. Like gone! Pompy, I says to myself, that was one helluva hungry oke.'

Jackson, whose secret dream was to be a member of Hell's Angels, was in his element. It was seldom he held such a captive audience.

'Anyhow,' he went on. 'This big oke sees the kids around his truck, and he gets up and walks around the back, like in the dark.' He points to the bushes behind him.

'Did the boys see him?'

'See him? Huh! Never.' Jackson shook his head vigorously. 'As big as what this oke is, he moves like a leopard in the night. I says to myself, Pompy, I says, if this oke is not a hunter then my name's not Pompy Jackson. One minute he's here, next minute he's gone. Just like that! Next thing he's standing on the other side of his truck, and he listens to everyfing the kids are saying. Then when the kids go back to their bike this big oke goes right back to the bench he was sitting on before. Then he makes like a big show, and a lot of noise and he walks right past the two kids, making like he's never seen them. He goes straight to his truck, and he's off.'

'And the two youngsters?'

'Very strange,' said Jackson. 'They sommer gobbles up their food, stash the cokes in the bike and start to follow this big oke.'

'Are you sure?'

'Are Sloppy Joe's hamburgers lekker?' exclaimed Jackson. 'The big oke drives off, and the kids follow him. Just like I says.'

'Which way?'

'That way.' He pointed, then leaned closer. 'You know somefink? That big oke must be thick if he can't see those kids following him. It was so, so like obvious.' Pompy beamed with pride at his mastery of such a big word.

'Thank you very much,' said Captain Peterson. 'You've been very helpful.' He got up and walked back to his car accompanied by Jackson. Opening the door, he turned to him. 'I may need you to identify that truck driver. Would you recognize him again?'

'Of course. Like I says.' Jackson replied confidently. 'Anyone would recognize him. He's so big. A big oke wif a high voice.'

'A high voice?' Captain Peterson's eyes narrowed.

'Just like a woman.'

'Thank you very much.' The policeman got into the car, slammed the door and took a slow, thoughtful drive back to the station in Randburg.

One thing was certain. The boys had been both ambushed and kidnapped or ... He refused to contemplate the alternative. In a way, he owed his life to Rampha Singh, and he would not leave any rock uncovered until he found them.

At his desk, Captain Peterson pressed the intercom button.

'Yes, Captain?' crackled a voice.

'I want an all points bulletin put out for two missing schoolboys.'

'Missing, believed dead?'

'No!' gritted the policeman. 'Just missing, that's all.'

'Be with you in a second, Captain.'

Captain Peterson took a deep breath and exhaled slowly. Now he could only wait for wheels to turn and the investigation to take its course.

In the meantime, however, he had the very unpleasant task of informing their parents.

TWENTY-SIX

FRIDAY 21H00

Bernard Patterson sat on the front patio step of his home in Morningside and gazed absently at the pool cleaner randomly gulping and shaking its way around the murky pool like some droll leaf-eating fiend. He was over one-point-nine meters tall and lean with thick dark brown hair tinged gray at the sides. Dressed in a pair of shorts and a vest, with several days' beard growth, he looked older than his fifty-one years. He toyed loosely with an almost empty glass of double scotch and lemonade, his fourth. He hadn't bothered to shave or get dressed.

What for? His life had become meaningless since his retrenchment.

He had worked for Delaware & Co. for twenty-five years, and all he had to show for it was a paltry severance package and an ulcer. He thought his future was secure. He was sure he was earmarked to head the company in another few years, and his whole life was geared towards that goal. Delaware manufactured the best tools in Africa and had recently started exporting to Australia. Bernard skilfully nurtured the company over many daunting obstacles to reach that point.

Now everything had changed. He was without a job, without a future and, at his age, unemployable. He still couldn't figure out what had gone wrong.

He had the feeling either Jack Springer, his boss, or the Government's new policy of Black Economic Empowerment, or a combination of both, had something to do with it. Or maybe it was something more sinister. There were some awkward questions concerning the Government's interpretation of the contract that suddenly turned sour.

The tender was Bernard's baby, and he knew it was meticulous. His figures were spot on. Margins were cut to the bone, and the document was weeks ahead of deadline. Delaware had poured hundreds of thousands into research and development, and Bernard was convinced no competitor could ever match their submission or their expertise.

But the tender fairy had other plans.

Theirs was rejected in favour of a little-known competitor who came in at almost twice the price. It made no sense and pointed to blatant corruption.

He focused on the edges of the pool. Algae were beginning to take hold. But, guess what? Quite frankly, he couldn't give a damn. He was mildly surprised at his unfamiliar careless attitude and grimaced listlessly.

Six months before, his reaction would have been to get down on hands and knees and vigorously scrub the offending edges till original colours shone through.

Lately, however, he was hardly able to muster the energy to get out of bed, never mind clean the pool. He drained the whiskey and made his way back to the liquor cabinet for a refill. His mind kept returning to his predicament.

His only son was going to have to face the fact they could no longer afford an expensive school such as Woodlands. He loved Paul with an intense ache in his heart. He felt even more devastated knowing he was about to let his son down. Paul would be crushed.

He felt powerless and really had no idea which way to turn.

Then there was Martha. The day before yesterday, they had engaged in a senseless, raging, verbal battle over an insignificant issue. He could not even remember what it was. She had taken herself off in a huff, to her mother, in The Wilderness, in the Cape. He was left to fend for himself. Not that it mattered. He could not blame her in the least. He knew he had become impossible to live with.

He had even vaguely contemplated suicide. But A. he was too much of a coward and, B. there was a non-payout clause in all his insurance policies that prohibited his taking such an extreme measure.

He realized too that Paul had not been to visit for weeks, probably out of fear of having to take sides.

Their only son.

What a heavy burden the child had to endure because of his useless father. He took another sip of his fresh drink and felt the welcomed fuzziness creep into his brain.

The gate buzzer rang.

Bernard Patterson wondered who on earth it could be this late. It was probably some beggar, he thought. No, someone was testing to see if anyone was at home. If he ignored it, it would no doubt go away. He was in no mood for people with their idle chatter. Not now, not ever.

It buzzed again.

He swore out loud. He would not answer the intercom. It could never be Paul. He had his own key and remote. But what if he might have lost it?

No, Paul would have phoned first.

One thing about the two of them, he thought wryly, was the way they connected. They were so very much alike the two of them. No, it would never be his son. In any event, he would really hate Paul to see him in this state.

The buzzer sounded longer and more insistently this time.

He put down his glass, made his way slowly to the intercom and lifted the handset. 'Yes?'

'Mr Patterson?'

'Yes, what do you want?' He demanded. His tongue felt thick. How on earth did they get his name?

'May I come in for a moment?' the male voice had the distinct Cape accent. 'I have to discuss something with you.'

'If you're selling anything, I'm not interested and furthermore do you know what time it is?' he slammed down the receiver. The nerve of these people, he thought, invading your privacy on some or other lame excuse.'

The gate bell rang again.

'I told you,' Bernard Patterson shouted. 'I don't …'

'Mr Patterson, I have to talk to you about your son, Paul,' the voice interrupted.

'Paul?' he felt a chill. 'Is he…? Who are you?'

'I'm from the police. You have to let me in, please, Mr Patterson.'

With a feeling of dread Bernard Patterson pressed the outside gate remote button and made his way to the front door. As he stepped onto the patio, a police car drew to a stop, and a plainclothes man stepped out. Was he the bearer of some dreadful news?

'Mister Patterson?' he said and approached with his hand extended. 'I'm Captain Peterson from the Security Branch. May I come in?'

'Of course,' Bernard Patterson, deeply worried, took his hand as he stepped aside. 'Come in, please.' Security Branch! His mind reeled as a sinking feeling of impending doom gripped him. Security Branch? 'Is my son okay? Why are you here? Why the police?'

'Is Mrs Patterson here?'

'No, she's away.' He was trembling as he confronted the policeman. 'Please tell me, has anything happened to Paul?'

'I think we'd better sit down,' said Captain Peterson.

Bernard Patterson went pale. His knees buckled as they sat down at the dining room table.

'First of all, Mr Patterson, I would like to stress that there is, as yet, no cause for alarm.'

'As yet? You mean he's not harmed in any way?' Paul's father swallowed bleakly. 'What do you mean?'

The policeman's penetrating blue eyes searched the worried face of the man opposite. This gut-wrenching chore was what he hated most about his job. To confront families of victims was the pits. He had been taught the direct approach was the only way.

'We have reason to believe your son and his best friend, Rampha Singh *may* have been kidnapped.' He announced.

'Kidnapped?' Mr Patterson sputtered. A fleeting expression of relief flashed through his brain and across his countenance to be replaced instantly by disbelief.

'What...I mean, how ...?' He was shocked and fully sober now. His heart pounded in his throat.

With a measured tone, Captain Peterson related the whole story from the beginning to the end. He spared no detail but sprinkled positive and encouraging comments along the way. He did not want to unduly alarm the man.

'But why were we not contacted sooner?' Bernard Patterson wanted to know. He felt a slow anger rising through his bloodstream as his pulse rate hit red alert.

'We are the child's parents for Pete's sake.'

'Mr Patterson,' said the policeman. 'That is precisely what we have done. Given that we became aware of their disappearance, only late yesterday afternoon.' He calmly met the furious but fearful gaze of the other man. 'We had to undertake certain investigations. Having done so, you were first on our list.'

His anger assuaged somewhat; Bernard Patterson rose and paced up and down. 'Sorry,' he said, 'But what do we do now? How can we find them? Where do we start?'

He stopped pacing and leaned on the table facing the policeman. 'I want you to know and understand something. I don't care what it takes, money, anything else.' His fists punched the table emphasizing every phrase, his voice rising. 'We must do everything in our power to find him, er, them. I'll sell my house, I don't care. Whatever it takes, it must be done. Is that understood, Captain Peterson?'

The policeman nodded. 'You can start by giving me some recent photographs of your son. We'll circulate them through the media.'

Bernard Patterson's anger subsided. 'I've got plenty,' he said. His spirits lifted fractionally as the prospect of doing something positive crept into his psyche. 'Wait a minute! Did you say that the other boy is Rampha Singh?'

Captain Peterson nodded.

'Well, I believe I've got a very recent picture of the two of them. They're best friends, you know. I'll fetch it now.' He rushed off and returned a few seconds later with the photograph and handed it to the policeman.

'Yes, this is a very good picture. We most certainly can use it.' He rose from the table. 'Can I offer you something to drink.' Mr Patterson's words tumbled out as he remembered his manners. He was very flustered. 'Would you like some tea?'

'No thank you,' Captain Peterson produced one of his cards and handed it over 'We'll be in touch. And you should really call your wife.'

Bernard Patterson's hand flew to his mouth. 'Oh my gosh! Of course, I almost forgot.' He hurriedly ushered the Captain to the front door and saw him out.

Captain Peterson turned. 'Will you be available if I want to contact you?'

'Anytime, Captain Peterson.' He thought for a moment. 'Would it be possible for me to come with you now?'

'I first want to tie up a few loose ends, but if it becomes necessary, I'll call you right away.'

When the police car left, Bernard Patterson ran into the house and fell to his knees at the dining room table. Sobbing uncontrollably, with a terrible pain that engulfed his entire being, he began to pray. He earnestly beseeched God, to protect Paul and Rampha.

Rising tearfully, he went to the phone and dialled a number. 'Mom,' he said, as his mother-in-law' answered, 'Is Martha there?'

'It's the middle of the night for Pete's sake, Bernard! Where's your consideration? Besides, she doesn't want to speak to you, until you're ready to apologize.'

'Mom, please, I'll do anything, just get her on the line.'

'Martha,' her mother called. 'It's him.'

'What is it, Bernard?' The soft, sleepy voice of his beloved wife came on the line. It stirred him. 'Martha,' he said, trying hard to control his emotions. 'Paul's been kidnapped. You must come home right away.'

After trying desperately to pacify his wife he replaced the receiver and made his way to his bedroom. There, once again he went to his knees and prayed desperately.

FRIDAY 21H00

Sam Kentridge could not sleep. He spent the best part of the evening cleaning his video equipment. He shifted his gaze to Hank Bass on his back snoring contentedly in the narrow cot next to his.

He still could not believe what had happened earlier. He felt a coward for not speaking up at the time. But the more he considered it, the more he resolved not to go through with this insane operation. His mind kept returning to the wounded lioness wandering about out there in the bush.

The poor animal would be suffering terribly at this moment.

He had an idea. He would go to Tiny's hut and try to persuade him to abandon the hunt.

He carefully packed the video equipment into the appropriate bags and sliding on his Mac he eased himself out of the door and went next door. He saw a crack of light under the door and knocked gently.

There was no answer.

Just then he heard footsteps approaching. It was Tiny carrying a torch.

What on earth was the man doing wandering about in the rain, Sam wondered?

'What's the matter, Mr Kentridge?' Tiny wanted to know.

'Do you mind if I come in?' he replied. 'I'd like to speak to you for a moment.'

'Okay, come in then.' Tiny hoped that he was not going to ask for his money back.

'Tiny,' he began as he sat down on a cane chair. 'I've been thinking about what happened this afternoon.'

'You don't have to worry Mr Kentridge,' Tiny said, flicking the wet from his arms. 'We'll go out first thing in the morning and find them.'

'No, no, that's just the thing,' said Sam Kentridge. 'I really don't want to continue with this hunt.'

'But we've already had all these expenses,' said Tiny as he saw all his money flying out the window.

'I'll give you another ten thousand if you call it off.'

Tiny was too stunned to say anything. What's with these crazy Americans?

'Look,' the man continued, not noticing Tiny's expression. 'You can make some or other excuse tomorrow morning and maybe lead us away from the lions.'

Tiny remained silent. This was all so confusing, and he did not know what to say.

'Anyhow,' Sam Kentridge said rising, 'I'll have the package ready for you tomorrow, the rest up to you.'

He opened the door and left.

TWENTY-SEVEN

FRIDAY 21H30

'I wonder how far it is to the river?' panted Paul as they jogged side by side. 'Then from there to the tar road.'

'From the dirt road turn-off, I would say it's about two-hundred and eighty, three-hundred k's,' replied Rampha. His body was now thoroughly warmed up. 'But to the river from here, it can't be more than say, twenty, thirty, forty at most. I really can't tell.'

'That's a helluva distance,' said Paul. He was also well into his stride. 'How long do you think it will take us to get there?'

Rampha had already worked it out. At an estimated average of seven K's an hour, it would take them roughly six hours or so. 'We should be there by the time it starts getting light, about four-thirty, five.'

'I just hope we can keep up this pace,' said Paul. He felt strong enough now, but to keep this up for six hours? That was a different story. As they ran on through the rain, their eyes became accustomed to the dark. They could distinguish a little better, the two muddy tracks of the road before them. The surrounding bush was deep and thick on either side.

'If our shoes weren't so soggy,' said Paul, 'This would be a breeze.'

'You're right,' puffed Rampha. 'What we really need now are some nice comfortable Nike's.'

'You're right. I'll never take anything for granted again, ever,' Paul said passionately.

'Yup, me too,' Rampha panted.

They cantered on in silence, each lost in his own thoughts.

'I bet they've started a search party.' said Rampha after a while.

'Cut it out,' said Paul. His athletic body moved easily and rhythmically in time to his measured breathing. 'No bets.'

'I guess.'

'Okay then, I wonder what the girls are up to?'

'Probably fast asleep,' Rampha said. But he did not believe that for one second. He knew Ayesha would be chronically worried about him. He was sure she would put a bomb under the police to find them. Right now he would give anything to feel her softness. She was without any doubt the best thing since sliced bread and cream cheese.

Ahead the twin tracks seemed endless.

TWENTY-EIGHT

FRIDAY 22H00.

The search party was not yet ready, nor on its way. But the strands were steadily being gathered together one-by-one. Logistics began to take shape.

After Captain Peterson had interviewed Pompy Jackson at Sloppy Joe's, he was convinced the boys were in real trouble. The media were very helpful. Radio and television broadcasts countrywide had appealed to the public to come forward with any information. Of course, any news remotely connected to the widely publicized escaped lion saga was manna to the media. Stories and speculation were given top priority.

FRIDAY 22H30

Japie van Rensburg was of medium build with a sharply-pointed face. His supper comprised a fried impala steak shot by Tiny and two eggs. He was watching television when the appeal was made.

He was horrified to learn of all the drama that had happened since he helped Brett and Tiny capture those lions. Things seemed to have gotten out of hand. He knew, of the two of them, Brett would show no mercy to those kids. He would get rid of them in a hurry. He was reasonably certain Tiny was no murderer. But Brett, with his temper and his drinking, was a different barrel of sharks. Japie really did not want to be implicated in anything like this.

But what should he do?

After supper, he lit a cigarette and sat deep in thought.

Since he stopped chopping stolen cars for parts, he never needed to market his skills. He liked being legitimate. He was even building up his insurance work with word of mouth referrals. He knew exactly how to undercut more legitimate businesses and submit claims to insurance companies. It also didn't hurt too much to have Simon Zambha of National Assurance as his friend.

It was a win-win situation.

His was a highly successful one-man operation, but for those few little blots on his sheet in the past. He had also been caught, a few years before, trying to defraud an insurance company with a bogus claim. He was lucky at the time, to get off with no more than a hefty fine. He now sat with the real possibility of a criminal record if Tiny and Brett got caught.

He wasn't a criminal.

But this news on television about the missing boys was disturbing.

He had been to Brett's farm many times in the past, helping out with this and that and being rewarded with a small buck or two for freezing and for the pot. Poaching was one thing, but kidnapping, that was an entirely different ball game.

At last, he made up his mind. He would go to the police and tell them everything he knew. In this way, if anything went wrong and Brett did involve him, which he would do without hesitation, he Japie, would turn State's witness. In fact, he might even be rewarded or something. Everything was negotiable these days. Of course, Brett would come after him with guns blazing, but he could always lie low till the dust settled. He would never be found. Besides if Brett was in jail what harm could he do?

FRIDAY 22H30

An old lion from a pride of eleven jogged up the dirt road heading north. His left ear was slightly torn, and his flank revealed deep gashes where dried crusted blood showed the marks of an opponent's claw.

The pride had become too small for two males each with testosterone bristling. He was the older and unluckier one that had been defeated. His instinct now was to find his own nomadic females and with any luck, start his own pride, age permitting of course.

Earlier he crossed over the river where it was shallow. There his nostrils picked up a strange faint scent of a female. He could not understand why the smell was not more pronounced. This was the fourth time he had wandered up and down this very road, but he could not seem to pinpoint their whereabouts or the direction they were travelling.

But definite traces of their scent hung in the air like inviting whiffs of tantalizing perfume.

He stopped and looked around for a moment, then lifted his head gave a mighty roar to proclaim as his territory this part of the bush.

As the downpour increased he eased himself into a thicket next to the road with his back to the rain and lay down, waiting for it to subside. Later, he would hunt for a meal.

FRIDAY 22H35

Captain Peterson was having a bad time with the reporter from the Daily Dispatch. He was about to explain why they had no leads when Japie van Rensburg's call came through.

'Yes, this is the investigating officer.' The Captain listened intently then said. 'Very well, I'll meet you there right away.' He looked triumphantly at the reporter. 'You'll have your statement later tomorrow. Now if you'll excuse me.' He grabbed his jacket from behind the door and hurried out.

Ten minutes later he met Japie at Sloppy Joe's and five minutes after that he knew the man's entire life history.

Yes, Captain Peterson would see what could be arranged regarding immunity from prosecution if he came clean. No, it was not a police trick. Yes, he would be protected.

'I suppose there could be a reward when those missing boys are found?' Ventured Japie hopefully.

Captain Peterson leaned over and grabbed the man by the shirt and pulled him roughly towards him. 'Listen here, you pathetic piece of mechanical garbage, don't push your luck. You'll tell me everything I want to know and cooperate fully.' His eyes penetrated deeply into Japie's very soul, 'or I'll make your life such a misery you won't know your gearbox from your spark plug. Do I make myself clear?'

'I just thought…'

'Never mind that.' Captain Peterson looked at him with contempt. 'You're coming along to show me where your friend lives,' he said.

They arrived at Brett's house shortly afterwards. As they mounted the stairs, the automatic security lights flashed on, flooding the entire outside area. After knocking loudly on the front door and getting no response, the Captain used a skeleton key to open it, and they both entered.

218

'Your mates live very sparsely, from the looks of things,' Captain Peterson observed as they checked from room to room. Apart from the furniture, there appeared to be no other signs of usual daily habitation in the house. None of the customary assortment of home comforts was to be seen. It looked almost like a lock up and go kind of place. A temporary station. They entered the living room.

'Nothing here either,' the policemen muttered as he switched off the lights and locked the door behind him. They looked around outside. There too, was nothing of any significance. The double carport was empty.

The outbuildings stood a little way from the main house. These comprised stables, an empty sheep pen and a chicken run occupied by a few scrawny looking birds. Further along, there were the usual staff quarters. These too were deserted.

As they trudged back to the car, Captain Peterson turned to the man beside him. 'What other vehicles do they have, besides the truck?' he wanted to know.

'Well, there's Brett's Jeep,' Japie said tentatively. 'It's an open …'

'You can give me details later on. In the meantime,' Captain Peterson gripped a surprised Japie by the shoulder and turned him around to face him. 'In the meantime,' he repeated, emphasizing each word with a corresponding jerk, 'I want you to tell me exactly where you think they might be, right now.'

Japie got the message loud and clear. This cop meant business.

'They have a farm in Botswana near the border, where they take clients to hunt,' he said hastily.

'I see,' said the policeman coldly. 'Go on…'

'I think, I mean they could have taken the lions there.'

'Don't play games with me, you scumbag,' he said. He gripped Japie tighter. 'You know very well they took the lions there. They've probably got the boys there as well.'

'I suppose they could have them there,' Japie stammered.

The Captain savagely pushed the man away from him. 'And how do they get across the border? Do you know how to get to the farm?'

Japie averted his eyes. He had been hoping it would not come to this – a face-to-face encounter with Tiny and Brett? They would kill him! Of that he was sure. His days could be numbered. On the other hand, he was in no position to argue. 'There's a small track that crosses the river a few K's away from the border post. They use that.'

The policeman turned and headed for the car with Japie following like an obedient puppy.

'We'll first go back, get some more men, then contact the Lion Park people,' announced Captain Peterson as he climbed in behind the wheel. 'Then we'll all go and give your friends a nice, pleasant surprise.'

Japie swallowed hard. 'We?' he asked in a small voice.

'Yes, we,' snarled the policeman. 'You and me!'

They drove towards the gates and were almost out of the property when Captain Peterson suddenly jammed on the brakes.

He jumped out and ran a little way into the grass verge at the side of the road. Bending over, he picked up the red object he had spotted in the headlights. It was distributor cable. The lads had been on their motorcycle, according to the man at Sloppy Joe's. It all added up. The poachers must have ambushed them and ripped the cable from the bike to prevent their escape.

The Captain walked over to the gate and searched around. Sure enough, motorcycle tracks were clearly visible leading from one of the gateposts. He wondered what happened to the bike.

Pocketing the cable, he returned to the car and headed towards Woodlands School. As he drove, he spoke to headquarters on the car radio. 'Tell Martin Resnick to meet me at the school, A.S.A.P. and get hold of Mr Patterson and tell him to meet us there as well.'

Almost immediately the message came back, 'Martin Resnick and his team are already there, waiting.'

Ten minutes later the police car swung through the gates of the school and pulled up outside the office alongside the Lion Park truck. Captain Peterson switched off the engine and turned to his passenger. 'You'll still be here when I get back, won't you?' he smiled pleasantly at Japie van Rensburg, but his cold eyes sent a different message. He got out and strode to the office.

Knocking once, he walked in. Martin Resnick was watching Mr Banner pacing the floor, followed by clouds of pipe smoke. The policeman greeted them briefly.

'I have a firm suspicion the boys have been taken to a farm in Botswana near the border,' he said.

'Botswana?' Mr Banner queried, surprised. 'Are they safe?'

'I don't know yet. We'll have to get a rescue party up there right away.'

'Well, we're all packed and ready to go,' said Martin Resnick. 'I'm going to save as many of my lions as I can and bring them back.'

Captain Peterson looked at the Lion Park official and flashed a smile. 'You really are attached to them, aren't you? However, when we leave here, you can bring up the rear in your own good time. I'm not going to be hampered by any slow-moving convoys.'

'I understand,' said Resnick. 'But, I'd appreciate it if you can tell me how to get there.'

'I'll let you know in a few minutes. Just wait here.' With that, he turned and made for the door.

'I'll be pleased when all this is over, and the boys are safely returned,' said Mr Banner, trying to make small talk.

'Yes,' said Martin Resnick. If they're very lucky, he thought.

Banner re-ignited his pipe and sucked furiously as Resnick got up and moved away from the offending fumes.

Captain Peterson returned shortly with a sheet of paper. 'I have this rough map, courtesy of my guest in the car,' he said as he spread it on the desk. The three of them bent over to study it.

Martin Resnick copied the map and made notes on a fresh sheet. 'Perhaps you can leave some sort of a marker at the turnoff, in case we miss it.'

'I'll put a police pointer board there.' Captain Peterson straightened up. 'You should be careful about twenty K's along the dirt road – apparently there's a river bed that runs full during rainy season.' He moved to the door.

'Just a minute,' said Mr Banner. 'I had a call from Mr Patterson before you arrived to say he was on his way here. What should I tell him?' Mr Banner glanced enquiringly at Captain Peterson.

'Yes, I got the station to contact him,' said the policeman. 'I promised to keep him in the loop.' He thought for a moment. 'When he arrives would you fill him in? Tell him I tried to contact Singh's parents but apparently, they're out of the country. Tell him also I can't waste any more time here. I have to get moving.'

'What if he wants to come along to Botswana?' asked Resnick.

'That's entirely up to you,' said the Captain. 'Look, it's fast approaching midnight. I've been running around for hours, and I can't waste any more time. My job is to locate the boys and if possible, get the kidnappers. I can't be held responsible for any passengers.' He went to the door. 'See you soon.'

'Good luck!' Martin Resnick called after him. Once again he was impressed by the confident approach and efficiency of Captain Peterson. He was a no-nonsense man and a credit to both the Force and the country.

FRIDAY (REWIND TO) 22H40

After more than an hour and a half of steady jogging, they were beginning to feel the strain. When Rampha suggested they walk for a while, Paul was greatly relieved.

'I haven't run this far since we did out last cross country,' he said breathing deeply.

'That was only ten K's,' said Rampha scornfully. 'We've done more than twice that already.'

They walked slowly to catch their breath. The rain had eased a little and the misty, cool night air penetrated their lungs with a sharp bite. The bush looked and sounded eerie with ghostly tree shapes looming either side of them. To reach their goal would not be as easy as they first thought.

'What would you say to a nice juicy Sloppy Joe's burger right now?' Asked Paul. He was feeling ravenous.

'Don't forget a few cans of Coke as well.' Rampha responded. 'But those things must wait,' he sighed. 'The most important thing is that we're free, and we must stay that way.'

'Yup, you're right about that.' Paul said and jumped back suddenly as a small spring hare darted across the road, directly in front of them.

'Hey!' Rampha gasped, gripping Paul's arm. 'That stupid bunny gave me such a fright,' he laughed nervously.

'Me too,' said Paul catching his breath. He was pent up and shaking all over. 'I just hope it's not being pursued by some big predator that grabs us instead.'

'Like a lion for instance?'

'Something like that.' It was exactly what Paul was thinking. But hey, they shouldn't talk themselves into a state of terror.

'We needn't worry,' Rampha reassured him. 'I read somewhere when lions are chasing prey, they remain focused on their victim. They would never change course in the middle of a hunt. Just imagine if they did, they'd never catch anything.'

'Come to think of it,' said Paul, feeling a bit better. 'I've noticed that too. In every Nat Geo documentary I've ever seen of a kill, that's precisely what happens.'

'Yes, when the lions are closing in, most other animals just stand around and watch.'

'Nature's got it figured,' said Paul thoughtfully.

'Survival of the fittest, I guess.' Rampha agreed with him.

As they strode on through the heavy darkness, bush sounds seemed to grow steadily louder and more ominous. It was one thing to run, with air rushing past their ears, blocking other sounds, but when they walked, they heard every syllable, every nuance of the bushveld's midnight symphony loud and clear.

Crickets screeched. Piercing sounds paused long enough to assess footsteps pounding past their hiding places, starting up again as the perceived danger passed. The throaty croaking and groaning choruses of myriad frogs followed the same pattern. Plovers, protecting their young, hidden amongst tufts of grass, would start their raucous, shrieking night watch alarm. First one, then another, bird would pick up the main theme and soon a glee club of wailing sounds filled the night air.

This bush telegraph was a super-efficient warning system. Their journey could not be heralded with greater fanfare and efficiency than any rowdy political rally could hope to muster.

'I think we should start picking up the pace again,' suggested Rampha, jogging once more.

'Right, let's go.' Paul said. He followed suite. It took a few minutes to get back into their rhythmic stride again. It was amazing, thought Paul, how quickly muscles became stiff then loosened up again once they warmed up.

They ran on in silence each engrossed in his own thoughts.

After a while, Paul said, 'I'm sure they'd be out looking for us by now.'

'Whatever,' said Rampha. The subject had become boring. 'The problem is how on earth will they know where to start looking?'

'That's also been worrying me.' Paul suddenly felt tired and depressed. 'Let's face it. No one knows where the hell we are.'

'Including us,' said Rampha. What a feeble attempt at humour that was.

Then it happened!

Rampha stumbled suddenly as he stubbed his toe on a protruding rock. 'Ouch!' he cried, hopping around on one foot.

'What's wrong?'

'My toe,' he moaned. 'I think I'll have to sit down.' The pain was excruciating.

'Here, let me help you.' Paul stopped and slung his friend's arm around his own neck. He gently lowered him into a sitting position on the wet ground at the side of the road and sat down next to him. It was a huge relief to rest their aching feet for a moment, even though the wetness soaked right through their trousers and into their underwear.

'Let me take a closer look,' Paul said.

Rampha removed his shoe and sock. The foot was beginning to swell quite rapidly. Paul leaned closer and surveyed it. In the darkness, he could not tell whether or not the toe was broken. 'Try moving it,' he suggested.

Rampha tried, but the agony was too much to bear. 'I can't,' he groaned, fighting back the tears.

'I'm not sure,' said Paul, 'but I think it's broken.'

Rampha put his hand on his big toe and tried to move it once more. He clenched his jaws tight to stop himself crying out. His toe was definitely broken. He could feel a crunching sensation in the joints. He sighed deeply. 'Yes,' his voice was despondent. 'I think you're right.'

Paul was silent. It would now take forever to reach the river where the beach buggy stood.

'I'm about to become a burden, aren't I?' moaned Rampha, reading his thoughts and grimacing as the stabbing pain throbbed upwards into his calf muscle.

'Hell, I'm really so sorry.' He lay back on the wet ground suddenly feeling utterly dejected and defeated. 'You go on alone.'

'Are you crazy?' Paul said. 'We just have to get you moving, that's all.' He stood up and peered into the thick dark bush. He had to think of something. But what? Slowly after a few minutes, it came to him. 'I've got an idea.'

'Yeah, what?'

'Maybe we can get you a pair of crutches.'

'Crutches?'

'Yes,' said Paul with far more conviction than he felt. 'But first, we have to do something about your foot. Where's that sock of yours?'

Rampha sat up and handed it to him. He began shivering. Wringing the water from the sock, Paul tied it tightly around his friend's foot securing the toe. He got up. 'You wait here. I'll see what I can find.'

He set off into the bush. Wet leaves and branches rustled as he trekked forward.

Seventy meters away two tawny ears pricked up. A large head covered with thick, dark mane sniffed the air.

TWENTY-NINE

After the full significance of the situation finally sunk in, Bernard Patterson emptied the remains of his drink down the sink. He was suddenly gripped by an overpowering sense of purpose. He would do something positive. For far too long he had allowed himself to become enveloped in a cocoon of negative self-indulgence and self-pity.

He made his way to the bathroom and stripped off his clothes. He stood, naked for ten minutes beneath an icy shower. A feeling of life and strength slowly seeped back into him and coursed through each fibre of his body. Afterwards, he stood dripping in front of the basin and shaved the several days' growth of beard from his face. He dried himself, opened the wardrobe and dressed in a clean pair of jeans, a denim shirt, and his mountain shoes.

He was going to find his son if it was the last thing on earth he would do. No more worrying about being jobless. When this was over, he would take the bull by the horns and start his own goddam business. Screw

Delaware, Jack Springer, and the entire corrupt Government tendering system. He began feeling better already.

But first things first.

He went to the phone and searched through his private phone book for numbers of any of Paul's friends. He came across the number of Debbie White. Wasn't she at his house only last month when Paul had his birthday bash? They'd given Paul a digital watch for a present. It was what his son always wanted. This girl Debbie was the pretty blonde one. If he remembered correctly, she and Paul seemed to be a bit of an item. Didn't they play music together? Perhaps she would know something the police may have missed. Bernard Patterson wondered if she might be home for the weekend. He hoped they wouldn't mind being disturbed at this late hour.

Well, too bad if they did.

This was an emergency. He called the number.

'Hello?' a sleepy voice slurred at the other end.

'Is that Mr White?'

'Yes?' White said. 'Who are you? This had better be good. Do you realize the time?'

'I do, Mr White,' said Bernard Patterson. He explained the situation and why he felt the need to speak to his daughter.

Cedric White knew all about the kidnapping from the newscasts and was more than willing to cooperate. 'In fact,' he said, now wide-awake and fully alert. 'Debbie and her friend Ayesha, happen to be spending the weekend with us. They've spoken about nothing else. Tell you what, give me your number. I'll wake them, and we'll call you right back. Perhaps you can come over or something.'

'That's kind of you. You sure it's not too late?'

'No problem at all,' said Mr White. 'We'd like to help in any way possible.'

'Great.' He replaced the receiver, and the phone rang almost immediately.

It was the police station requesting him to come to the school. There he would be brought up to date on the progress thus far.

Bless Captain Peterson, a man of his word.

The phone rang again.

'Patterson.'

'Cedric White here. I've spoken to the girls; they were both wide awake. They're eager to discuss this whole thing right now. Here's my address.'

Bernard Patterson wrote down the address. 'Hey, that's just around the corner from where I live. I'll see you in ten minutes.'

'I'll have coffee ready.'

He arrived at their house to find all the lights blazing and the front gate open. He rang the buzzer and was greeted by a tall, slim man in his early fifties with a head of prematurely white hair. He was dressed in a similar outfit to Bernard Patterson. Meryl White, an attractive woman in her late forties with a long blond ponytail and penetrating blue eyes, was in her dressing gown. After introductions, they sat down at the dining room table. A fresh pot of coffee was waiting.

Debbie and Ayesha, both dressed in jeans and sloppy pullovers, set about pouring several cups as they chatted solemnly about the kidnapping. Unfortunately, they could shed no further light on their friends' whereabouts.

'I've been summoned to the school right now to find out the latest developments,' said Bernard Patterson. 'Apparently, they have more information.'

Debbie and Ayesha exchanged glances. 'Can we go too? Daddy, please!' Debbie jumped up and hugged her father. He looked at Bernard Patterson with a raised eyebrow.

'Blackmail.' He turned to his daughter. 'It depends on what your mother thinks and what Mr Patterson wants.'

Meryl White smiled indulgently. 'I really don't have too much of a say,' she said in a soft musical voice. 'Looks like it's fait accompli.'

Paul's father looked from one girl to the other and nodded. 'I'm sure the boys would like to know their friends are so supportive. I certainly don't mind, if you don't, Mr White.'

'Not at all. In fact, I think I'll tag along as well.' He looked at his watch. 'It's almost Saturday, and I have nothing planned for today, er tomorrow and if you can use the help.'

'Oh, that I can,' said Bernard.

'And please call me Cedric.'

Bernard Patterson felt a surge of relief and silently sent up a quickie prayer of thanks.

SATURDAY 00H05

Soon after the police car left, headlights announced the arrival of Bernard Patterson and his entourage. They filed into Mr Banner's office. He was taken aback. 'Well, well, what have we here,' he said, looking from one to the other. 'A delegation no less?'

Martin Resnick was introduced but remained silent as Mr Banner apologized on Captain Peterson's behalf for his departure. He explained to Bernard Patterson where they suspected the boys might be at this moment and the necessity for prompt action.

Paul's father understood perfectly. His heart felt lighter, as hope for his son's safety flickered a little brighter. He turned to Martin Resnick 'Are you leaving right away?'

'Yes,' replied Resnick. 'I was just waiting to find out if you would like to drive there as well. We could travel in convoy.'

'Wild horses wouldn't keep me away,' said Bernard Patterson. 'If you can tell me which highway you're taking, I'll catch up with you. I first need to drop Mr White and the girls then make a detour back home for my passport and some fresh clothes and things for the boys.'

'Daddy?' Debbie looked pleadingly at her father as she tugged at his arm. 'Can we go too?'

Resnick looked sharply at her. 'Do you really think that is wise? I understand it's about a five-hour journey.'

Debbie looked crestfallen.

Cedric White shook his head vigorously. 'You most certainly can't go on a dangerous trip like that.' He looked questioningly at Mr Banner for support. 'What do you think?'

Mr Banner shrugged. 'I have no jurisdiction over the students whilst they're in their parents' care on weekends. But if you want my opinion, Mr White, I would say it's totally out of the question.'

Debbie and Ayesha exchanged disappointed looks.

Cedric White had a sudden thought. He turned to Bernard Patterson. 'Tell you what, I could come along if you like.'

'I could do with the support.' Bernard Patterson looked gratefully at him. 'Are you sure? Will your wife agree?'

'I'm sure she won't mind. In fact, if you drop the girls and me off at my place, I could rustle up some tea, food, and blankets for the boys and the rest of the Lion Park gang.'

'Done!' said Paul's father making for the door. 'Let's go.'

Martin Resnick shook his head as he followed them outside to Bernard Patterson's Opel station wagon. 'I just want you to know,' he said. 'I understand how you must be feeling about your son, Mr Patterson.'

'Bernard's the name,' said he. 'I appreciated your concern. And I must say you haven't had it easy either. Losing that youngster and all those lions.'

'Yes,' said Martin Resnick grimly. 'That was such a tragedy. And my lions, they're my children.'

Whatever rocks your boat, thought Patterson. He learned from Resnick which highway they would be taking and arranged to meet him at the first off ramp.

After dropping Cedric White and the girls outside their house, Bernard Patterson drove home. He threw some blankets and things onto the back seat, found his passport and hurried back to the White's residence.

In the meantime, Meryl White and the girls had prepared sandwiches, food, and drink for the trip. It looked enough to feed the entire South African Armed Forces.

The girls' disappointment had evaporated. They excitedly helped pack the back seat of the station wagon with many food baskets and more blankets.

'Hey, steady on,' Patterson laughed. 'I've got more than enough blankets and things for the boys.'

'Rather too much than too little,' said Debbie with a smile as she and Ayesha exchanged glances, giggling.

Cedric White, in the meantime, was pouring two cups of coffee for himself and Bernard Patterson to warm them for the trip.

'We'll say goodnight then,' said Ayesha yawning noisily. Debbie followed suit. She went over kissed her father then flung her arms around her mother and kissed her too.

'And all this sudden affection and hugging, Debbie?' Meryl White smiled, holding her daughter tight. 'What's with you guys?' Teenagers, she thought with pride in her heart. Was she ever as steadfast, at sixteen, as her daughter today?

The girls hurried off as Bernard Patterson and Cedric White finished their coffee.

Ten minutes later the two men climbed into the car and set off.

Cedric White glanced at the pile on the back seat and on the floor and the even bigger pile behind the back seat. He laughed. 'With everything you and the girls have packed,' he said as he buckled himself in and settled down. 'There's enough stuff back there for a trip to the North Pole.'

An hour later the Lion Park truck, followed by Bernard Patterson's station wagon, were both speeding on the open highway heading North towards Botswana.

SATURDAY 01H20

Minutes dragged by in agonizing adagio. The oppressive darkness hovered like a thick cloud over Rampha as he sat on the wet ground in the middle of the African wilderness nursing a broken toe. He felt utterly miserable and wondered, irritably, what was keeping Paul so long. What if he got himself lost in the bush?

What if they were attacked by wild predators that surely had to be wandering around here somewhere? How would they be able to reach safety before daylight? If that big thug discovered their escape, he would surely come after them. He would have to silence the two of them. He and Paul knew too much.

What would he do to them? Would they ever be rescued or even get out of here alive?

He was convinced by now a search party had to be out looking for them. But where would they start? How on earth would they begin to know where to look? He was pretty sure they were somewhere in the North Western district of South Africa. How would they ever find their way back to civilization?

It was becoming too much to bear.

Just then, Rampha heard a loud rustle in the bush to his left. It had to be Paul, he thought, and about time too.

'Paul!' he called in a stage whisper. 'Over here.' He waited. No answer. His friend probably had not heard with the noise he made walking.

'Paul?' he shouted, louder this time. 'For Pete's sake, I'm over here.'

The crashing sound continued, and as Rampha peered towards it, he froze. There, right in front of him appeared a pair of enormous elephants, no more than a few meters away. The two huge shapes ambled leisurely across the road into the bush on the other side, where they resumed their noisy devastation and feeding.

Rampha sat transfixed. He broke out in a sweat, terrified. How could they not have seen nor heard him? Unbelievable! Luckier still, had he been directly in their path, he would have been a trampled mess.

Deep in the bush Paul was almost done cutting a pair of crude crutches when he heard the noise. A pair of yellow eyes following his movements blinked. The lion had been waiting for the right moment to charge but was now distracted. He turned aside and gave way to the superior size of the pachyderms.

Rampha put his head between his knees, feeling quite nauseous. Just then, he heard more rustling in the bushes.

'Rampha?' a voice called tentatively. It was Paul.

Rampha almost wept with relief.

'Here.' He called in a strained whisper.

Paul hurried over. 'You'll never guess what I have just seen,' he said excitedly.

'Let me guess,' said Rampha. 'Elephants?'

'Two great big giant elephants!' said Paul. 'How did you know? Did you see them?'

'Not only saw them. They crossed over right next to me. I nearly fainted.'

'Me too,' said Paul. 'Whew! I thought I was a goner. I'm amazed they didn't see me.'

'Luckily for us, they've got poor eyesight.'

'Yeah, lucky all right,' said Paul, trying his best to control his fear. Little did he know just how lucky.

'Anyhow, I think you'll soon be mobile with these.' He gave Rampha the two sticks he was carrying. 'Here, let's see if you can use them,'

Rampha's foot ached badly, but he reached for them. They comprised two, almost straight, saplings, each with a prong at the top and another halfway down.

'Help me up,' said Rampha, biting his lip as Paul gently lifted him. The blood rushed to the foot causing renewed throbbing and anguish. The two prongs fitted comfortably under his armpits, and he was able to take the weight off his damaged foot.

'How on earth did you manage to cut them?' asked Rampha, trying like mad to take his mind off the pain.

'Just like our ancestors, the Flintstones,' replied Paul. 'I used a sharp rock.' He put his arm around his friend, guiding him. 'Can you manage?'

Rampha tried a few tentative steps forward, his sore foot suspended behind. It was an awkward gait, but at least he could move forward. His hands gripped the smaller prongs below.

'Okay,' he gritted after a moment, 'Let's go.'

Paul could only but admire his friend's courage and sheer determination. The going would be slow, but at least they were mobile once more.

He picked up Rampha's shoe and they set off once again into the night.

The pervading darkness felt heavier now. And although the rain had stopped, a thick fog had settled in. It had an eerie quality. The surrounding bushes loomed like ghostly apparitions out of the darkness.

Rampha was in agony with every step. The crutches under his arms became more and more uncomfortable until gradually the skin on his hands began to blister.

'I'm sorry to be such a nuisance,' he groaned after a while. He had to say something, anything, to distract his mind from the constant, biting pain.

'Rampha,' Paul encouraged him. 'Don't talk like that. It can't be much further. I just know we're going to make it.'

'If we're lucky enough to reach the beach buggy, we still have to travel all the way back home,' the injured boy said. 'Always presuming we're able to hot wire that car. What do you know about cars?'

'Don't worry we'll manage. I'm sure it can't be that difficult. Hijackers do it all the time.'

They struggled on in silence for a while, then Rampha stopped and sighed deeply. 'I can't. I can't do it anymore, Paul. Do you understand me? I simply can't go on!' He sobbed bitterly. He was close to the edge. Hysteria was knocking at the door.

'Okay, we'll rest for a bit.' Paul's tone was mild but compassionate. He thought it best to be matter of fact.

'I don't really want to slow us down,' complained Rampha putting his foot gently on the ground. 'But I can't help it.' He paused feeling desperate. 'Can't we do something to support my leg?'

Paul thought for a moment. 'I have an idea.' He peeled off his shirt, wincing as the rain and cold night breeze stung his bare skin. Using the shirt as a sling, he secured Rampha's leg behind him tying the sleeves around his waist.

The effect was immediate.

'Genius!' Rampha said. 'I have an idea this is going to be much better.' He tried a few steps. The pain was far easier.

'Okay,' he said. 'Forward march.'

'Great.' Paul was elated. His optimism soared. 'We're gonna make it.'

'And in the process, put that big guy behind bars where he belongs,' added Rampha. His voice sounded stronger as he matched the mood. 'I'll bet there's a search party out looking for us right at this very moment.'

'I'm sure there is. So the bet's off,' Paul laughed as he glanced at his watch. It was approaching one-thirty in the morning.

In the distance, the nomadic lion tried to interpret the sound of the voices. He was cautious after the encounter with the elephants. Humans too were bad news, and now there was more than one. But prey is prey, and he would follow them at a distance till the right opportunity presented itself.

THIRTY

They had been driving in silence for a while when Cedric White's cell phone jangled Mozart's Symphony No. 40. He preferred the original ring tone despite ragging from his wife and Debbie that he was old fashioned.

'That's Meryl,' he told Bernard Patterson. 'She wants to talk,'

He punched the green button. 'Hello, my love, can't sleep without your favourite hot water bottle?'

The voice on the other end was crying hysterically.

The girls!' she sobbed. 'They're not in their room!'

'Stop the car!' shouted Cedric White.

Bernard Patterson braked suddenly, swerved to the left and skidded to a stop at the side of the road.

'What's up?' He said.

Cedric White unbuckled his seatbelt and swung around to the back and in one swift movement lifted the blankets on the rear seat. Nothing.

He climbed over the front and kneeling on the back seat stretched over and pulled the blankets covering the big pile in the back. Curled up under the covers were Debbie and Ayesha. They were fast asleep.

'What are you doing here?' he roared in a fury.

Wide-eyed and dazed, the girls sat up, their hair rumpled, staring blankly into his face, contorted with rage. Remembering that he was still on the phone with his wife he spoke into the cell phone. 'They are here, Meryl, stowed away in the back of the car.'

'Thank God,' cried the voice on the phone. 'I'm so glad they're safe. Please don't be too harsh on them, Cedric,' she pleaded, knowing his temper.

Bernard Patterson stared in disbelief at the two frightened faces peeping from beneath the blankets.

'Harsh with them?' Cedric White shouted in a rage. 'What am I supposed to do? Dish out medals?'

Debbie was first to speak, her eyes brimming with tears. 'Sorry, Daddy,' she said in a small, choking voice. She hated upsetting her Dad. 'Please don't be angry, please Daddy.' She turned to Ayesha who was also weeping loudly. 'It was all my idea. A spur of the moment thing.'

'It's not true,' wailed Ayesha. 'Debbie had nothing to do with it.' She blinked away her tears and sniffed loudly between sobs.

'It was me, Mr White. I was worried about Rampha. I persuaded Debbie to hide in the car with me. Please don't punish her.' Her shoulders shook. 'It's all my fault. It really is, and I'm sorry.'

Cedric White turned his face away from the distraught girls and addressed both Bernard Patterson and his wife. 'We've got a problem.'

'I don't think there's much we can do,' said Patterson. 'We certainly can't turn back now; we've come too far. We have Resnick and his crew just ahead of us. Besides, it'll lose us at least three and a half hours.' He looked appealingly at his companion. 'I wouldn't like to waste that time. We have to find my son.'

Debbie's father sighed deeply and turned to the girls. 'I'm deeply disappointed in the two of you. Especially you, Debbie.'

'Cedric,' his wife's voice was soft and calmer now. 'Go easy on them,' She sighed. 'At least I can now go back to bed. I was so worried. But I know you'll look after our baby and take good care of her.'

'Of course, I will,' his voice subdued. He turned to his daughter. 'You're grounded every weekend till the end of the year. Is that understood?'

Debbie climbed forward onto the back seat and threw her arms around her father's neck with a fresh outburst. 'Thank you, Daddy,' she spluttered.

His heart melted as he felt her baby softness close to him.

'Thank you, Mr White,' put in Ayesha climbing over onto the back seat with her blanket. She looked at Paul's father. 'I'm really sorry for causing you all this concern, Mr Patterson. I promise we won't be any more trouble. Promise.' She drew the blanket closer about her and hung her head in shame.

'Let's forget it and keep going,' he said feeling rather emotional. 'It's no use pursuing this any further.'

The two men turned, looked at each other. Cedric White nodded to Bernard Patterson. He shifted into gear, and they pulled off.

'You go back to sleep now. I don't want to hear another peep out of the pair of you.' Debbie's father spoke sternly over his shoulder, buckling his seatbelt once more.

THIRTY-ONE

Early in the morning, Tiny woke with a start. Something at the back of his mind had been gnawing, worrying him the whole night. With all the amazing money being thrown at him from all sides, he had forgotten to feed his prisoners.

He really did not want to hurt them anymore than he had to. Although he would not hesitate to kill anyone who threatened his life, he was no cold-blooded murderer. His was a motto of live and let live. He was a hunter. All he wanted was to keep those brats out of his hair until the money from his clients was securely in his hands. Then he would set them free, somehow. Or blindfold them, and drop them off with their motorcycle, somewhere close to Johannesburg. They would never be able to find their way back here. He was pretty certain of that.

Getting out of bed, he lit the gas lamp on the table and went to the provisions cupboard. He selected a can of baked beans from the variety of stock kept there. Opening it with one of the can openers hanging from the shelf, he shoved a spoon into it then grabbing his flashlight, walked over to the rondavel where the boys were. He paused outside to listen for any sounds. All was quiet. Probably still asleep, he thought with satisfaction. Drawing the bolt on the door, he went inside.

The boys were gone!

Tiny stared. He could not believe his eyes. How could they have escaped?

He searched around with the flashlight then spotted the gaping hole in the middle of the roof. He guided the beam down the centre pole and saw the discarded ropes lying there. He tested his weight against the pole and found that it came away easily exposing a gap between its base and the ground.

So that was how they did it. The ground was saturated with rain from the hole in the roof, which meant that they must have escaped a long time ago. They could be anywhere by now. But where?

The obvious route for them to take would be towards the river.

Tiny walked to where the road led away from the house and shone the beam on the ground. He spotted their footprints right away. They were headed towards the river. He stood and pondered for a while. It would be silly to track them on foot. It would be much quicker with the Jeep.

But what about his two clients? Especially after last night when he had been approached by Sam Kentridge to somehow call off the hunt? That was easy to organize but what about the other guy, Hank Bass? He was not supposed to know about the whole deal.

He had promised them an early start and Hank Bass would be expecting that. But he could hardly wake them up now only to tell them that he would be back later. No. He must hurry after the boys, find them and bring them back and lock them up again before the Americans emerged for breakfast.

Then he had an idea. He would write a note and slip it under their door. He would say that he had gone out to track the lions, and they must wait for his return. Sam Kentridge would understand and probably interpret that he was going to make sure the lions were nowhere to be seen.

Tiny hated all this skulduggery. He liked things straight up and down.

Hurrying back to the house, he found a sheet of paper in Brett's briefcase and laboriously printed out the message. It read, 'I have gone to look for the lion tracks. Please wait for me till I get back, Tiny.'

Satisfied he folded it in half, walked back to their rondavel and pushed it under their door. He then made his way to the Jeep. After removing the plastic covering, he climbed in, started the engine and set off.

As he drove towards the open gates of the homestead enclosure, he opened the glove box and felt inside for the .38 special revolver he knew Brett kept there. Sure enough, it was still there wrapped in a yellow duster. Tiny checked the old gun. It was in mint condition and fully loaded.

Once through the gate, Tiny put his foot down. Those two troublemaking kids were going to pay for this; especially if he lost the second ten K deal with Sam Kentridge.

The Jeep sprinted along the muddy twin tracks with light raindrops stinging his face and gathering on the windscreen, just enough to keep the wipers working at intermittent speed. Periodically he would stop to make sure their tracks were still there. They could hardly be missed. The footprints were not very fresh, so Tiny knew that they were still some distance ahead of him. He determinedly gunned the accelerator. The Jeep responded and leapt forward in a surge of power.

He was hoping they would not have reached the river by now. But he did not think so. They were travelling on foot, and it would take them quite a few hours to get there. In any case, even if they did get to the beach buggy, they would not be able to start it without keys. Surely they would not know how to hot-wire an ignition. Or would they?

Surely not. They were only kids. He pressed his foot down harder.

SATURDAY 05H30

Paul and Rampha had made steady progress. In spite of Rampha's severe handicap, they had managed to keep walking practically non-stop. The damaged foot had continued to almost unbearable pain. To ease it a little, he alternated between having it hang down for a while, then putting it back in the makeshift shirt sling, when the throbbing became too intense. Also, by using both their jeans and Rampha's shirt as pads, they had solved the wear and tear problem the crutches were having on his raw and blistered hands and armpits.

Paul tried in vain to persuade him to stop and rest more often. Rampha would not hear of it. His willpower and determination were unbelievable.

'I can't understand why you don't want to rest for a bit,' Paul nagged him for the hundredth time. He also felt nearly on the point of collapse.

'If I stop now,' said Rampha desperately, 'I won't be able to get up again, ever.' He hobbled on blindly, one step at a time with robotic doggedness.

Earlier, they had exhausted their repertoire of songs to keep up their spirits. Now they spoke little, conserving as much energy as possible. Their only goal was to reach the river, the buggy, and safety.

Jaw thrust forward with determination, Rampha had to concentrate on every step. The pain was piercing, and he had to draw on every ounce of willpower to force himself forward. One step at a time. One step closer to the river. One step closer to freedom. One more step. Dig a little deeper. One more step.

One more.

Paul pushed his own limits too, as he trudged wearily beside his brave friend. The fear of being attacked by predators, a concern they had felt earlier, had long since dissipated. Wild animals had become the least of their worries.

How were they to know the nomad lion had been pacing through the bush parallel to them? He was waiting for the right open terrain to launch his attack. Without any female ambushing skills to assist, he had to be sure.

'Time to change.' Rampha said after a while, pausing.

Wordlessly Paul went to him and gently lifted his leg behind his body fastening it to the sling once more. And on they toiled.

It was becoming lighter now. The birds' loud declaration of their territories became increasingly bolder. Birdsong overpowered and gradually silenced the night sounds. The lighter it became, the easier it was for the boys to avoid potholes and rocks in the road. They plodded on in silence and approached the top of a little rise.

There, suddenly in front of them, was the river!

'The river!' shouted Rampha joyously.

'And the beach buggy,' yelled Paul, his spirits leaping. 'It's still there!'

'We've made it.' Rampha rasped, choking with emotion. 'We're saved!' He looked up heavenward. 'Thank you, God.'

Paul heard him and added his own silent prayer of thanks. He ran towards the river and shouted, 'I'm going on ahead to the beach buggy.'

He reached the water's edge and waded into the brown, swirling torrent towards the other side. The river had subsided a little he thought. Even so, the water reached up to his waist.

Yellow eyes alert, the lion hidden among the undergrowth, paused as his quarry parted. He watched one in the river leaving behind the other. He swung his head back and focused on the single prey, the wounded one. He crouched low and silently stalked forward as he prepared for a charge.

At that precise moment, a pair of headlights appeared over the rise and Tiny, behind the wheel of Brett's Jeep, smiled. He was just in time!

Lucky for him.

Unlucky for the lion. Unlucky for the boys.

THIRTY-TWO

Debbie was first to spot the marker.

'There it is,' she cried excitedly from the back. After a few more hours of sleep, she had forgotten completely their unfortunate confrontation earlier.

'What?' asked her father turning around, as Bernard Patterson eased his foot and slowed down.

'There on the left. The police pointer board.'

'So it is,' said Cedric White as Paul's father applied brakes and swung left into the narrow dirt road.

'I hope the Park guys found it too.' Ayesha ventured. She was wide awake. 'We haven't seen them for a bit.'

'Yes they were ahead motoring at quite some speed,' said Bernard Patterson. 'But I'm sure they wouldn't have missed it. Besides, we arranged to meet here at the turnoff.'

The closer they got the more nervous he became. What if something had happened to Paul? What if they never found him alive?

The thought produced a smouldering knot in his stomach. He would never be able to face life again if something bad were to happen to his son. His Paul.

Cedric White glanced at him and squeezed his shoulder. 'Try not to worry,' he said, noticing the anxiety. 'I'm sure everything will be fine.'

Bernard Patterson nodded. He was grateful for the moral support and the company of his unexpected passengers. What absolutely fabulous people - Mr White *and* Debbie and Ayesha.

'There they are,' he said as he spotted the Lion Park truck a little way ahead. He brought his car to a stop behind it. Opening the door, he climbed out and walked over.

Martin Resnick wound down the window and leaned out.

'Well, we're here,' he said. 'This road looks quite bad so I think I'll lead the way. If you can't make it any further in your car, you can travel with us.'

'Okay,' said Bernard Patterson. 'I'll follow you. We'll see how far we get.'

He returned to the car, and they set off, much slower this time, down the rough winding dirt road.

'Now we're really in the jungle,' said Debbie, ducking instinctively as some low Mopani branches skimmed the windscreen.

'I'm scared,' laughed Ayesha, leaning forward a little. 'What if there are lions and elephants roaming about?'

Cedric White chuckled. 'Even if there were, they're probably more scared of the car than we are of them.'

'Besides,' put in Debbie. 'We've got the best game rangers in the world right in front of us. I'm sure they'd know what to do if we came across anything dangerous.'

'I suppose they're hoping like mad their lions are still here.'

'You can bet on it,' agreed Ayesha. 'How can they tell their own lions from the wild ones?' she wondered.

'We'll ask Mr Resnick when this is all settled,' said Debbie's father. 'I'm sure he'll know. From what I understand, they're like pets to him.'

In the truck ahead of them, Martin Resnick was hoping he was not too late. Having lost two out of six was bad enough. It would really be such a tremendous loss of they had been already slaughtered. Humans are so destructive and short-sighted, he thought.

He looked at Joshua M'Laga sitting next to him. 'I really hope they're still alive,' he said voicing his concern.

'If they are, I hope they're not too hungry,' the warden said echoing his.

'I hope the police catch those thieves and put them away for life,' said Joseph.

'Never mind the police,' responded Resnick grimly. 'If I catch them, I'll put a dart into each one of them.'

The men laughed at the thought of it.

'One thing is for certain,' he continued. 'I'm not going back without my lions - dead or alive.'

THIRTY-THREE

SATURDAY 06H00

The suped-up two-litre Toyota Corolla jerked as it struck a big pothole. Captain Peterson flinched, gripping the wheel tighter. 'It'll have to go in for a major overhaul when we get back,' he muttered to the man sitting next to him.

'I'll book it in,' the sergeant said, wondering why they had not taken the police Landover instead.

'I would have taken the Landover,' said the Captain reading his thoughts, 'But it was only due back and available in the morning; besides this car is faster.'

Not on these roads it isn't, thought sergeant 'Spore' Kaaimans. He had never worked with Captain Norvel Peterson before. But he was chosen for this job because of his extraordinary tracking ability. As his nickname, Spore, (meaning tracks, in Afrikaans) suggested, he was the best Bushman tracker in the force.

Seated in the back of the car, with not too much to say, sat a very worried Japie van Rensburg wishing for the hundredth time that he had never gone to the police. What a stupid decision.

'How much further, van Rensburg?' Captain Peterson demanded, looking at the digital clock on the instrument panel. Outside the wet gray dawn showed faint tinges of light.

'To the river about another ten K's.'

'Let's hope we can get across,' said Captain Peterson. 'With this rain, who knows?'

'When it floods, it usually goes down again pretty quickly,' said van Rensburg, trying without much success, to be friendly and helpful.

'And from the river to the farm?'

'About another twenty.'

'And the road, what's that like?'

'A little better than this section, I think,' came the reply. 'But I haven't been there for at least six months.'

'No doubt on another illegal hunting expedition,' commented the policeman, sarcastically.

As it grew steadily lighter, they could see more clearly the road ahead. The twists and turns demanded total concentration and driving skill. Captain Peterson was pleased to occupy his mind with the task at hand. He had allowed the pressure of this case to get to him. Not a good thing for a policeman. The closer to their destination the more he worried. So far there were two casualties. Two too many. He did not want more, especially either of those boys.

He wondered where they could be right now.

SATURDAY 06H15

The steadily approaching police car was less than ten kilometers away. At that moment Paul, wading chest high, was halfway through the river. Rampha, on crutches, had almost reached the water's edge. He swung around at the sound of the Jeep behind him.

He realized he would likely be hit so he flung himself towards the side of the road into the bushes. His foot, bound in the sling, struck a tree trunk. An agonizing pain shot up through his leg and tore through his whole body,

'Run, Paul, run!' he shouted as he hobbled deeper into the bush.

If the big guy followed him, he thought, Paul might just make it to the other side if he was lucky.

Paul turned 'round and assessing the situation, pushed with all his might through the water towards the beach buggy on the other side. He caught a glimpse of his friend heading into the bush, and he wondered who their captor would pursue first.

He glanced back once more to see what was happening. The Jeep had entered the river and was coming straight for him. Then he heard a splash in the water right next to him, followed by a loud gunshot from behind.

The man was firing at him from the Jeep.

The saga had now become deadly.

Taking a deep breath, Paul dived under the water. It was the only way he could think of to get away. As he felt the muddy water closing over him, he heard another gunshot, more muffled this time. Staying under the water, he allowed the current to carry him along. After a while, when he felt his lungs would burst, he slowly emerged, lifting only his head out of the water.

He looked back. He had drifted downstream quite a long way. The Jeep was still behind him, but now some distance to his left. So far, so good, his luck was holding.

He took another deep breath and slowly submerged again. It was not too deep, and he felt his feet touch the bottom. There were plenty of boulders down there. He would have to be careful.

With his feet and hands touching the sandy riverbed, Paul felt himself drifting further and further downstream. At last, he could hold his breath no longer, and he rose again slowly to the surface.

The Jeep had stopped in the middle of the river and the big guy, holding the gun high over his head, was wading through the water towards him. Near the bank of the river was a huge boulder.

Taking another deep breath, Paul ducked once more into the water and made his way blindly towards it. He slowly emerged once again right next to the rock and concealed himself behind it.

He somehow had to reach the buggy without being seen. But if he exposed himself, he knew that the big man would not hesitate to shoot.

Suddenly another shot rang out, the third. Paul's first reaction was to run. Then, he realized that he had not heard the sound of the bullet. The big man had obviously shot in another direction. Paul was puzzled and scared stiff. His stalker was dangerous and very cunning. He decided he would not move from this spot where he felt safe for the moment.

He crouched there, half submerged, clad only in his underpants and shoes.

Paul wondered how his friend was doing.

Rampha was not doing so well. Paul's shirt, which had served as a sling, had come off, and his leg was suspended without support as he struggled deeper into the bush. He had seen Paul dive under the water when the big man went after him.

Good old Paul! He had a good head in an emergency.

He then heard the first shot, and his heart sank. After the second one, a deep depression gripped and overwhelmed him. It permeated his psyche.

Paul was to be the sacrifice.

If Paul had not been hit by the first shot, then surely the second would have got him. But Rampha dared not investigate because one of them had to try for freedom. They had agreed on that. If he then would be the one, it was his duty not to get caught.

A sudden overwhelming tiredness gripped him.

He decided to snatch a tiny rest for just a brief moment. He reasoned that with renewed energy he would push ahead stronger and continue his escape. The idea took hold. It was the sensible thing to do. In his present state, the best thing to do at this moment was rest and renew his energy.

Just a short rest.

He laboured a little further into the bush and found a suitable patch next to a tallish Mopani tree. He eased himself gently onto the soggy ground and stretching his aching leg in front of him leaned back against the trunk.

Perhaps Paul had not been hit. Perhaps the big guy had missed his target. After all, to fire a handgun accurately over a long distance was not easy. He had read about it somewhere, very recently. Somewhere. A feeling of incredible relief washed over him.

Paul was safe.

He let out a deep sigh and allowed his eyes to close for just a moment. One moment.

One sweet precious moment.

Within seconds his consciousness departed.

A hundred and fifty meters away, Paul squatted shivering behind the boulder on the far bank, half submerged in water. He spotted the man again. He was wading directly towards him, the revolver above his head. Paul held his breath. The man seemed to be looking right at him. This was it!

He was trapped!

Suddenly the big man swung around, firing another shot to the left. He seemed to have fired at what looked like a half-submerged log.

So, he had not been seen.

The hunter turned around once more, his eyes searching the surrounding water. Paul did not move. The man's gaze swept towards the boulder. Paul froze. Any movement now would surely give him away. He wondered desperately if he should make a dash for it. He was reasonably confident he could outrun the man. But he was certain he could never dodge a bullet. So he stayed where he was.

He could not understand how his pursuer had not seen him. He felt completely exposed. The hunter now less than thirty meters from him was moving closer every minute.

In no time at all, the big man stood almost directly above the boy.

Paul was stunned.

He could easily reach out and touch him, but still the big man had not seen him. What was happening? Now the man was standing right next to Paul, waist deep in the water but facing away from him, his gun arm still held high.

Then suddenly everything became crystal clear.

The big man simply lowered his free hand into the water and Paul felt a vice-like grip on his upper arm.

It was the oldest hunting trick in the world. Every hunter used it. Every magician used it. Even predators and plants in the wild used it; the art of distraction and misdirection.

It was such a simple ploy. So very effective.

Paul fought and beat the man with his fists. It was hopeless. He was dragged struggling towards the Jeep in the middle of the river. 'Leave me!' he shouted. 'Let me go, you're hurting me!' he yelled, close to tears.

'You're going nowhere,' muttered Tiny in his high voice. 'You've given me enough trouble.'

He dragged Paul to the Jeep, dumped him in the front seat and pushed him roughly over to the passenger side. As he held him with one hand, he slipped the gun into his shirt pocket and felt at the back of the seat for a rope, which he pulled out.

'If you try to escape again, I'll shoot you,' he hissed as he tied one of Paul's hands to the steering column. It would have to do until they got back to the farmhouse.

Tiny closed his door and started the engine. He reversed slowly out of the water.

Paul's hand throbbed. It was very tight, and his circulation had stopped. His body was in a very awkward and uncomfortable position.

'Put your other hand on the dashboard where I can see it,' commanded the big man as he backhanded Paul a painful blow to the side of his head. 'And don't forget what I told you. No tricks! Do you understand?' his eyes glared coldly at the boy.

Paul nodded sullenly. He turned his face away. He did not want his captor to see the tears stinging his eyes. This cruel, kidnapping ogre meant business.

Tiny stopped the Jeep on the riverbank. He got out and headed towards the bush where Rampha had disappeared.

SATURDAY 07H00

At that precise moment a beige Toyota Corolla with roof lights flashing appeared on the opposite bank. It stopped alongside the beach buggy.

Paul saw it immediately and waved his free hand high in the air.

An arm appeared through the driver's window and waved back. He had been seen!

He beckoned desperately for his rescuers to come and get him as he struggled in vain to free himself.

SATURDAY 07H10

At the farm in the camp where they had been left, the four lions were very much alive. Except for the female who had a slug in her flank, they were all in pretty good condition.

Earlier that evening they had managed to catch a small stray duiker. This had satisfied their hunger for a while.

They had not wandered too far from the clearing where they encountered the hunters and were huddled together in an overgrown gully, well hidden. The injured lioness was reclining on her side licking her wound. The bullet, embedded in her rib cage, was beginning to work loose and was very painful.

One of the others rose slowly, stretched herself to her full length and yawned widely, her four-inch canines flashing white. She walked around a little, returned and flopped down next to the others.

They were content to stay put in this area of safety for the present. In time, left to their own devices, they would probably adopt this as their own territory. They were unaware of two drenched Americans close by, but upwind of them. Due to the gentle rain, pug tracks were clearly visible in the soft earth.

'Look,' said Kentridge in a low voice, pointing. 'There's another one.' His eyes were fixed on the ground where the tracks were very obvious. Hank had forcefully persuaded him to continue with the hunt, and there was no way out of his dilemma. The only thing to do was to go along, track down the wounded lioness, put her out of her misery, then wrap up this whole sick business.

'Yeah,' said Bass. 'I don't think it's such a big deal to track lions.' He fished out a hip flask and took a huge slug.

'Nothing to you is a big deal,' chided Sam Kentridge. He glanced with disapproval at his companion. There was no better place to discern character than right here in the bush, he thought.

'What exactly do yuh mean by that?' Bass glared at him through bloodshot eyes.

Kentridge turned away. 'Forget it, you'll never understand.' He changed the subject. 'I wonder what's happened to Tiny.' He said to keep himself in the clear. 'And I keep wondering where old Van has disappeared to. Tiny said he would be here on the farm.'

'He's a weirdo that one,' said Bass, unwittingly describing himself. 'He's gonna freak when he finds out we didn't wait for him.'

'Well, we should've,' said Kentridge. He knew the note was according to their arrangement last night. He had tried in vain to dissuade Bass from going out.

'We'll just tell him we never saw the note.'

'Yeah, we'll tell him that,' said Bass. 'This trip is costing me a fortune anyhow, and we can't wait around all day. I want them lions.' He took another swig.

'We should just focus on the wounded one,' said Kentridge. He hoped his partner would lose the urge to shoot any of the rest of them. 'And I think if we don't see them shortly, we'll go back.'

He was sure that he would have to employ stronger tactics to dissuade Hank Bass from this mission. He was determined to do whatever it took.

He also felt a little hungry and anxious to get this whole thing over with quickly as he could manage, with as little killing as possible. They would get back to base and get stuck into a healthy American breakfast, then leave for Johannesburg and back to the States.

Bass, however, had other ideas. He wanted to get in a couple of good shots, especially at the big male. He would then leave the cleaning up and skinning for the big guy and Van, his so-called invisible mate. Hell, after all, they had to earn the huge fee they were charging, even if Kentridge was footing most of it.

He thought about his den back home and how the head of each lioness would occupy three of the corners. The male lion with the huge mane would be mounted on a special pedestal right in front of the entrance. He smiled with relish as he thought of some of his cronies coming around for a drink and seeing this great big African lion glowering at them from close-up.

Especially Randy Cotswold, the old buzzard, always ready to flaunt one bigger and better. That'll shut him up for good. The expression on his face would be worth every cent of this expedition. He could hear old Randy trying to bring him down. 'Say, Hank where did you *buy* that one?'

'Didn't buy it Randy. Shot it myself! Have another drink?' He smiled as he savoured the thought. He quickened his pace. This was going to be his lucky day.

THIRTY-FOUR

SATURDAY 07H45

Captain Peterson lowered his hand. 'That's the one boy,' he said triumphantly. 'I wonder where the other is?'

'I'll see who this is,' the sergeant said as he fished on the floor for the binoculars. He removed the instrument from its case.

'Give me that,' said Captain Peterson snatching it out of his hands and putting it to his eyes. 'It's Patterson. Looks like his one arm is tied up,' he said.

He got out of the car and looked despairingly at the river. How he wished he'd brought the land rover. He glanced inside the beach buggy. There were no keys in the ignition. Besides, it was far too low slung to make it through the water.

It would have to be the Corolla, he thought grimly as he hurried back to the police car. Signalling for Paul to wait, he opened the hood. Sergeant Kaaimans stood next to him.

'Do you think it'll get us through?' he asked.

'I don't know much about cars, but I don't think this one will make it through there. They stared helplessly at the engine when Japie van Rensburg joined them.

'I can make this car swim,' he said, putting his head under the bonnet.

The two policemen regarded him sceptically.

'Show me,' said the Captain.

'I'll need two plastic bags, some string, and a tire lever

'I've got some in the glove box,' said the sergeant. He rummaged in the car and produced a bundle of plastic bags bound tightly with several rubber bands. It was standard equipment in all police cars.

'Will these do?' He asked, giving them to van Rensburg. Captain Peterson handed him the tire lever he had removed from the boot.

'Perfect,' said Japie, pleased to be finally of some assistance. 'And the rubber bands are just what I need.'

He covered the distributor with a plastic bag, securing it with one of the rubber bands. He then turned to Captain Peterson. 'Could you please start her?'

The Policeman got in the car and started the engine.

Using the tire lever, with a swift movement Japie popped the fan belt off its three pulleys. The car was now running on battery power. He slipped another plastic bag over the alternator and held it in place with another rubber band. Fixing the loose fan belt to a protruding bolt, he emerged from the bonnet and closed it.

'Okay,' he smiled with satisfaction. 'It should get us through.' He wiped his hands on his handkerchief. 'But you'll have to drive carefully. If the plugs get wet, we've had it.'

'They should be high enough out of the water,' Captain Peterson curtly nodded his thanks to Japie. 'Let's go.'

Keeping the engine at high revs, the policeman gently guided the car into the river. As the water became deeper, he gripped the wheel and his knuckles whitened;.

As they moved forward, water seeped in through the sides of the doors, slowly filling up the floor.

From the Jeep on the opposite bank, Paul was waving encouragement.

Just as they were about half way across the river making good progress, Tiny emerged out of the bush carrying Rampha. He was headed for the Jeep.

'There's Tiny! shouted Japie van Rensburg from the saturated back seat of the police car.

'And he's got Rampha,' exclaimed Captain Peterson with a mixture of consternation and joy, gripping the wheel even tighter.

'If only this thing would go faster!' he clenched his teeth and leaned out of the window. 'Hey you!' he bellowed, honking the horn.

Tiny turned and cried out in surprise, 'What the ...' With one quick movement, he dumped Rampha onto the ground and rushed for the Jeep.

Captain Peterson leaned further out of the window. 'Stop! Police!' he yelled.

The big man ignored him and leaped into the driver's seat, started it and jamming it into gear. He wheel-spun the Jeep forward.

Paul flung himself on the man, but a huge hairy arm swiped him on the chest sending him reeling against the door and jerking his tied arm in the process. He cried out in pain as the car slewed ahead.

Rampha, still lying on the ground where he had fallen, saw the blow that Paul had received. He propped himself up on one arm and shouted after the receding Jeep. 'You pig! You'll pay for this!'

With all four wheels whirling and mud flying high into the air, the Jeep took off in the direction of the farmhouse.

'Damn!' Captain Peterson swore softly under his breath. They still had about thirty metres to crawl through the water. But on the bright side both boys were alive. He was elated.

Rampha watched, relief flooding through him, as the police car drew nearer. The pain in his toe had eased slightly after his short, unintended rest. His ordeal was nearly over. But Paul's life was still very much in danger.

'Hurry!' he whispered impatiently under his breath.

When they reached the riverbank, Captain Peterson manoeuvred the car out of the water and stopped close to Rampha. They opened all the doors, and a flood of water poured out.

'Fix the car and get rid of that water,' he instructed Japie, as he ran over to Rampha and gently lifted him up.

'Are you okay, Champ?' The policeman's eyes made a quick assessment of the boy's condition.

Rampha nodded vigorously. He was overcome with emotion and could hardly speak. 'I never thought I'd be so pleased to see a policeman.' He swallowed with difficulty and sniffed away the threatening tears. 'I'm okay except for a broken toe. But I'm worried about Paul.'

'You're safe now,' Captain Peterson said gently. He turned to his sergeant. 'Bring me the first aid kit,' he ordered. He examined Rampha's foot. 'And you don't have to worry about your friend. We're gonna rescue him soon as possible. How many kidnappers are there?'

'Only the big one, as far as I can tell,' replied Rampha. 'But there are also the other two hunters.' He pointed to the buggy on the opposite bank. 'They followed us in that thing over there. But I don't think they could get through the river with it. I don't know where they are right now.'

'And the lions, did you see them?'

'They were in the camp yesterday,' Rampha said. 'But we've been locked up most of the time. Except for last night, when we escaped.'

'Look, Champ,' Captain Peterson spoke soothingly to Rampha as he began expertly applying a bandage to his damaged foot. 'I know what you've been through, and we can talk about that later, but right now, I've got me a kidnapper to catch. So I'm going to ask you, if you have the strength enough to get to that beach buggy, to wait for Martin Resnick. He can't be too far behind. You can fill him in on all the details. Then you guys can come and find us.'

Rampha was clearly disappointed.

'We've got a chase on our hands, and I don't want you getting hurt any more than you already have. Okay?'

'Okay,' sighed Rampha softly. He was in no mood to argue. 'Just promise you'll get that big guy and give him one for Paul and me.'

Captain Norvel Peterson looked steadily at him. 'You can bet on it, and it'll be my pleasure, trust me.' He strode back to the car. 'And don't worry if your bandage gets wet. As long as it keeps your foot firm, it'll be fine.'

The policeman climbed in behind the wheel. The other two were already in the car. It was idling nicely after Japie had restored the fan belt.

In a spray of mud, they sped off after the Jeep.

THIRTY-FIVE

SATURDAY 08H15

As the police car disappeared over the ridge, Rampha picked up his homemade crutches and hobbled off to the water's edge. Slowly he made his way through the river, step by small step. The pain had eased considerably as his foot, thrust out in front of him, half-floated near the surface. He was grateful that the water was relatively slow-moving and sluggish. He was pleased also to have the bandage around his foot, even though it began pulling tight as it soaked up and absorbed water.

He finally emerged on the other side and limped to the beach buggy. Gingerly easing himself into the back seat, he sank into the soft wet cloth. He propped up his leg onto the front seat, closed his eyes and once more slipped into a deep sleep.

He did not hear the approach of the Lion Park truck nor the car that followed behind. Nor did he hear the seven people who emerged from the two vehicles and stood around the beach buggy gazing down at him.

'Is he okay?' murmured Ayesha, trying hard not to cry and trying even harder to avoid looking at his almost naked body. His steady breathing confirmed he was in no danger.

'He certainly looks it,' replied Debbie, feeling the same as her friend.

Bernard Patterson said, 'I think we'd better wake him and find out what's going on.' Leaning over he gently shook the boy's shoulder.

Rampha opened his eyes to find himself surrounded by many familiar faces. For a moment he was totally confused.

'Where am I?' he asked in a daze. 'What are you all doing here? Ayesha? Debbie?'

He pulled himself up into a more comfortable position and looked around at the others. 'What's happening?' He frowned. He was clearly startled.

'You were asleep in this beach buggy,' explained Mr Patterson. 'We've only just arrived. Is Paul all right? Where is he?'

It all came rushing back to him. He looked up into the worried face of Paul's father. 'Paul has been captured by the big guy,' he told him. 'But Captain Peterson has gone after them.'

'Do you think ....?'

Rampha shook his head. 'I'm sure everything is going to be okay, Mr Patterson.' He turned and looked at Martin Resnick. 'Captain Peterson said that the moment you arrive we are to follow him.'

Martin Resnick nodded. 'Yes, we'll do that. But tell me, do you know whether or not my lions are safe?'

Rampha quickly told them everything that had happened. 'But I think we should go after them right away,' he finished off. He was very worried about Paul.

'We'll have to try and squeeze into my truck,' said Martin Resnick. 'I don't think you'll make it across the river with your car. You can leave it here, next to the beach buggy.'

'I think you're right, said Bernard Patterson. 'I don't want to take a chance. Your truck is a better bet.' Turning to the girls he said. 'Why don't you two get all our things out of the car and load them into the truck?'

Flashing broad grins at a mighty confused Rampha, Ayesha and Debbie ran over to their car.

'I'll help,' offered Cedric White, following.

'Okay,' said Bernard Patterson bending over Rampha. 'Put your arm around my neck and I'll carry you to the truck.'

'Here, let me give you a hand,' said Martin Resnick.

'Hey! I'm not a cripple, you know,' protested Rampha, with not too much conviction. 'I can manage.'

'Relax,' said Mr Patterson. The two men hoisted him out of the buggy and carried him to the truck where they deposited him on the front seat.

'Tell you what,' suggested Martin Resnick. 'Let the girls ride up front with us in the cab. You two can rough it at the back with my guys.'

'Good idea,' agreed Paul's father.

They put all the baskets of food, the blankets, and various other items on the floor of the cab. Everyone clambered into the Lion Park truck, and they set off through the river.

Rampha gratefully wrapped one of the blankets around himself. He felt better covered. With the two girls on either side of him, he revelled in the unexpected luxury even though it was difficult to fathom how they got here.

It had seemed an age before they climbed out on the opposite bank. Then, Martin Resnick put a heavy foot on the accelerator and picked up speed as they headed north. They all chatted excitedly and wondered what they would encounter at the end of their journey.

THIRTY-SIX

SATURDAY 08H30

Captain Norvel Peterson was an excellent driver. Apart from the many stock car rallies he won, which was his hobby, he was also an advisor and consultant to numerous advanced driving schools in Johannesburg.

As the Corolla hurtled along, Japie van Rensburg's grudging admiration increased with every swiftly passing kilometre. But his mouth was dry and his stomach in a knot as he clung desperately to his seat and braced for bumps.

'We should be getting close now,' ventured Sergeant Spore Kaaimans. He did not seem to mind the terrific speed at which they were travelling.

Fool, thought the man in the back, now he'll go even faster.

Sure enough, the speed increased dramatically. Japie closed his eyes and prayed silently.

'There he is,' shouted Captain Peterson, spotting the Jeep ahead of them. 'Hold on tight, everyone.'

Japie's heart sank. Would this nightmare never end?

In the distance, the back of the Jeep disappeared into the next dip.

'Just a few more minutes,' muttered the grim-faced policeman. 'And we'll have him over a barrel!'

'How are we going to stop him?' Sergeant Kaaimans wanted to know. He had his gun out, ready for action.

'We'll see what happens when we get there,' answered the Captain, putting his foot down even more. 'There they are,' he shouted triumphantly. The Jeep ahead of them now came into full view. It was moving pretty fast! The big man was a good driver, but he was hampered by the vehicle's rigid suspension. Each time it hit a bump, all four wheels lifted off the ground then landed back on the dirt road. Hard!

Paul was in agony. His hand tied to the steering column was numb. He could hardly see the road ahead and could not anticipate any bumps that sent shockwaves through his body. He tried to keep his eyes on the road behind to see as much as he could.

Suddenly, he spotted the police car in hot pursuit, and he watched eagerly as it drew closer. His grim-faced captor was concentrating very hard on the road ahead and hopefully, was not yet aware of them.

Paul wondered what he could do to help.

As they approached a right-hand bend in the road, Paul felt his pulses race. He had been waiting for just such an opportunity.

Just as the Jeep went into the bend, Paul twisted his body around and with all his might kicked his feet up against the steering wheel, dislodging the big man's grip for an instant.

Grabbing the wheel with his free hand, he jerked it towards him.

Tiny was caught totally unawares as the wheel slipped from his grasp for a second.

It was enough to send the Jeep careening wildly off the road and straight into the bush ahead where it crashed against a tree trunk in the thick undergrowth, coming to an abrupt halt.

Paul managed to hold on to his seat and the steering column, but his captor was flung sideways out of the open door and onto his back in the branches of a thorn bush. The big man quickly disentangled himself and took his gun from out of his shirt pocket, he fired a pot shot at the rapidly approaching police car. He then turned and disappeared into the bush.

The Corolla skidded to a halt. The two policemen jumped out and ran towards the Jeep.

'Are you okay?' Captain Peterson called out as he climbed over the broken branches to get to Paul.

'Yes,' shouted Paul happily. 'I'm fine. Just get me out of here.'

Captain Peterson bent to examine the rope as Sergeant Spore Kaaimans stood by, waiting for instructions.

'After him!' ordered the Captain. 'But be careful. He's big and dangerous, and there are lions as well, out there somewhere. But bring him back.'

'I think the homestead's no more than a few K's further on,' said Paul helpfully, pointing northwards.

'Great!' said the policeman. 'So we'll see you back there then, Spore. Go, get him! And good luck.'

The diminutive Spore Kaaimans just grinned at them and set off after his quarry. He was now in his element. The bush was his habitat.

The policeman fished for his pocketknife and cut the rope around Paul's hand. 'I'm very pleased to see that you're still in one piece,' he smiled. 'Feeling better?'

Paul nodded.

Captain Peterson turned his attention back to the Jeep. 'In the meantime, we'll see if we can get this Jeep going.' He grinned at Paul. 'I have an idea we might be able to use it in the bush. If we can't start it, we'll tow it.' He beckoned to Japie van Rensburg.

'What about Rampha? Where is he?' Paul wanted to know rubbing his swollen hand.

'Don't worry,' said the Captain. 'He'll be fine in a day or two.'

Paul was so relieved he wanted to cry. 'What happens now?'

Sergeant Kaaimans will take care of the big guy. He's the best tracker in the world. We'll try and get this Jeep going and then get to the farmhouse. The others should also be here shortly then we'll see if we can round up this whole sorry gang.'

'The others?' Paul was curious.

The policeman regarded him a while, a smile playing on his lips. 'Oh, the Lion Park man and his crowd.'

'Mr Resnick?'

'That's right.' Captain Peterson walked back to the car, chuckling. 'Come! Let's get you out of the rain and get our mechanic busy.' He nodded to Japie who was standing by.

After clearing the undergrowth and working at it for about forty-five minutes, they managed to disentangle the Jeep and tow it backwards out of the bushes and onto the road where Japie got busy working on it. There was surprisingly little damage and after a while, the engine sprang into life. Captain Peterson was ecstatic. Now he would be able to drive anywhere in the bush to apprehend the kidnappers. It was going to make his job much easier.

SATURDAY 09H30

Just then, the Lion Park truck arrived and stopped behind them, Paul got out of the police car and went to greet Martin Resnick.

As he approached the truck, he stopped suddenly and stood there transfixed as he saw Ayesha and Debbie emerging from the cab. A limping and beaming Rampha followed close behind.

'What?' he looked wide-eyed from one laughing girl to the other. 'What are you guys doing here?' He could hardly believe his eyes. He turned to Rampha. 'Please tell me I'm not dreaming.'

Debbie ran up to him and gave him a big hug. 'Don't be silly, Paul. Do I look like a dream?'

'You sure do,' he said, his voice unsteady. Tears were perilously close. Stepping back, Debbie blushed scarlet.

Ayesha laughingly gave him a cuddle and said. 'We were wondering who would take care of the two of you. So Debbie and I decided to come and see for ourselves.'

Rampha hobbled up to a nonplussed Paul and hugged him too. 'I'm so glad to see you safe. When I heard those shots by the river, I really thought you were a goner.'

'Well, I must tell you…' Paul said, still in a very befuddled state. He looked disbelievingly at the two girls. 'But I still don't understand why …'

'There's more to come, my dear flustered friend,' interrupted Rampha mysteriously. 'Ta Dum,' he waved expansively towards the rear of the truck where Paul's father and Cedric White stood, dusting themselves off.

'Dad!' shouted Paul and ran to his father and flinging his arms around his neck, fiercely embraced him. Tears flowed without restraint as father and son unashamedly held each other. After a while, Paul withdrew and gazed steadfastly into his father's eyes.

'Where's Mom, Dad?'

'She'll be home when we get back…'

'But, what about …?'

Bernard Patterson held his son at arm's length. 'Look at me, Paul.' There was a new inner strength shining from his brightly glistening eyes. 'I'm really sorry about everything, Son. But from now on, things are going to be different. I've been very selfish, but all that has changed.' He sniffed tearfully. 'I'm going to make it up to your mother and you.'

'But Dad, there's nothing to be made up,' Paul coughed, his body shaking uncontrollably as he sobbed.

'Oh yes, there is,' Bernard Patterson said softly as he pulled his son towards him once more. 'Oh yes, there is.'

SATURDAY 10H30

They joined the others and soon three vehicles, led by the police car, were on the road once more, travelling in convoy with Japie driving Brett's Jeep.

It started raining again, and when they arrived at the farmhouse, they found the place deserted. As the others disembarked, the policeman did a quick review to find which building would be the most suitable to occupy.

Taking charge, Captain Peterson decided to make the kitchen of the main rondavel their temporary headquarters. They moved in with all their baggage and equipment, and he ordered that Rampha be given first priority. He was to be given proper treatment using the first-aid kit from the police car.

'Right,' said Captain Peterson after he was satisfied that everything was under control. 'I'd like to look around to see if Brett van Jaarsveld or anyone else is here.' He turned to Paul. 'You can come and show me where you two were held prisoner, and you Van can show me the rest of the place.' He looked coldly at Japie.

'We'll also come along,' said Martin Resnick. 'You never know just where my lions might be.' He checked the rifles and the dart guns his wardens were carrying.

'I'm coming along too if you don't mind,' said Bernard Patterson. He did not want Paul out of his sight without him especially after his ordeal.

Cedric White looked on. He knew where he wanted to be. 'I'll stay here and take care of the girls and our patient,' he smiled, looking at Rampha.

The party went outside.

Ayesha and Debbie were eager to play nurse and apply all the necessary bandages and dressings under Cedric White's supervision.

'I'm not a baby,' protested Rampha as he was forced to remain seated with his leg up on another chair.

'Be quiet,' instructed Ayesha as she gently removed the wet bandage from his foot. 'You really don't have much say in the matter.'

'But I want to go with Paul and them,' he moaned. 'It's not fair.'

'It's out of the question,' said Debbie firmly. 'You're in no condition to go anywhere.'

'You'll just have to put up with us,' teased Ayesha. She deftly sorted through the items contained in the first aid kit and began working on his foot. 'Besides,' she went on. 'I'm sure you'd like something to eat.' The two girls exchanged glances and Debbie went over to the cooler box and brought out one of the many packets of sandwiches as well as the tea things.

At the mention of food, Rampha suddenly realized just how hungry he was. Neither he nor Paul had eaten anything for many hours, or was it days? Oh, what the hell!

'I'm not eating till Paul gets back,' he said stubbornly.

'Don't worry. We'll keep some for him. There's enough here to feed a regiment.' Ayesha handed him a whole-wheat cheese and lettuce sandwich.

Rampha sank his teeth into it with relish. It tasted heavenly.

Just then Paul arrived back with Captain Peterson, Martin Resnick, Mr Patterson and the others. They found no sign of anyone.

'Are you sure there was no one at the farm besides Tiny Terblanche, your kidnapper?' Captain Peterson asked the boys.

'We only saw him and the two people who followed in the buggy,' said Rampha with his mouth half full.

'There was no one else,' confirmed Paul. He looked longingly at the packet of sandwiches lying on the cooler box.

'Help yourself, Paul, you deserve it.' Cedric White offered with a wave of his hand. 'Sandwiches and tea everyone?' There was a chorus of approval from everyone except Captain Peterson who made for the door. 'You carry on; I'll be back shortly. Van Rensburg, you come with me.'

The food was most welcome, and everyone began tucking in heartily.

As Japie and the policeman got outside, Captain Peterson turned angrily to face him. 'I want some straight answers out of you my friend. I want to know where your mate, Brett has disappeared to. He can't be walking around in the bush. His Jeep is here, his truck is here, his guns are here, but he's not here.'

'I don't understand it,' wined Japie. 'I saw the two of them leaving when I called 'round at Brett's place early the next day.'

'And why did you call?'

'They owed me some money, and I also thought that I would be coming along with them to the farm.'

'So you weren't invited. But you actually saw them leaving?'

'Yes, they even asked me to close the gate after them.'

Captain Peterson was silent. He did not like it. Brett seemed to have vanished. 'Let's go and take another look. Come!' He strode off with Japie following behind.

Fifteen minutes later Captain Peterson returned. His face was ashen. Japie behind him was walking as if in a trance. They were both drenched to the skin. Everyone looked at the Captain expectantly.

'Something wrong?' Martin Resnick asked.

'I'll say,' he said grimly. 'We've got a murder on our hands!'

There was a stunned silence.

'Murder?' Rampha was the first to speak.

'What appears to be Brett van Jaarsveld,' said the policeman. 'Or at least his remains. It's not a pretty sight. It seems the lions in that small camp out there must have gotten hold of him. We found his mangled head in the far corner. I don't think he walked in there by himself.

Someone chucked him in. And I think I know who that someone might be. We found the rest of his leftover bones scattered about. His face was grim.

They all felt sick.

He looked at Rampha. 'Wasn't that what Tiny did when he let you out of the truck?'

The boys nodded.

'It seems like this was his modus operandi.'

'What was the reaction of the lions when you found yourselves in their enclosure?' Martin Resnick asked the boys.

Paul thought for a moment. 'They weren't very interested. They just stood and looked at us.'

The girls giggled nervously and Captain Peterson glared at them, his jaw set. He turned to Martin Resnick. 'This means that your lions have become man-eaters. All of them.'

Martin Resnick was pale. 'I'm very aware of that,' he replied testily. 'When we find them we'll decide what has to be done. In the meantime, don't you think we should concentrate on finding your man?'

The two men looked hard at each other as tension between them mounted.

Captain Peterson spoke first. 'I've got the best tracker in the business on the job.' His face relaxed a little. 'But I do think we should go out there and find those two beach buggy owners. I presume they're also out there wandering around in the bush somewhere.'

He turned to the others in the room. 'I don't want a repeat of what happened earlier at the Lion Park, so I'm ordering you all to stay put right here until we get back. Is that clearly understood?' His eyes scanned around at the serious faces gazing back at him. 'When this is over you can throw your party,' he smiled. 'Okay?'

In the general hubbub that followed, Captain Peterson organized a hunting team. He went outside fetched his spare standard police Vector from his car. He gave it to Bernard Patterson.

'This is for your protection in case this guy comes back to the house,' he said and showed him how to release the safety catch. 'If you are threatened in any way, don't hesitate to use it.'

'If I'm protecting my son and the others, trust me, I'll use it.' Bernard Patterson said firmly. He was not about to throw away his newfound lease on life. Paul glanced admiringly at his father, hero-worship shining from his eyes. The rest of them nodded their approval.

The Captain addressed Martin Resnick. 'I want you and your men to come with me,' he commanded, drawing his own service pistol and checking it. 'And check your rifles and other equipment.'

His gaze focused on the Ruger hunting rifle hanging against the wall. He walked over and lifted it off the hooks and held it, balancing it in his hands and checking the chamber. It was fully loaded. 'Nice gun,' he said. 'I think we might be able to use this out there in the bush.'

Japie van Rensburg, having recovered somewhat, said, 'What about me? Can I help?'

The Captain gave him a stony look. 'You can stay put. Mr Patterson and Mr White are in charge here, and you are to follow their instructions in all circumstances. Do I make myself clear?'

Japie nodded with eyes averted.

Captain Peterson made for the door. 'Let's go,' he said.

He left with Martin Resnick and his wardens.

THIRTY-SEVEN

SATURDAY 12H30

Tiny was making steady progress. He was very sure there was no man alive who could equal him in the bush. He had only one thought in mind, and that was to get away from the police as quickly as possible. He did not relish the idea of being caught. Life in prison would finish him. He would surely perish if his freedom were taken away.

To keep within the borders of Botswana, he would have to travel northwards. That meant he would be passing close to the homestead. If it were at all possible, he would sneak into the house and collect the money the Americans had given him as a deposit. Then there was the Ruger, his beloved rifle that he hung on the wall. He could not bear the thought of leaving it behind. It was his baby.

After that, he would keep heading north and start a new life.

Damn and blast those kids to hell!

Sergeant Spore Kaaimans had a particular dislike for criminals in general and poachers in particular.

His home and traditional way of life as one of the few remaining true bushmen, living and surviving in the harsh Namib desert, had been disrupted one terrible night twenty years before. He remembered that day as if it were yesterday.

Some poachers, drunk with White man's spirits, had arrived at his meagre hut one early evening. One of their motor vehicles had broken down in the desert. They carried with them a cargo of rhino horns, hacked from the animals they had decimated days before, demanding with sign language, that Kaaimans point them towards the nearest town.

Wishing only to be friendly to strangers, he agreed. However, since it was late and dark, he invited them as was his tribe's custom, to spend the night. It was a night that scarred him for life and would live in his memory forever.

He was rudely woken in the night, overpowered and bound hand and foot by his guests. They then proceeded to ravish and gang rape his wife and his sixteen-year-old daughter. Having satisfied their evil lusts, and leaving utter devastation in their wake they disappeared into the early dawn.

He could still hear his family's screams. His wife never recovered from the shame of it. She died eighteen months later. His daughter left home soon after, to seek solace in the big city.

After moping about for the next six months, Spore's agony had congealed and hardened into a deep silent anger. He set about approaching wildlife organizations in South Africa and anti-poaching bodies offering his services as a tracker. After several successes, his reputation grew, and he was headhunted by the new ANC government to become part of their dog tracker unit of the South African Police Services.

This case he was assigned to under Captain Peterson, was right up his street. Tracking a poacher in the bush was all that he could ever wish for. No colleagues, no dogs, just he and his quarry.

As he read the signs: a leaf here, a twig there, his disdain for this low-life poacher, evolved steadily into reluctant admiration with each passing kilometre. This big white man's sheer skill in bushcraft was awesome. He moved like a shadow over the difficult terrain, leaving little trace of his passage.

Spore saluted him, he was a worthy opponent, but he was not the best and would not get away.

Not easily!

He quickened his pace.

SATURDAY 13H30

Captain Peterson stumbled over the hundredth rock hidden in the long wet grass and swore under his breath. How he wished Spore Kaaimans was with them. They would have been much further by now. He also hated himself for being justifiably super critical of Martin Resnick's tracking ability. Twice they had gone in a complete circle and arrived back at the same place again. He was sure he could have done better. The Mopani trees were high, and the thick grass and undergrowth looked pretty much the same, especially where the terrain was flat, and one could not see over the tops of the trees. It was like walking in a maze.

It had started raining again, and although it was only afternoon; it was relatively dark with heavy clouds hanging low over the bushveld.

Suddenly, without warning, they came across the two American hunters in a clearing. There they sat huddled together under a tree with their rifles leaning against the tree trunk.

Captain Peterson drew his gun.

'Don't move! You're both under arrest,' he called.

They surrounded the two. Martin Resnick raised his rifle, pointing at them.

The two men looked up in surprise, offering no resistance. The fat man stood up, brushing rainwater and leaves from his drenched clothes.

'Who are you, and what are you arresting us for?' he demanded.

'Poaching, for starters,' retorted Captain Peterson. 'And how about murder for seconds?'

'Now just a cotton pickin' minute,' Kentridge objected indignantly, jumping up and looking at the policeman. 'We ain't poached nothing yet, and we don't know nothin' about no murder. Who are you anyhow?'

'You mean you haven't shot anything yet?' interrupted Martin Resnick, ignoring his question.

'D'you see any carcasses lying around?' replied the American.

Martin Resnick relaxed visibly, his eyes lighting up.

'One of them is wounded, though,' put in Kentridge. 'That was the one he shot yesterday.' He indicated Bass. He felt mighty relieved at this unexpected turn of events.

'Bring me those rifles,' Captain Peterson ordered Joseph m'Lapa and when they were in his possession, the policeman lowered his gun. 'Okay,' he said. 'For now, we won't press the poaching issue. The most important thing right now is whether you know anything about Brett van Jaarsveld?' He looked searchingly from one man to the other.

'Old Van?' said Hank Bass. 'He was supposed to have met us back in Johannesburg. He took our initial deposit, and we haven't seen or heard from him since. He sends his muscleman, Tiny to bring us here, then, after we handed him the rest of the down payment, he does a disappearing trick.' He looked at the policeman. 'This rain, their unprofessional attitude, this whole doggone mess.' He went into a tirade of bitter complaints. 'If you find him, I would like to speak to him.'

Captain Peterson interrupted him impatiently. They seemed to be telling the truth. 'Where are the lions?' he asked, changing the subject.

'Oh, there are plenty of them out there. Not too far away either, I reckon.' Kentridge waved his arm in a general direction. 'We've been stalking them for hours, but they always seem to stay just ahead of us.' He sighed deeply. He did not want to appear too mollified with this turn of events. The arrival of these policemen whom, he assumed were genuine, was so in his favour. Now at least, no more lions would have to be slaughtered.

'This guy Tiny was supposed to be our guide,' Hank Bass Informed Captain Peterson. 'But he left a note under our door saying he was going to look for tracks,' said Sam Kentridge.

'And what's more, we paid him the rest of the money up front as per our agreement. Hell, looks like we've been taken all the way,' piped up Bass. 'We thought their operation was legit. I've just about had enough.'

'Me too,' responded Kentridge, a mite too quickly. 'And another thing,' he changed the subject. 'We've had nothing to eat since last night. Our meals are supposed to be included.'

'I'm taking you two back to the farmhouse,' Captain Peterson said, wondering vaguely why the taller man seemed so relieved. 'And don't forget you're still my prisoners until we've sorted this whole thing out.' He turned to Martin Resnick. 'It's up to you now to find your lions and do what you have to. I'll see you back there later.'

'Okay,' said Martin Resnick, pleased by the suggestion and feeling in a much better frame of mind. His lions were safe, and that was all that mattered. He would deal with the man-eating aspect of it later. Right now all he wanted was to capture them safely and take them back to the Lion Park.

Captain Peterson was now certain that Tiny Terblanche was responsible for Brett's demise. He hoped sergeant Spore Kaaimans would soon bring back his prisoner. He was confident he would.

He wondered where they were right now.

THIRTY-EIGHT

SATURDAY 14H00

Tiny Terblanche, at that moment, was no further than a hundred meters from the farmhouse. He had decided to risk going back there after seeing the policeman and his party heading off in a westerly direction away from the house.

His thoughts raced. They were probably looking for him, or the lions, or the Americans. But they were fools to think they could intercept him. He had heard them long before he spotted them. Human voices carry great distances in the bush. They were raw city slickers, the whole lot of them.

Now, as they appeared to be far enough away from the house, he decided that he would risk recovering his rifle and the cash the American had given him.

The only entrance to the house was through the kitchen, but Tiny did not want to take a chance and blatantly walk in on someone who may have been left behind there.

He crept 'round to the bedroom section that was linked to the kitchen via a passageway. Climbing through the window, he moved stealthily to the cupboard where he had put the cash with the rest of his belongings. The door leading to the kitchen was closed.

He could hear voices. They sounded like those two goddam boys, but he was not unduly worried. His instinct was right.

But his Ruger was still in there. It was a desperate situation that called for desperate measures. He thought for a moment then decided. He would burst open the door, grab his rifle from the wall and dash out before they, whoever was in there, realized what had happened.

He took his rucksack from the top shelf and felt for the money. It was still where he had left it. He stuffed the cash back into the bag then started to pack a few of his things on top of it. Lastly, he removed Brett's revolver from his belt and put it into the bag as well, shoving it deep towards the bottom.

He was so intent on the job that he did not hear the silent approach of Spore Kaaimans.

Suddenly the tracking policeman was at the window, gun in hand.

'Freeze Mister!' came the command.

Tiny's heart almost stopped. It was not possible! There was not a man alive who could catch him unawares. Why had he not heard anything?

His hand, halfway into the rucksack, fumbled quickly for the revolver he had just put there.

'I said freeze,' said the voice once more. 'Now turn around slowly.'

Tiny's hand found the gun, and as he turned around, he brought the rucksack up slowly and squeezed the trigger.

The shot rang out, and the bullet tore through the canvas and with a thud buried itself into the earth wall a few centimetres from Kaaimans's head. Tiny was not a very good shot with a handgun at the best of times, and the handicap of the rucksack made it worse.

He pulled the trigger once more, heard a shot, but did not feel the gun jerk in his hand. Why was that?

Instead, he felt an impact like a huge blow to his shoulder. He had been hit!

Still clutching the rucksack, he turned with amazing speed, jerked open the kitchen door and dashed into the kitchen.

There were people everywhere!

He looked up to the wall where his rifle usually hung. It was gone.

He heard the policeman in pursuit behind him.

Sergeant Spore Kaaimans had leaped through the window and given chase, but he had to hold his fire when he saw the crowd in the room.

Debbie screamed as Tiny pushed past her, sending her crashing into Ayesha. Cedric White aimed a blow at his chest. It was like hitting a block of wood. The impact sent him spinning.

Rampha half lying on the couch could do nothing. 'Tackle him!' he yelled. Paul put his foot out but fell headlong as his other leg was kicked out from under him.

Bernard Patterson pointed the police gun at him and shouted, 'Stop!' But Tiny's momentum simply sent him crashing to the floor, still clenching the gun. Kaaimans following close behind tripped over Paul and went sprawling.

As the big man reached the door, his glance rested for a microsecond on Japie van Rensburg. Recognition flashed in his eyes and Japie cringed into his corner as he saw his death written there.

Tiny burst through the outside door and disappeared into the bush. On his way across the clearing, he noticed the truck from the Lion Park.

'After him,' shouted Paul quite unnecessarily as Sergeant Spore Kaaimans disentangled himself and ran outside.

Because of the many tracks surrounding the rondavel, it took a good few precious moments to pick up a spot of blood on the ground. Then, Kaaimans was on the trail once more. His quarry had a good start, but he was at a disadvantage. He was now wounded and bleeding.

Minutes later, Captain Peterson arrived back with the two Americans. Paul quickly told him everything. 'Your tracker left about a moment ago. He's following the big guy,' he finished off.

'Which way did they go?'

Paul pointed to the undergrowth. 'Thataway.' It sounded just like the movies.'

The Captain handed the two Winchester .375 rifles to Cedric White. 'Guard these two, but first give them something to eat.'

'We're not going nowhere,' said Kentridge, blowing his nose. 'Just show me that food.'

Captain Peterson set off into the bush following Paul's directions. 'All of you stay put,' he shouted over his shoulder as he disappeared into the thicket calling for Spore Kaaimans.

In the meantime, Martin Resnick and his party had tracked down two of the lionesses and his pet male, nKunzi. In fact, it was the other way 'round.

The lions had tracked them when they responded to Martin Resnick's voice calling to them. They had approached the wardens without fear, to appear within sight of them. After a few minutes, they had all been successfully darted.

'While the tranquilizer is taking effect, let's spread out and look for Queenie,' Resnick suggested. 'You can go back meanwhile and fetch the truck,' he instructed Joshua.

The warden hurried off.

Fifteen minutes later, they still had not found the remaining missing lioness.

'She must be the one they wounded,' said Resnick when they rejoined each other once more.

The tranquilizer had taken effect, and the three animals were lying down comfortably but dazed. Martin Resnick went over to them and petted them and spoke to them in a soothing voice. 'Never mind, my babies,' he said. 'We'll have you back home in no time.'

About twenty minutes later he heard the truck approaching, its engine whining as it crashed through the bushes and tall grass. Shortly after, with their usual efficiency, the wardens loaded the animals safely onto stretchers and into their custom built, automatic loader truck.

'If we can't find Queenie, maybe we can let the rest of them out into that camp again until they've recovered' suggested Joshua as they were driving back. 'They will call her.'

'It could work,' agreed Resnick. 'I'd hate to lose her.' His eyes searched the surrounding bush. 'I'm sure she can't be too far.' He murmured thoughtfully.

He was right.

The wounded lioness lay, hidden in some tall grass, not fifty paces away from where they had picked up the others. She had become wary of humans and trusted them no more. Her yellow eyes, roused with anger and resentment had watched her wardens as they loaded the rest of her pride onto the truck. Even though she was familiar with Martin Resnick's voice and the sound of the Lion Park truck's engine, she no longer wanted to be associated with any part of it.

Her pain was too fresh.

SATURDAY 15H00

Tiny Terblanche also heard the distinctive sounds of the dart guns. In a slight daze, he too heard the Lion Park truck approach. He had followed the sound of its engine as it made its way through the bush, to the right and in front of him.

He was bleeding profusely from the wound in his shoulder and feeling a little light-headed. Try as he may, he could not stop the blood flowing. His shirt front was drenched with a mixture of blood and rainwater, and his pace was slowing.

He heard the truck stop some distance ahead, and he had to negotiate a wide arc around it.

After a while, he heard it start up again, and the throb of the motor gradually faded into the distance. Tiny assumed correctly that the lions had been picked up. This was a relief to him; for now, he did not have to worry too much about a chance meeting with any of them.

What worried him infinitely more was that Bushman policeman who had tracked him down. He was very good to have caught him in such a way. Who was he? Was he still following? Under different circumstances, Tiny mused, he would love to have worked together with such an expert tracker.

He had to be an incredible hunter.

It was a disturbing thought.

Spore Kaaimans was still quite a way behind his target.

After he had spotted the blood on the ground, he had picked up the trail quite easily. It was then that he heard his superior calling to him. He felt duty bound to wait for him. Reluctantly! Another few valuable moments were lost.

'He can't be too far now,' said the Captain breathing heavily as he caught up and joined his sergeant.

'We'll catch him,' said Spore confidently. 'You'll see.'

Captain Peterson knew that this was true. Bushman trackers were by nature formidable in the bush, with reputations to match. However, Spore Kaaimans was a cut above the best of them.

The little man bent down then came up with a drop of blood between his thumb and forefingers. 'He's not too far now. He will not get away.'

THIRTY-NINE

The wounded lioness watched with interest as the big truck drove away. She was aware that the rest of her pride had been captured. The sounds of the engine died, and the normal bush sounds descended once more. She growled lightly, calling to her companions. There was no answer. Still wary and suspicious, she limped silently in a detour, to the clearing where they had gathered earlier, sniffing and grimacing as she went. The man-smell hung heavily in the damp air. There was a familiar tinge to the mixture of scents that reminded her of her home in the park. She moved forward carefully, her every instinct on the alert.

Tiny was feeling more and more lightheaded from loss of blood, as he pushed on through the bush. He had become less concerned about moving with caution and stealth, his prime objective being to put as much distance as possible between himself and his pursuer.

But somewhere in the recesses of his psyche, something nagged him, something he had forgotten. His mind sifted through the preceding events, but the gnawing thought kept slipping elusively, just out of reach.

His hazy feelings and reflections were interrupted when unexpectedly he tripped on a jutting root and sprawled headlong. That was really careless and clumsy. He simply never tripped, ever. He was always so sure-footed, especially in the bush.

He dragged himself up slowly, feeling a little dizzy. Probably from loss of blood, he thought. His shoulder felt numb, and he was sure that the policeman's bullet was still lodged deep within the muscles. He had no choice but to attend to it a little later.

He was just about to take another step forward when he stopped dead.

In total disbelief, he shook his head as he tried to focus his slightly blurred vision.

There, not more than ten paces in front of him stood a lioness her smouldering eyes regarding him in silence. It was not so long since she had tasted human flesh and the smell of fresh blood and the excitement of an easy target coursed through her wounded body, heightening her senses.

Then, everything seemed to happen in slow motion.

With one smooth movement, Tiny's right hand thrust into the rucksack and his fingers curled around the smooth butt of the revolver, gripping it firmly. The bag dropped, and the gun was free. As his left hand swung up to clasp the other wrist, he felt a sharp jolt shoot up through the arm. He ignored the pain and took careful aim. He knew that he had only one chance. He waited.

The same nagging thought swept once more into his subconscious. Something he had forgotten. The doubt persisted. But there was no time for that now. He would deal with it later.

As the lioness began to move, Tiny aimed at her left eye. A brain shot was the only thing that would stop her. Closer and closer she came, her powerful muscles rippling in waves under the tawny hide.

Tiny paused.

He knew most hunters, much to their regret afterwards, always shot too soon at a charging animal. He would never make that error. He stood his ground. He had to be sure.

No mistakes!

His adrenalin pumped through his veins at top speed clearing his vision somewhat. He could see deep into those fast approaching bright yellow eyes.

Now - he thought.

He squeezed the trigger. The revolving mechanism turned the next chamber, and the hammer fell.

Click!

With total disbelief, Tiny jerked at the trigger three more times in quick succession.

Click – click – click!

The revolving chambers were vacant!

The nagging doubt that had been plaguing him, now crystallized into a terrifying revelation. In a flash of absolute horror, Tiny realized that he had spent all his ammunition earlier, on those boys and the policeman.

His gun was empty!

In desperation, he flung the useless weapon at the charging lioness. It bounced harmlessly off her tawny body, now in mid-flight.

Tiny went down in a flurry of claws and teeth as the huge animal, incensed by the smell of blood, sank her jaws into his soft flesh. He heard a scream and realized it was his own.

He fought desperately, but his strength was sapped.

Then at last one huge paw with razor sharp claws fully extended attached to his face. The other embedded deep into his chest. The lioness's wide jaws closed, clamped tight over his exposed throat, and held. Tiny thrashed about wildly, then with a final desperate spasm gave up the unequal struggle.

The last thing Tiny Terblanche felt before blackness fully engulfed and overcame him, was a curious sensation of well-being as he succumbed to the justice of the wild!

Captain Peterson and Sergeant Kaaimans arrived at the scene, minutes too late. They looked on helplessly as the lioness, proud of her kill, raised her gory head to consider this latest intrusion.

The men looked at each other silently, and Spore Kaaimans nodded.

The Captain raised Tiny's rifle and taking careful aim, squeezed the trigger.

Queenie sank next to her victim as the report of the Ruger .375 was echoed by a peal of thunder pounding about the cloudy African sky.

FORTY

Mr Banner stood on the stage and cleared his throat several times as he waited for the applause to fade.

'Thank you, thank you,' he beamed, as though the praise was his to relish. 'That was a very noble gesture from our visitors from the USA.' He beamed again as his eyes followed the triumphant Kentridge and the sullen Bass as they stepped off the stage.

The Woodlands Debutantes Ball would not get underway before all the speeches were over and done with. The headmaster always enjoyed these speeches as a precursor to these gala evening festivities.

'And now I should like to call Mr Rampha Singh and Mr Paul Patterson,' Mr Banner announced proudly.

The boys walked towards the stage amidst thunderous applause.

'I'll bet you ten bucks he talks for more than five minutes,' Rampha whispered to Paul.

'You're on. Synchronize watches.'

They did this as they mounted the steps to the stage. Mr Banner, his arms outstretched, welcomed the boys and positioned them on either side of him.

Silence fell.

He began. 'You are all aware of the bravery of our two Woodlands students, and I shall not elaborate or dwell on it any further, as much as I'd like to.' He cleared his throat and paused for effect. 'As you have heard, our American friend, Mr Kentridge has generously donated a substantial grant to the Rhino Anti-Poaching fund.' He raised his hand to silence the ripple of applause that followed. 'They have also donated a generous sum to the Lion Park to be channelled specifically for the acquisition of more lions and the wildlife work being carried out there.

More applause.

'But now, the highlight of the evening,' Mr Banner looked around the audience, still beaming. 'The Department of Wildlife Conservation in conjunction with the Department of Justice would like to present an award to our two students.' He cleared his throat once more.

Rampha glanced at his friend and looked at his watch. 'Thirty seconds left,' he whispered from the side of his mouth.

Paul sighed. He never won. Simply never!

'I'd like to call on Captain Peterson and Mr Resnick to present the award.'

As the two men went up to the microphone, Paul nudged Rampha. 'You've lost, mate.'

Captain Peterson spoke. 'It gives us great pleasure, on behalf of the Police Department and the Lion Park to award bursaries for the completion of their secondary and tertiary education, to Rampha Singh and Paul Patterson, in recognition of their services to the community.'

Martin Resnick presented them with certificates, and the hall erupted with more applause. Rampha and Paul were overwhelmed.

Looking around at the sea of faces in the audience, the boys caught sight of Ayesha and Debbie. They sat together in the front row with their respective parents amidst an ocean of coloured handkerchiefs dabbing damp eyes.

Rampha looked scornfully towards Paul, 'Girls!' he said.

But Paul's eyes were fixed on his own parents sitting next to them. They were holding hands. His heart leapt, and he felt a lump in his throat.

'Speech, speech,' roared the crowd.

Paul laughed, but his smile froze as Captain Norvel Peterson thrust the microphone into his hand.

'You go first,' he smiled.

Paul swallowed hard and opened his mouth.

Nothing came.

THE END

ABOUT THE AUTHOR

BIO OF MICHAEL DU PREEZ

Both writing and music have always featured prominently in his life and career. Working as a professional pianist/singer at night left him ample time to pursue his writing. This stood him in good stead during his eight-year stint at the SABC as a writer/director of many TV variety programs. Fortunately, he is now in a position where he is able to perform less, and focus more on writing, which is fast becoming his all-consuming passion.

PUBLISHED WORKS (BOOKS)

1. **Television through the Front Door**, published by McGraw-Hill, a 'how to' booklet.
2. **'A Comprehensive Guide to Improvisation, Composition and Arranging', Part 1.**
3. **'A Comprehensive Guide to Improvisation, Composition and Arranging', Part 2.** Both the above Light Music Textbooks requested by the Department of Education in South Africa, are currently in use in some high schools.

COMPLETED NOVELS

1. **'Justice of the Wild'**, an adventure novel depicting and exposing 'canned hunting' in South Africa.
2. **'Teach Yourself – Basic Music Literacy'**, an eighty-page self explanatory, 'how to' book.
3. **'Forty-Five Babies'**, a dramatised, true life novel about Lenise Hamilton who fostered, mothered and nurtured discarded infants from the time they were rescued, till they were ready for adoption.

MUSIC RECORDINGS

1. **'No Ordinary Man'**. Composition. A full length forty-eight minute recorded SATB Cantata, with Choir and Soloists. The Cantata tells the story of Jesus' final days in Jerusalem, from His Last Supper to His Crucifixion and Resurrection.
2. **'In Casual Style'** Volumes 1, 2, 3 and 4. Light Music Piano CD albums, featuring more than eighty popular songs.

COMPLETED MUSICAL WORKS

1. **'The Sermon on the Mount'**, a full length, 50-minute SATB Music Cantata with Choir and Soloists.
2. **'A Different Dance,'** a full length, South African Musical.
3. **'The Wandering Jew'** a short Ballet.
4. **Numerous Gospel Songs and Anthems.**

WORKS IN PROGRESS

1. **'Carruthers'**, a fantasy novel about a young, spiritual, super-sleuth with the ability to communicate, via ESP, with animals, humans, plants and other creatures.
2. **'Adam Tas'**, a full length South African Grand Opera based on the Historical facts and events in Cape Town, from 1688 to 1710.
3. **'Island of Enchantment'**, a full-length Musical based on Homer's Odyssey.

Other Faraxa Titles

Poems

Young Adults

Non-Fiction

Fiction

70822819R00173

Made in the USA
Columbia, SC
15 May 2017